DOMINION

NICK WALTERS

Published by BBC Worldwide Ltd,
Woodlands, 80 Wood Lane
London W12 0TT

First published 1999
Copyright © Nick Walters 1999
The moral right of the author has been asserted

Original series broadcast on the BBC
Format © BBC 1963
Doctor Who and TARDIS are trademarks of the BBC

ISBN 0 563 55574 2
Imaging by Black Sheep, copyright © BBC 1999

Printed and bound in Great Britain by Mackays of Chatham
Cover printed by Belmont Press Ltd, Northampton

For my father, Alan Robert Walters

Acknowledgements

Steve Cole – endless thanks for this wonderful opportunity!

Jac Rayner – for support at the eleventh hour, and tireless efforts in sending me the proofs of the excellent cover.

Paul Leonard – for read-through duty, continuity notes (Fitz's hair!), and for believing in me.

Paul Vearncombe – read-through duty, and invaluable help in conceptualising the Ruin and other creatures. And for helping me maintain a reasonable level of sanity throughout a difficult time. And for spotting Fitz's bear before it did any damage.

Jon Blum and Kate Orman – for sending me *Unnatural History* (wow!).

Mum and Dad.

Brian and Vicky Elliott – for the most alcoholic holiday I have ever experienced. Oh sunny Isle of Wight, how I yearn to return.

Richard Everson – for the sofa.

Bristol Fiction Writers: Christina Lake, Simon Lake, Paul Leonard, Mark Leyland, Innes Newman – read-through duty and support.

Bristol SF Group – Christina and Simon again, Paul Leonard again, Doug, Richard, Tina, Nathan, Tim, Brian, Jane, Sue.

Jane Hilton – best wishes for Baby Jane.

Naiem Iqbal – IT expertise, without which this book would never have been finished.

Jim Mortimore – inspiration.

Ian Morris – always take Pride.

Mark Phippen and Helen Fayle – for not hating my 'Sad Professor'!

Andrew Shattock – discussions on which is the best Cardigans album, boozy nights past and – inevitably – to come.

David Tee – move to Bristol! You know you want to!

Jonathan Way – for Cosmic Fugue 2 and the joy of hearing Colin and Lis read my stories.

Book One
Loss

Chapter One
The Lake at Midnight

Beneath the surface of the lake Kerstin's world was a deep, blurry blue, and the pressure sounded as a roaring in her ears. She loved the way the water caressed her body, leaving no part of her untouched. The way she had no weight, as if she were floating in space. She liked to see how long she could stay under, her chest bursting with the effort, until a sudden thrill of need would make her kick her feet and haul herself to the surface, gasping, treading water, her heart pounding, limbs tingling as her lungs filled with air.

Although it was nearly midnight, Kerstin could see the cabin clearly. Beyond, the land rose in a shallow incline to the dark mass of forest that surrounded the lake. Under that dense canopy it would truly be night, dark and humid.

Kerstin floated on her back, staring up at the starless sky. It wouldn't get any darker. She enjoyed the long, light summer nights. At this time of year in Stockholm or Eskilstuna it was perfectly possible to read a book outdoors at midnight, without artificial light.

She heard a splash from over by the cabin, followed by precise, cutting strokes.

Johan.

She slipped down into the water, so that her eyes peeped across the gently rippling surface.

His purposeful shape arrowed towards her. He would soon join her and start fooling about.

But he had to catch her first.

Kerstin struck off for the middle of the lake, enjoying the game, pulling herself along with powerful strokes. She prided herself on her high level of physical fitness. No point having a well-trained mind and carrying it around in a flabby frame.

1

Kerstin was tall, with well-muscled legs, strong arms and small breasts – a swimmer's body.

Johan was even more of a fitness fanatic. Even on holiday, he still worked for several hours a day on the farm, helping old Björn do the things he couldn't do any more. Leaving her alone to study, daydream and think about her life. She was twenty-one now, they both were, both about to complete their final year at Uppsala. And after that?

She swam harder, exorcising the feeling of self-doubt. Johan was catching up. Time for a change of tactic. She dived deep down, then surfaced, shaking water from her short blonde hair, blinking. Had she lost him?

Hands grabbed her ankles. No such luck!

She wriggled free and bobbed up to face him. He was laughing, his dark hair plastered to his forehead, chin dipping up and down as he trod water. He had dark eyes, an angular face. People said he always looked rather morose. But, when he smiled, his whole face lit up.

He was waiting for her to say it. Every night, the same thing. Their ritual.

She flicked water at him. 'Race you to the shore!'

It was a close-run thing but Johan won. She watched him splash out of the lake, his body pale, statuesque. She followed in a more leisurely fashion, trotting up the narrow beach to the cabin. Although the air was warm, she shivered as the water dried on her skin. Moths fluttered around the outside light. She could hear the fierce hiss of the shower from inside. He couldn't wait to soap his muscles, wiping the condensation from the body-length mirror so he could admire himself. Always did love himself. She didn't let it get to her – no, she enjoyed his body almost as much as he did. And he said he loved her, every night. Usually afterwards, sometimes during, often before. But did she love him? That was the big question. And she was putting it off, which wasn't fair on both of them.

She joined him in the shower, and then the sauna, and forgot her doubts for a while.

But later that night they returned, as doubts always do, bigger, stronger and with their older brothers in tow. Kerstin lay awake on the rumpled sheets of their bed, thinking about another man, another lover, from another country. James, who never exercised and couldn't swim. Not for the first time, she wondered what he was doing now, whether he had found someone else, or if he still thought of her.

Next to her, Johan stirred, bringing her back to the undecided, hazy present.

'Are you hungry?' he said. 'There's lots in the fridge. Sausages, smoked fish. Brie and beetroot.' He embraced her again, his hands delving down her stomach, whispering across her skin.

She pushed them away, troubled.

He sat up, leaning on his elbow. 'What's wrong?'

Kerstin turned over. 'Nothing.'

She heard him sigh, and squeezed her eyes shut. Not an argument, not now, not tonight.

'What are you thinking?' he said, his voice light, apparently unconcerned.

I'm thinking about whether or not to dump you. I'm thinking about what to do when I pass my finals. I'm thinking about moving to England. 'Nothing.'

She heard him slump back.

She swung out of bed, suddenly irritated with him, and even more irritated with herself. Something had soured, in the hot evening air. She stomped out of the bedroom.

'Where are you going?'

'To get food,' she called back.

The wooden two-storey holiday home was like a thousand others in southern Sweden. The bedroom, small and functional like all the rest of the place, took up the front half of the ground floor, with the shower, sauna and a second, smaller, bedroom behind. Over the front bedroom was a lounge with great views of the lake, and behind that the kitchen with its chipped mugs, stout saucepans and an old but serviceable electric stove. It was Kerstin's parents' cabin and this was the second year she and Johan had stayed there. Kerstin loved its remoteness, its silence.

Kerstin padded up the stairs to the kitchen and started towards the fridge. She never got there. There was a huge, deafening crunch – a thunderclap? – right inside the house, deafening her, throwing her across the kitchen to land in a heap on the floor.

She shook her head, trying to clear the ringing in her ears. What the hell? She got to her feet, turned round, and –

It just wasn't possible. Where the living room had been…

Kerstin closed her eyes, took a deep breath, opened them again. The whole front of the house was… just gone, completely vanished. Where the outer wall had been, there was nothing but a view of the still, silent lake. Splinters of wood were falling from the exposed timbers in the roof and raining down below like falling leaves on –

What about Johan?

She ran to the edge, looked down to where their bed should be.

There was nothing, only a crater in the earth.

The stairs were listing, ready to break away from their supports. Kerstin picked her way down. Impossible, all impossible! But she was standing on the brink of it – a circular crater about six metres across.

That thunderclap – it must have been an explosion. But that made no sense: an explosion large enough to destroy half the cabin would surely have killed her. Perhaps this was some force of nature – a freak lightning effect? That didn't make sense either. Kerstin stumbled outside, and walked around to what had been the front of the cabin. It had all gone – the veranda, the balcony outside their bedroom, gone.

As she circled round, bare feet scuffing the short stubby grass, she realised that this could not have been any conventional explosion. There was no wreckage – no wood littering the grass, no sign of the missing walls at all. And, as she approached tentatively, she could see that the wooden wall of the cabin had been somehow *torn*. Not charred, but torn. The missing section was roughly spherical; the remaining walls had a concave profile in line with the crater that had been their bedroom.

Shivering, Kerstin turned and looked out over the lake. What had once been a peaceful, comforting landscape now seemed like the arena of a nightmare. The smooth lake, its waves lapping the shore, the dark line of forest, the pale sky, all seemed to be watching her. She began to feel an odd dislocation from reality – a floating sensation, as though she were deep inside the lake again.

And then she thought of Johan, and collapsed on to the grass, choking back tears. She was going to ask herself if she loved him, she remembered. Now he was gone, she knew the answer. She let herself cry until her chest hurt. And then she stood up, unsteadily, and walked on shaking legs towards the cabin.

What should she do? Call the police? But the phone had been in the lounge, and the lounge was gone. Get dressed? Most of her clothes had been in the wardrobe in the bedroom, and those were gone too. Of course, there was a bag of spare stuff in her car. Mechanically, she walked past the cabin towards her little red car – such a normal, cheery sight that she began to cry again.

She tried to open the door, and then remembered that her keys were in the cabin. She felt a crushing feeling in her chest. That was the last place she wanted to go.

Steeling herself, she ran back into the cabin, up the teetering stairs. One stroke of luck – the keys were on the kitchen unit next to the kettle, where she'd thrown them last night. She grabbed them and ran back outside. She opened the boot. Johan's sports bag nestled next to her rucksack. Controlling herself with an effort, she took out a T-shirt and a pair of shorts. She dressed, stumbling on the dry ground, and then sat in the driver's seat, composing her thoughts. What to do? She could go to the farm, wake Björn. But she didn't like the melancholy old farmer, and he'd probably be drunk. Cold comfort in this crisis.

No, it had to be the police.

Kerstin fumbled the keys into place and started the engine, and drove away from the cabin.

Behind her, the lake remained placid and calm.

Björn Andersson woke abruptly, gasping, blinking away the remnants of a dream. He hated waking up in the small hours. Never could get back to sleep again. He swung out of bed, moving his large frame with difficulty, wincing as familiar aches and pains asserted themselves. He grunted as he knocked over a bottle of whisky. Empty, he noticed. Again. There was a glass on the carpet next to it, also empty.

He glanced absently around. He'd forgotten to draw the blinds, so the small room was washed in sickly, pale light. The ornate wardrobe, Nina's dressing table, and above that the framed photographs on the wall opposite the bed – he could make them all out clearly. Björn didn't like the lightness of the summer nights. He preferred the depths of winter. Easier to sleep in total darkness.

He sat on the edge of his bed. No point trying to sleep again. Perhaps a glass of water and some bread, read a book. Or perhaps go over the plans for the new barn. Plans he knew would never become reality. He felt his mood sinking. Why had he woken? Then he remembered. The generator wasn't working, and he'd been trying to fix it. He'd lost his temper, and started on the whisky. He glanced ruefully at the bottle, and then at the clock on the wall. Three in the morning. Might as well get up now.

He went to the wardrobe, fishing out a denim shirt and canvas trousers. He put his boots on, puffing as he bent to tie them. He left the bedroom and went down the narrow staircase to the kitchen, his boots clumping on the wooden stairs.

He stepped out into the cool night. The farmhouse was a square, wooden building, with three rooms downstairs, and three upstairs. The doorway opened on to a glass conservatory, cluttered with boots and rakes and an old lawn mower, which gave on to a long curving drive which ran down to a rickety gate.

The farm overlooked an arm of forest which hid the lake from view.

Björn walked down towards the gate, breathing in the fresh air, feeling the muzziness in his head clear a little. The gate gave on to a concrete yard, surrounded on three sides by farm buildings. On the right was the tractor shed and equipment store, his old truck parked outside. Facing the gate was an arch-shaped building under which the track ran out to join the road to Strängnäs. Here Björn kept timber and sawing equipment. On the left was the long, low livestock enclosure.

He frowned. Something was wrong. He opened the gate and walked down the path. He could hear a noise. A screaming, coming from within the pen. The pigs were screaming.

What in God's name was happening?

Scared, Björn ran back to the house, stumbled into the kitchen. He opened the case bolted to the wall, and heaved down the shotgun. It was still new – used only once, on tin cans perched on a bale of straw as a test. Every time he touched it, he recalled what had happened as vividly as a photograph. Touching this new shotgun made him feel sick, physically sick.

But something was in there, with the pigs. He couldn't just leave them.

He ran back outside, down the path and to the enclosure, panting with exertion. He keyed in the combination and hauled the heavy door open. The familiar musty animal smell hit him as he stepped inside. Light from the doorway cast a knife shape on the straw-strewn concrete floor. The squealing was louder now, a terrible sound which quickened his heartbeat.

He reached round for the light switch. Nothing happened. Of course – he hadn't fixed the generator. Next to the light switch was a torch on a hook. Björn took it down. Encased in rubber, it was reassuringly big and heavy. He clicked it on, sending the bright white beam up and down the rows of pens. The pens were waist-high and built of breeze blocks. They were spacious and clean. Björn took good care of his livestock.

The screaming was coming from one of the far pens.

Björn walked down the central aisle, sending the torchlight before him. There was another sound, a low growling. A wolf? But how? There was simply no other way in apart from the entrance door he'd come in through, and the wide barn doors at the other end. Both operated by electronic locks to which only he knew the entry code.

Björn shone his torch in the nearest pen, and shouted in anger. This pen had contained a large sow and her litter of twelve. Now the jerky movements of his torch picked out a mass of torn flesh, and blood, blood *everywhere*, over the walls of the pen, over the floor. He couldn't make out anything recognisable.

He staggered backwards, almost dropping the torch. No animal he knew of was so vicious, so wasteful.

Then he saw a movement, and turned to see something leaping over the wall of the pens at the far end of the barn, landing to crouch in the shadows. He squinted. That humped shape was no wolf. They just didn't move like that. As he watched it shuffled closer.

He raised the torch. He had time to pick out two sinewy, reptilian legs, a slimy body covered in cactus-like spines, and a flash of white teeth before it leapt at him, hissing.

Björn dropped the torch. It went out. He turned to run just as the thing cannoned into his shoulder.

He fell on his side, hands scrabbling on the concrete floor. He tried to get up and felt a stabbing pain as the thing clawed at his thigh, tearing the flesh. He yelled in agony.

He kicked the beast away, and rolled into a sitting position. There – the torch. He picked it up, flicked the switch, shook it – it came on. In the beam, he caught a glimpse of teeth like needles in a champing, circular mouth, and a row of black pitiless eyes. What on God's Earth was this thing?

Almost blacking out from the pain, Björn managed to shuffle backwards against the wall of the pen. He raised the shotgun, but he didn't have time to fire: the thing leapt and the barrel of the gun entered the creature's mouth, forcing the butt into Björn's chest, winding him.

He watched, hypnotised, as sharp white teeth gnashed down on the metal barrel, making a juddering clicking noise, saliva spraying from the round mouth. Though bigger than a Labrador, the creature was surprisingly light.

Björn closed his eyes and squeezed the trigger.

There was a muffled blast, a howl of pain and a splattering, crunching noise.

The recoil hit Björn in the chest and he slumped against the concrete floor, winded.

He felt himself slipping away. He reached down. His trousers were soaked with blood. Perhaps he would die; perhaps this demon carried poison in its claws. In which case the last thing he would ever hear would be the squealing of the pigs.

Björn looked at the creature through blurring vision. Its rear half was a mass of torn flesh – shotguns always leave a messy exit wound. Its two powerful legs jerked in a futile hopping motion, a wheezing escaped from its maw, and then it was still.

Then Björn passed out.

Chapter Two
Emergency Landing

Fitz wandered along the curved corridor to Sam's room, rehearsing what to say, hoping that there was something he could say that would make her forgive him. If he was going to stay in the TARDIS at all – if he wasn't going to just get off at the next stop – he had to patch it up with her. Deep down, he didn't want to believe that Sam thought he was capable of killing without remorse.

And the truth was, he didn't want to believe it about himself, either.

He arrived at Sam's room and knocked on the door. No answer. He knocked again. Still no answer. He'd have to barge in, which would only make things worse. He splayed his fingers and ran them through his hair. It was still short, a painful reminder of the events of the last two years: the Revolution Man. Om-Tsor. Leaving the TARDIS with Maddie. Being brainwashed – *brainwashed!* – into working for the Chinese Army.

He frowned. His head still felt mucked about with. Could he be sure he was all right now?

As he stood, prevaricating, a strange sound boomed from all around him. It was like a bell, sounding from deep underwater. He'd never heard it before but he could tell it meant something bad was up. It was that sort of sound, along with creaking doors and the release of safety catches.

Then he heard something that jolted him into action. The sound of Sam yelling her guts out.

He yanked open the door and tumbled inside, holding on to the handle to steady himself. By now the TARDIS was vibrating, and everything in the room was whirling around, spiralling towards a swirling tunnel at the far end. He gaped. It looked like a whirlpool, but instead of water it seemed to be made of golden-white light.

Fitz could feel himself being pulled in, so he grabbed on to the door handle even harder, his feet skidding against the smooth floor.

Sam clung to her bed as it was dragged towards the whirlpool's mouth. He yelled her name, aware of how futile this was. The bed gave a sudden jerk, until its far end was actually over the lip of the whirlpool. Sam scrambled backwards, shoving the duvet in front of her and tumbling off the bed, which was snatched away down the white, pulsing throat.

'Sam!' yelled Fitz, but it was too late because in the next heartbeat Sam followed, her arms and legs flailing.

And then, abruptly, the whirlpool vanished.

Magazines and pages from books fluttered slowly to the floor. A few chess pieces rolled about, a reminder of their abandoned game. All was silence except for the tolling of the bell, which was beginning to speed up. And something was happening to the roundelled walls. They were warping, like wet cardboard.

Whatever this was, it wasn't over.

Fitz backed out of Sam's room. Where the whirlpool had been there was now a ragged hole, filled with grey, crackling static. He staggered along the corridor towards the console room, the floor listing under his feet. The sound of the bell had speeded up to a high, keening whine which invaded his skull, tormenting him. Guilt as well – he could have tried to save Sam. He could have followed her into the whirlpool. But what was the sense in getting them both... killed? He swallowed hard, pushing the thought to the back of his mind.

After what seemed like miles of corridor, Fitz made it to the console room. He felt sick and giddy, about to throw up at any moment.

The Doctor was standing on the console, arms wrapped around the glass column in the middle, the blue neon fingers inside meshing and unmeshing jerkily. His eyes were closed, and he was muttering, operating the controls with his stockinged feet.

12

'Doctor, Sam –'

The Doctor looked up. 'Fitz! My shoes! Get my shoes!' he bellowed. 'And then get up here with me!'

Fitz just stood there.

'Quickly! Or you'll sink!'

Fitz ran across the console room to where the Doctor's brown brogues were waiting on his plush Regency chair. When he stopped running, his feet started to sink into the floor.

What was that the Doctor had said?

Heart in mouth, Fitz grabbed the shoes and bounded on to the console, slipping on the polished brass and wood, flinging his arms round the central column. His breath misted the glass, but he could still see the Doctor's face, his usually calm features wild, his hair a mess and his eyes wide. The blue fingers inside the column had now become fixed in one position.

The Doctor reached around and grabbed the shoes. 'Thank you, Fitz.' He slipped them on while maintaining his position on the console.

Then things started to get worse. The air around them seemed to shimmer and vibrate, and a tremendous tearing, screaming noise rose from the console, as if the TARDIS were in pain. 'Doctor, what the bloody hell is happening?'

'The TARDIS has been invaded,' cried the Doctor above the din. 'She's defending herself.'

Invaded. The thing in Sam's room. 'Doctor –'

The screaming noise suddenly rose in pitch. Fitz saw the Doctor's mouth move but caught only a few of his words. 'Emergency landing… fingers crossed.'

Fitz's boots slipped on the console. He reached round and held on to the column, his face pressed against the cool glass. He could see that the floor of the TARDIS had become a churning, porridgey mass. The girders supporting the console seemed to be *bending*, stooping inward, and beneath his feet the console itself seemed to be mutating into a giant marshmallow toadstool. Above them the entire ceiling of the TARDIS was a sickly green, and the tower above the console was beginning to melt, dripping dark splats of matter. The library, the filing cabinets and the stone walls of the console room had all run together like a watercolour left out in the rain.

The Doctor was frowning as he operated the melting controls with his feet. 'Fitz, reach round and give that little blue switch a kick, will you?'

Fitz craned round and saw the switch. It was rapidly losing its solidity, wilting like a dying flower. He touched it gently with the toe of his boot and the TARDIS gave a sickening lurch. They both grabbed on to the glass column – the only thing that still seemed to be solid.

The screaming sound was dying, fading to a disturbingly human-sounding moan. A wind sprang up from nowhere, ruffling his hair.

'And by the way,' said the Doctor, his piercing blue eyes locked on to Fitz. 'Where's Sam?'

Fitz opened his mouth to speak – and the console gave way beneath him, collapsing like a soggy sponge cake. Fitz tried to grab something but there was nothing solid left and he fell, plunging into the grey goo that had been the TARDIS floor. He let out a yell as he sank deep into the stuff, but it wasn't like being underwater. Strangely, it wasn't wet, and he could breathe. He floated in a grey void, which crackled with blue sparks. The Doctor's VW Beetle floated past, followed by a tandem, a shopping trolley and a whole procession of books.

The Doctor appeared before Fitz. His mouth was moving but all Fitz could hear was a buzzing in his ears. He was pointing with one hand and grabbing Fitz with the other. His intention was obvious. They had to get out.

Together, they half swam, half floated towards a square of light, flanked by two huge, melting slabs of chocolate which Fitz realised were the TARDIS doors. As he watched, the doors lost all solidity and joined the murky soup that had once been the TARDIS interior. He began to lose all sense of perspective. Sometimes it felt as though he were falling slowly down towards the doorway; sometimes it felt as if he were swimming upward. He decided on the latter because it made him feel less dizzy. It was therefore a bit of a surprise that, when they finally reached the doorway and hauled themselves out of the TARDIS in what Fitz thought was an upward direction, they fell sideways on to soft ground.

Fitz lay, panting, staring upward at a dark canopy of trees, bright sunlight filtering through spiky branches. After he regained his breath, he sat up.

The Doctor was lying nearby, his eyes closed, his hand clasped across his chest, breathing slowly, regularly.

Fitz sat back on his haunches, getting his bearings. Clearly, they were in a forest. Looked perfectly normal. Could even be Earth. He inhaled. A sharp, tangy dampness. But he could breathe. What were the odds of the TARDIS making an emergency landing somewhere that would support life? He shuddered to think.

To Fitz's surprise, the TARDIS looked perfectly normal, with no outward sign of the turmoil within, its dark-blue paintwork, square windows and stacked roof just as they always were. He'd spent the last two years away from the TARDIS, away from the life it had opened up for him. Now he'd just got back and it had spat him out, like a nasty taste. He shuddered. The experience had reminded him that the TARDIS was an unimaginably powerful, totally alien machine – no, more than a machine: almost a being in its own right. How much did even the Doctor know about it?

The Doctor suddenly sat up. His velvet frock coat looked pristine as ever, his cravat neatly tucked into his padded waistcoat. He grabbed Fitz's arm, his gaze pinning him down. 'Where's Sam?'

Fitz swallowed, his throat dry. 'Something in her room – a sort of whirlpool thing.'

'Tell me exactly what happened. Leave nothing out.'

So Fitz told him.

At the end, the Doctor sat there, staring into the distance, his face blank.

'Doctor?'

But the Doctor remained silent. He suddenly stood up, brushing bits of twig from his coat, and walked over to the TARDIS. He put both hands flat on the doors, closed his eyes and raised his head. Then he let out a full-throated yell which made Fitz leap to his feet and run to his side.

The Doctor was breathing hard, staring at nothing.

'Are you all right, Doctor?'

The Doctor leaned his face against the TARDIS. 'She's in pain. Something invaded her, tore right into her. It's damaged her, badly. She's going to take a long time to heal.'

Bad news. That meant they were stranded. But at least they were alive. 'What about Sam?'

The Doctor's face tensed. 'From what you describe it could be anything – vortex infarction, time scoop – but none of those should be able to penetrate the TARDIS, theoretically.'

'What about Sam?' said Fitz again, unable to keep the anger from his voice.

The Doctor looked away from Fitz, and pursed his lips. 'I don't know. I expect she'll turn up sooner or later.' Then he walked away into the forest.

Fitz set off after the Doctor, angry at his seeming lack of concern. As he caught up, the Doctor stopped walking, and looked up at a beam of sunlight which had found its way through the branches. 'I know what you're thinking. Sam is missing. She may be dead, she may be alive, but there's nothing we can do for the moment.'

Fitz felt numb. Sam, dead? It was only just beginning to sink in. But the Doctor was right: there was nothing they could do for her now. With a monumental effort, Fitz brought his attention to bear on their surroundings. 'So where are we?'

The Doctor seemed to sniff the air. 'Earth.'

'Are you sure?'

'I think I know Earth well enough, Fitz.'

The Doctor sounded miffed, but Fitz couldn't believe he could tell just like that. 'How can you tell, just by sniffing the air?'

'More than that, Fitz. There's gravity, air pressure, air density –

each planet has its own intrinsic set of characteristics, as individual as a fingerprint.' He smiled, briefly. 'It's rather like wine tasting. Trust me, this is Earth. Which is nice. Emergency landings can be tricky – we could very well have ended up on Skaro. Or Telos.' He stepped over a fallen branch. 'Or worse.'

Fitz was beginning to sweat under his long coat so he took it off, throwing it over his shoulder. The atmosphere was hot and sticky and insects buzzed constantly around his head. 'OK, so we know where – how about when?'

The Doctor paused. To Fitz's amazement he licked a finger and held it in the air as if testing wind direction. He nodded decisively. 'Late twentieth century, judging by the pollutant content.'

'Pollution?' said Fitz incredulously. 'Here, in a forest?'

The Doctor nodded gravely. 'You may not be able to smell it or taste it but we Time Lords are sensitive chaps.'

He set off again at a pace. Fitz followed. How late in the twentieth century were they? How long after his time? No way of telling at the moment. The forest seemed to go on for ever, in every direction. The ground underfoot was uneven, strewn with twigs and stones and unpredictable hummocks. It was heavy going and Fitz and the Doctor kept bumping into each other as they walked.

'So, what's the plan?'

The Doctor sighed. 'I'm afraid all we can do is find somewhere civilised, and hole up there for a while.'

'How long might that be?' asked Fitz, dreading the answer.

The Doctor shrugged, raising his hands level with his head. 'Depends how long the TARDIS takes to heal. Could be days, months, or even years. Or never. Don't worry, Fitz, with any luck we're in your time, near enough. You're the fortunate one.'

He had a point, thought Fitz. If they were on Earth, near his own time, and the TARDIS was banjaxed for good, how would the Doctor feel? The eternal traveller, forced to hang up his hiking boots for ever.

Suddenly something buzzed past Fitz's head, and he flinched.

'Hey!'

The Doctor stopped. 'What is it?'

The thing careered off into the distance. What was it, a dragonfly? Weird wings if it was – seeming to radiate in four directions. It certainly wasn't like any Earth insect Fitz knew of – so perhaps the Doctor was wrong. Fitz gave chase, crashing through the undergrowth.

He lost it. It must have gone up into one of the trees, or landed among the ferns and bracken.

'Is this what you're looking for?'

Fitz turned round to see the Doctor nudging something with his toe, out of sight behind fern leaves. He went over and looked to see what the Doctor had found.

It was the insect. Certainly no dragonfly – too big, for a start, about the size of a seagull.

'It must have collided with a tree,' said the Doctor. 'Pity. It's a beautiful thing. Or rather, it was.'

Its body was black, shiny and bottle-shaped, with a long, slender neck. Its four wings were thin and tapered, coloured blood orange with a tracery of red veins. They looked far too insubstantial to support the body. At the 'head' end was a round hole, pouting like the mouth of some bizarre musical instrument. Surrounding this were about a dozen bright-blue buttonlike things which could have been eyes.

'Doctor,' said Fitz, 'am I right in saying that nothing like this does, or has ever, or ever will, exist on my planet?'

The Doctor nodded. 'Mmm. Yes, yes, yes.'

'So we're not on Earth?'

'Oh, we're on Earth. Trust me.' The Doctor wagged a long bony finger at the dead creature. 'But *you* shouldn't be!'

He set off through the forest again, and Fitz followed. 'How did it get here?'

'That's what I intend to find out. Aha!'

The Doctor had stopped at the edge of a track. It was pitted with potholes, and the caked mud bore the unmistakable imprint of tyre tracks. On the other side was a pile of logs, dead bark peeling and showing the yellowish wood beneath. The track led off in either direction, slightly curving away from them. There was no indication of which way led to civilisation, and which deeper into the forest.

'Tricky one,' murmured the Doctor, as if reading Fitz's mind. 'But there are only two choices, so what shall we do? Toss a coin?'

Fitz shrugged. 'Well if one of us chose the way we'd have someone to blame when we find ourselves even more lost than we already are. If that's possible.'

The Doctor shook his head, his brown curls catching the sun. 'I've got a better idea – we'll trust in my infallible sense of direction. We go –' he paused, pointing first one way, and then the next – 'that way.'

They set off along the track. It was only slightly less hard going than the forest floor. It couldn't have rained for a while because the orange mud was baked rock-hard. Above them, the sky was a bright, startling blue; looking up between the treetops was like gazing down a deep canyon on to a river.

Fitz was about to mention this to Sam when he remembered she wasn't there.

They trudged on in silence for a while, batting away insects. Presently they emerged on to a field of sun-yellowed grass which sloped down towards a cluster of buildings.

'Look – civilisation!' cried the Doctor.

'We hope.' Fitz shaded his eyes and peered into the distance. A square wooden building stood out brick-red against the surrounding green. There were a few long, low barnlike buildings clustered a little way from it. The place was unmistakably a farm of some sort.

'Judging from the architecture, I'd say we're in Scandinavia – Sweden, probably. Yes, this has the feel of a hot Swedish summer.'

Fitz wiped the tide of sweat from his forehead. 'Sweden? Thought it was a pretty cold country.'

The Doctor shook his head. Fitz noticed that he wasn't even

sweating. 'Swedish summers are short, but very hot. Just be thankful we're not here in the middle of winter. We'd have died of exposure before now.'

'Instead of sunstroke.'

But the Doctor had already started striding across the field towards the farmhouse. Fitz hefted his long, heavy coat and set off after him. After a few paces he stopped, looked at the coat in wonderment. Why the hell had he been carrying it for so long? Without a second thought he slung it on the grass and hurried to catch up with the Doctor.

Chapter Three
The Thing in the Barn

Kerstin awoke from a dream of drowning, and for a few seconds she had no idea where she was. And then she remembered. She was in Björn's spare room. The police had brought her here after she'd fallen asleep in the police station in Strängnäs. She had let herself in, not even bothering to look for Björn, and gone straight to bed.

She remembered last night.

Johan.

Negative thoughts crowded in on her and she hunched into the blankets, pulling them over her head, wanting to blot out the light, crawl away from reality. But, after barely a minute in the safe darkness, she surfaced again, blinking, shoving the sheets away from her. It was too stuffy. She was prickly with sweat and badly needed to shower.

The sun was streaming through the window into the tiny room. There were pictures of farm machinery on the walls, an old filing cabinet in one corner and a clapped-out computer on a dark oak bureau along one wall. The wallpaper was faded and peeling, the whole room thick with the air of neglect. The bed was shoved against the far wall, as if shrinking from the clutter. This was the room where Björn kept anything he wasn't using, and the very occasional guest.

This place must seem terribly large, living here on your own, thought Kerstin. Downstairs, there were two living rooms, one which Björn used as an office, the other for drinking and reading. Especially drinking. Upstairs, three bedrooms: this spare room, Björn's room, and the third bedroom, which was used as another office. All rooms were decorated in the style of ten years ago. It was as though Björn wanted to stop everything at the point Nina died. He even kept the farm going, at a loss, she suspected, as a monument to his wife's memory. It gave Kerstin the creeps – she never liked coming here. Johan didn't seem to mind, but now Johan was gone, perhaps for ever. What would Kerstin do to keep his memory alive? Her heart seemed to shrink within her at the thought of living with grief as Björn did. She would never be like that. She loved Johan, but she would get over him. He would always be a happy memory, but she would go on. Wouldn't she?

She swung herself out of bed, her bare feet encountering the sun-warmed planks of the floor. What time was it? Her watch had gone, along with all her clothes. There was a small travel clock on the bureau, showing 12.00. Midday. She'd had six hours' sleep, more than enough. Time she got back to the police station, or at least phoned them.

She padded out of the spare room on to the landing, downstairs to the kitchen. She could do with some breakfast, to start her brain going. No, call the police first. They had told her they would call as soon as they had any news, but how could she be sure? What if they were too busy? Or perhaps they'd found Johan's body and were wondering how to break the news to her – no, best not think about that. Anyway, far better to ring them.

She dialled the number on the phone in the kitchen, trying to stay calm, half hoping that there would be no news of Johan, dreading what she'd find out if there was. The phone rang for ages and Kerstin's agitation increased.

Then the phone was answered, and a voice said flatly, 'Inspector Nordenstam.'

Her breath caught in her throat. 'This is Kerstin Bergman. I reported a missing person last night, and I –'

Nordenstam spoke again, his tone stiffly sympathetic. 'Ms Bergman, I'm sorry. There's no news of Johan as yet.'

Voices in the background.

Kerstin's heartbeat quickened.

'Black coffee, please,' called Nordenstam.

Kerstin's heart slumped. 'Are you sure there's no news?'

'Of course I'm sure.' He sounded stressed and tired, as if he'd been up all night, with only his precious coffee to keep him going. 'No news of any of them.'

She heard him catch his voice at the end of the sentence. 'What do you mean – "them"?'

She heard him take a sip of coffee.

'Inspector?'

'Keep this to yourself,' he started, then he swore. 'There have been other disappearances, as well as Johan. Five other people.'

Kerstin gripped the phone, trying to digest the import of his words. 'Where… where from?'

'All from Strängnäs or Harad, within a five-mile radius of the forest. Look, Ms Bergman, I'd really rather you kept this to yourself for now.'

Kerstin nodded, and said, 'OK.' She didn't feel like talking any more. 'You'll call me if there's any news?'

Nordenstam promised he would, then hung up.

Kerstin put the phone back down, her heart thumping. So whatever had happened to Johan had happened to others. What was going on? Mass kidnappings? She shook her head, telling herself to be rational. Be rational and patient and all will be explained in time – she could almost hear her father saying it. More than that, she *wanted* to hear her father saying it. Independence could go to hell, this was a crisis and she needed comfort.

She dialled her parents' number, holding her breath as the line connected. She imagined the big cream-coloured telephone in the house in Stockholm, her father walking along the hallway.

But it was her mother who answered, and from the tone of her voice Kerstin could tell that she knew. 'Kerstin? Are you all right?'

'Hello, Mama.'

There was a choked sob from the other end of the line. Kerstin felt cold. Perhaps this was nothing to do with her. Perhaps something else had happened. 'Mama, are you all right?'

The sound of mother controlling herself. 'I'm just… so

worried about you. Mrs Svensson – she's in shock. They've had to take her to hospital.'

The coldness intensified, spreading through her whole body. So they knew. The police had told Johan's parents – as of course they would – and now Kerstin's parents knew.

'I'm sorry,' Kerstin said. Then the tears came.

Now it was her mother's turn to soothe her. 'There's nothing for you to be sorry about. It's not your fault.'

'I know, Mama. I'm all right, really.' Maybe if she said it often enough it would be true.

'Do you want us to come down?'

That was the last thing she wanted. 'No, really, I'm all right.' Kerstin promised to phone later and hung up, feeling vaguely annoyed. She didn't like the thought of her parents worrying about her. She walked to the kitchen table and sat down. She didn't feel hungry any more, but there was no point making herself ill. If she was going to get through this she was going to have to keep herself in shape. She went to the fridge and got out some orange juice, pouring herself a glass.

As she sat sipping the juice, she became aware of a sound from the bathroom, beyond the kitchen. She knew from past visits that it was tiny, hardly much larger than the shower cubicle it contained. All this land and mucky livestock and a room the size of a matchbox to clean yourself up in.

The sound was a male voice, lowing in pain.

Kerstin got up. It must be Björn. Was he drunk? It was early in the day, even for an old soak like him.

She knocked on the bathroom door, realising that it was the first time she had thought of Björn this morning. She peered through the cracked pane of frosted glass. She could just make out a figure, hunched over the sink.

'Björn? Is that you?'

The blur moved, and there was the clink of glass against glass. 'Go away.'

What was up with him? 'Björn, are you all right?'

'Yes, I'm fine!' His voice was dragging with pain, or drunkenness.

She began to get angry with the old man. She hammered on the door. 'Björn, you're not well. Let me help.'

There was a muttering from inside, and a clattering of things in the sink that sounded plastic. Pill bottles? And then the door opened.

Björn's red, lined face was creased in pain. He was wearing a vest and pants. There was blood in the sink. He was clutching a small bottle of whisky, a mouthful of the amber liquid slopping about inside. 'What the hell are you doing here?'

He turned back to the sink and Kerstin glimpsed a deep gash on the back of his leg, above the knee.

Kerstin gasped and took a step back. Of course, he would have no idea what had happened to her last night. Obviously, he had other concerns. 'What happened to you?'

'I had an accident,' he wheezed.

Kerstin appraised his injuries. His left thigh had three deep gashes. He'd been trying to apply ointment to them. In the sink was a bottle of painkillers.

She winced, almost feeling the pain of his wounds for herself. 'Accident? What happened?'

He looked at her, his pale-blue eyes milky, afraid. 'I'm not sure I want to tell you.'

Half an hour later, Kerstin had sterilised Björn's wounds, applied dressings, helped him dress and calmed him down a little.

She'd had a shower and put on a pair of white shorts, a loose yellow T-shirt and a pair of old trainers she'd dug out from the boot of her car. Johan's spare clothes were in there as well. They hadn't got round to unpacking fully. She pushed such thoughts to the back of her mind and went into the kitchen.

Björn was still there, large hands clamped around a glass of whisky. He didn't look up as she entered, as she sat down at the table opposite him.

What could have happened to send him into such a state? Ever since the death of his wife he'd been a lonely, depressive alcoholic, but everyone in Strängnäs who knew him always said he preferred it that way, liked wallowing in grief and lakes of whisky. But he didn't look depressed or drunk now – he looked frightened.

Perhaps some of the local lads had decided to play a prank, breaking into the farm and doing some damage. Wouldn't put it past them. In which case, the police would have to know. 'Björn?'

He looked up. 'Hmm?'

'Are you going to tell me what happened?'

He looked back down into his glass, shaking his head.

Kerstin sighed, trying not to get angry with him. 'OK. I'm going to tell *you* something. Something that happened to me last night.' And she told him, watching his face sag in disbelief.

When she finished, he took a gulp of whisky, his hands shaking. He looked up at her, his eyes searching her face. 'I'm sorry, Kerstin. I had no idea… What's going on?'

Telling him had made the events somehow less real, as if they'd happened to someone else. She felt numb. 'I don't know, but if anything weird happened to you last night I think you'd better tell me about it.'

He took another sip of whisky, draining the glass. 'I still don't believe it myself.'

She reached out and held his hand. 'Go on.'

He looked at her as if assessing her, his pale-blue eyes a sharp contrast with his sunburned face. He clasped his big hands together around hers. She could tell he was deciding whether or not to trust her, so she kept quiet. Eventually he sighed and stood up. 'Come with me. I have something to show you.'

It was cool and dark inside the tractor shed. The smell of petrol stuck in the back of Kerstin's mouth. She brushed her hand through her hair. It felt matted and sticky. She'd need another shower soon. Still, later she could go for a swim with Johan –

The thought had formed in her head, and she even felt a glow of anticipation, before she remembered.

Björn limped to the other side of the shed, manhandling a bulky object wrapped in a grey tarpaulin into the middle of the concrete floor. It was rolled up untidily, over a large irregular lump about the size of a human torso. Kerstin shook her head, perturbed by the morbid thoughts that were gathering within.

Björn bent down to unroll the tarpaulin, his gaze on Kerstin. There was a pleading look in his eyes, as if he needed her to believe him.

She felt uneasy, as if he were about to show her something she'd deeply regret.

He smiled, as if noticing her fear. 'It's dead. Don't worry.'

As if anything wrapped up like that could be alive. Kerstin stepped closer. The tarpaulin made a thick, crackling sound as Björn unrolled it. Kerstin gasped when she saw what was revealed.

It was like nothing she had ever seen, and a feeling overcame her, the same swimming feeling of dislocation she'd had when she'd been faced with the 'explosion' at the cabin.

Björn was speaking in a low voice, his face averted, as if confessing to some crime. 'It killed one of the pigs and her piglets. It was so savage, so strong.'

The rotting-fish smell of the thing crept over her and she gagged. She forced herself to examine the thing, one hand clamped firmly over her mouth. There wasn't much left of it. She could make out thick-muscled legs, like frog's legs, ending in black claws. Its body was taut and powerful, greenish flesh bristling with cactus-like spines. Some sort of lizard? But the head... It wasn't like any animal she'd ever seen. It was round, almost spherical, tapering to a round maw at the front, lined with sharp white teeth. Around the mouth were nine black, spiderlike eyes.

Kerstin stood up, walking back outside to get some air. Björn followed her, limping on his injured leg.

'Where did it come from?'

'It was in the barn, with the pigs. How it got in...' Björn shook his head.

They looked at each other. He spoke first. 'There must be a rational explanation.'

She nodded, glad he'd said this. She really wanted to believe it. 'Why didn't you take it to the police?'

He looked around sharply. 'I don't want anyone here. You know I like my solitude. If people find out about this, that would be the end of it.'

She understood his reluctance. This creature was weird enough to bring the police, the media, UFO hunters and all sorts of nutters to the farm. It would be the end of Björn's hermit-like existence and probably his sanity. She thought of the little farmhouse, frozen in time since 1989, a shrine to the past.

But this creature could be a link to what happened to Johan. It had appeared inside a locked barn without explanation; Johan had disappeared without explanation. There must be a link. She had to take it to the police.

She made a decision. 'I'll take it. On my own.'

Björn shook his head. 'No.'

'I'll tell them I found it by the roadside, miles from here. No connection with you at all.'

He waved a hand at her, suddenly angry. 'Do what you want with it. It's dead, and that's all I care.' He trudged out of the tractor shed towards the farmhouse without a second glance at her.

She watched him go, restraining her anger. Well, she'd have to do it herself.

She went back to where the dead thing lay in its grey shroud. The smell was worse now; there was no way she could go near it. She looked around, found a spade and used it to lollop the tarpaulin around the creature. That done, she grabbed the edge farthest away from the lump in the middle and dragged it outside. Her car was parked beside the porch, the police had kindly driven it here for her. This meant dragging the thing all the way up the drive. In this heat. But she had no choice, and set to the task. It wasn't heavy, but it was unwieldy – and that smell…

Perhaps this was an undiscovered species, living at the bottom of the lake for centuries, emerging only now and then. She stood up, wiping her brow. The red, square shape of the farmhouse, with its white-framed windows and shutters, seemed to be peering down at her, mocking her efforts. She bent and grabbed the tarpaulin again, taking it across the yard towards the gate that led to the driveway. Bits of the creature were falling out of the other end of the tarpaulin, leaving bright green smears on the ground. She suddenly felt sick and wondered what the hell she was doing.

Then she felt a hand on her shoulder.

She stood up, startled.

There stood Björn, a look of contrition on his face. 'We'll use the truck. Don't want to stink up your car.'

She blinked, wiping sweat out of her eyes. 'OK. You sure?'

He nodded, and grabbed the tarpaulin, swinging it round towards the old Ford truck, stationed outside the tractor shed.

As she helped him manhandle the tarpaulin and its grisly contents into the truck, she asked him what made him change his mind.

'I was thinking, in the house.'

Drinking as well, if his breath was anything to go by.

He shaded his eyes against the sun. 'You've lost someone. I know what that feels like. From now on, I'll help you.'

He gave the tarpaulin a final shove and it fell with a thump into the back of the truck.

Chapter Four
In a Hole

Fitz followed the Doctor across the field towards the farm, the long dry grass rustling against his legs. 'What exactly are we going to say to them?'

'We'll tell them that we're travellers, and we're lost,' said the Doctor. 'It's the truth. With any luck, they'll offer us tea, and maybe cake – if we're lucky.'

The mention of refreshments made Fitz realise how thirsty he was. He licked his parched lips. Wow. It was hot, a dry, penetrating heat from which there was no respite. He looked ahead to the farm, hoping there was someone there to feed and water them. Beyond the farm was another arm of forest. To their left, more forest. And there was no telltale traffic noise. Probably nothing but fields and pine forests for miles around. Fitz was beginning to get the measure of the TARDIS's little quirks. Emergency landing – huh; couldn't have put them down anywhere useful, could it? Like in a modern, prosperous city. Had to be the middle of bloody nowhere.

Fitz was about to say something about this when the ground fell away beneath his feet and he fell straight down, shouting in surprise, hands shooting out to clutch at clumps of grass. He landed with a jolt, bending his knees, falling over on his side. It had happened so quickly that he didn't have time to be scared, and he stood up blinking, waiting for his eyes to adjust to the darkness. Clumps of mud and turf fell on him from above.

'Are you all right?' came the Doctor's voice.

Stupid question. 'Oh, fine,' called Fitz. He looked up from where he had fallen. Above him, just out of reach, there was a ragged Fitz-sized hole, a fringe of stubbly grass framing the blue sky.

'Don't worry – I'll get you out.' He could hear the grass rustle as the Doctor hurried away.

A shaft of sunlight defined a dappled circle on the soil beneath his feet. He seemed to be in a spherical chamber about twelve feet across. There was no way out other than the one he'd accidentally made. What the hell could have made this, just below the surface of the ground, so that his weight as he walked across it would cause it to cave in? Was it a trap? He spun round, heart thumping, but he saw quickly that there was no one and nothing in here but himself. He tried jumping out, but the grass-fringed hole was too far above to reach. He calmed down, and tried to reason out what he'd fallen into. Could it be the den of some weird creature? If it was, where was said creature? Perhaps it was a natural phenomenon – soil erosion? He was no expert on geology. Perhaps the Doctor would know.

At least it was cool down here. Fitz touched the curving wall; it was only slightly damp.

At length Fitz heard footsteps from above, and a strange scraping noise. 'Are you still there?' came the Doctor's voice.

Another stupid question. The Doctor had to be joking. 'No, I've gone shopping.'

Something brushed against the opening of the hole. There was a metallic scraping noise and a succession of metal bars passed over the hole. It took Fitz a moment or so to work out that the Doctor was sliding a ladder across. Of course, if the Doctor walked over the top the whole thing would cave in and they would both be trapped – he was using the ladder to distribute his weight.

The Doctor's head appeared between the rungs, his face in darkness, his brown hair made golden by the sun. 'Hello!' he said. 'I'm – oops!'

Fitz crouched into a ball and covered his head with his arms as Doctor, ladder and an avalanche of soil and turf fell on top of him.

When he opened his eyes it was to see the Doctor, head downward and feet pointing up into the sky, still clinging on to the ladder, the top of which was rather conveniently resting on the lip of what was now a bowl-shaped crater. The ceiling of the spherical hole had completely collapsed.

Fitz clapped slowly and, he hoped, sardonically.

The Doctor scrambled off the ladder. 'Not quite what I had in mind.' He walked up the ladder. Fitz followed quickly. He looked back down into the hole, which was now a crater big enough to park a car in.

The Doctor grimaced. 'Hope the farmer's a reasonable fellow.'

Fitz brushed bits of dirt from his hair. 'What could have caused it?'

The Doctor shrugged. 'Don't know. One of the things strewn in our way to annoy us, I suppose.' He smiled. 'A metaphor for our predicament – we're in a hole, a very deep one.' His face became sad and he gazed back towards the forest. 'A very deep one indeed.'

They stood in silence for a while, as a welcome cool breeze ruffled the grass and played over their faces.

Then the Doctor said, 'Come on, we'd better take the ladder back to the farm. There's no one there, by the way, so we'll have to forgo tea.'

Fitz felt a sinking feeling of disappointment as they walked up to the farm. From the looks of it, it really was in the back of beyond. The farmhouse itself was small and square, almost too cute and perfect. It was wooden, painted rust-red, and its quaint little windows sported white-painted shutters. It looked ridiculously small; why have such a tiny place with all this land? Probably to conserve heat in the freezing winters, he reasoned.

The Doctor leaned the ladder against the wall. 'Perhaps they're working in those barns down there,' he muttered, pointing down the slope, to where a cluster of farm buildings bordered a courtyard. They walked down the sloping gardens, the Doctor still irritatingly cool-looking. Fitz was already drenched in sweat.

'Hello!' cried the Doctor. 'Anyone at home?'

His voice vanished into the heat and brightness of the sun. Fitz squinted and shaded his eyes. No doubt about it, the place was totally deserted. Just great.

He turned and walked back up the slope towards the farmhouse. The area around the house was littered with bits of machinery, boxes, wheelbarrows and junk. There was a wired-off chicken coop containing some threadbare hens. The whole place had an unsettling air of loneliness.

Fitz followed a gravel path to the back of the house, which was shaded by a copse of fir trees, growing apart from the main body of the forest. Parked on a wide gravel driveway was a shiny red car. It looked futuristic to Fitz, like something out of a Dan Dare strip – all smooth curves, with no extraneous parts. But as he looked he could see it was a logical extension of the vehicles he was used to in his own time.

Furthermore, its presence meant that there could be somebody around.

The entrance to the farmhouse was through a small glass conservatory. Fitz tried the door, hammering on the peeling green paint, but there was no response.

He sighed.

Back in the coolness of the shade, he took out his cigarette lighter and Camels. He lit up, leaning against the bonnet of the car.

He took a few puffs, and felt instantly relaxed. He closed his eyes, trying not to think of Sam spiralling away down that impossible whirlpool. But it was no use. The guilt wouldn't go away. He could have saved her, if he'd –

The sound of footsteps crunching on gravel interrupted his thoughts. He opened his eyes to see the Doctor standing before him, hands on hips.

'What are you doing, Fitz?'

Fitz felt like a schoolboy caught smoking behind the bike sheds by the headmaster. Indeed, at that moment the Doctor did resemble a rather cross schoolteacher. 'Having a smoke.'

The Doctor frowned.

'Helps me relax,' Fitz added lamely.

The Doctor opened his mouth as if he was about to deliver an anti-smoking rant. Then he seemed to think better of it and held up his hands. 'Whatever helps, Fitz. Right now I could do with a cup of tea. Does the same thing for me.' He flashed a smile.

'Come on, we've got to find the nearest town.'

Fitz was reluctant to leave the shade. He patted the bonnet of the car. 'We could use this.'

The Doctor shook his head. 'No, we couldn't. Stealing would only land us in trouble with the local police.'

'So what are we going to do?'

'Walk!' said the Doctor brightly. 'Can't be far.'

Fitz sighed. 'Bet it's bloody miles,' he muttered, and then set off after the Doctor.

As it turned out, they didn't have to walk far at all. The rough track led to a tarmac road, which in turn gave on to a wide dual carriageway. Rather fortunately, a steel-grey bus was waiting at a stop, and they boarded it gratefully.

Fitz hung back, let the Doctor do all the talking.

The bus driver, a young blond-haired chap in a sleeveless shirt, spoke English, and the Doctor ascertained that they were in Sweden, some fifty miles west of Stockholm. There was a bit of bother about paying their fare; luckily, the Doctor found a couple of ten-krona notes scrunched up with some other items of currency in his waistcoat pocket. Fitz half suspected that the Doctor's pockets had TARDIS-like attributes.

As Fitz boarded he noticed the driver give them a funny look. He smiled back, thinking that he'd better get used to funny looks – probably wouldn't be the last he got today. He joined the Doctor at the back of the bus, and they set off along the dual carriageway.

From peering at a newspaper the passenger in front was reading, Fitz saw that the date was 31 July 1999.

So he was in the future. Sam's time, near enough.

They got off at the first town, Strängnäs, and went to a small café off one of the narrow cobbled streets. The Doctor's money bought them sandwiches, cakes and tea.

Fitz was feeling out of place. As well as being over three decades in his future, Sweden was a country he had never visited and knew little of. He couldn't speak a word of Swedish.

Usually, the TARDIS telepathic circuits would translate – but not this time. The TARDIS was too badly damaged. Fortunately, so the Doctor said, almost all Swedes spoke English as a second language. Well that was certainly a relief.

Fitz gulped down a mouthful of rye bread. It was question time. 'What do you think is going on? I mean, that alien insect. And that hole I fell into. What would that have to do with what happened to the TARDIS? To Sam?'

The Doctor's eyes grew distant-looking. 'When you've travelled as far and as wide as I have, Fitz, then you'll begin to see the beauty and the delicate sadness of the interconnectedness of all things.' He spoke quickly, whispering, leaning across the table towards Fitz. 'Everything that has happened since this morning is all part of some plan, some scheme, some terrible course of events that we're smack bang in the middle of.'

Despite the oppressive heat, Fitz felt a chill. He looked around the café, at its pale-cream walls and dark oak furniture, the other customers in their summer clothes. It all looked normal, but a sense of dislocation crept over him as so often happened when travelling with the Doctor. 'How do you know?'

'Believe me, I know.'

There was a hard edge to the Doctor's voice. Fitz knew the Doctor well enough to know that he could pretend that things weren't affecting him, but the plight of the TARDIS and Sam was obviously taking its toll.

The Doctor put down his cup, smiling widely, his mood changing in an instant. 'That was a splendid cup of tea.' The simple things in life always seemed to please him. 'Come on, let's find the best hotel in town!'

There was a problem with this, thought Fitz. 'Have you got any more money?'

'Er, no,' said the Doctor as he opened the door of the café. 'But we'll work around that,' he added airily.

Back outside, the summer heat hit Fitz again. Strängnäs was a picturesque, tranquil, lakeside town. The buildings were immaculate, with orange-red tiled roofs, pastel or white walls, and tiny square windows. They all had a similarity to each other, as if the whole town had been designed by one architect. But Strängnäs, the Doctor told him, was a very old town, with roots in the pagan history of Sweden.

The most impressive feature, in Fitz's eyes, was the red-brick tower which loomed over the town from the top of a small rise. Black birds, probably crows, fluttered around it and Fitz could see dozens of them perched on dark windowsills.

They walked along a street lined with shops, banks and cafés. At the end was a busy lakeside marina, a boat trip just setting off. A conical red-brick windmill peered out from behind the houses at the water's edge.

And on the other side of the street Fitz saw Sam.

He stopped dead, hardly believing it. Sam. She was alive, she was *here*!

She was getting into the passenger seat of an orange farm truck. It was parked outside a rather severe-looking red-brick building and was revving up to go.

Fitz ran across the road, dodging traffic, yelling Sam's name. He was vaguely aware of the Doctor shouting, but he kept on running as the truck pulled away. But Sam hadn't seen him, and soon it had disappeared around the corner of the street.

Fitz stood in the middle of the road, panting, his shirt sticking to his back with sweat.

He felt a hand on his shoulder. 'I'm sure that was her, Doctor,' he muttered, but when he turned round it was to see that the owner of the hand was an unsmiling police officer.

Fitz put on his best, most disarming grin. 'Sorry, officer. Thought she was a friend of mine.'

The officer said something in Swedish and Fitz allowed himself to be led gently towards the building the van had been parked outside.

The Doctor suddenly appeared by his side, right up close to Fitz. 'Are you sure that was Sam?'

Fitz nodded. But was he? He'd seen a girl with blonde hair.

Not uncommon, especially in this country.'No.'

The officer led them both into the station.'Like it or not, we're going to have to explain ourselves now,' said the Doctor, a note of resignation in his voice. Then he brightened. 'But this could be the very place we want to be.'

Fitz frowned. 'How do you mean?'

'Well if anything odd is going on, then the police are the most likely people to know anything about it.'

Not in Fitz's experience, but then, these were the police of a foreign country three decades into his future. Efficiency and integrity may well be their watchwords.

Inspector Bengt Nordenstam finished his fifth cup of coffee of the day, and wished he'd had something substantial for lunch. He sat in the office of the District Chief of Police in Strängnäs. The District Chief himself had gone back to the farm with Andersson and the girl. Leaving him with the thing they'd found. It was in the mortuary now, stinking out the place. He tried not to think about it, and turned his attention to the laptop computer on the desk in front of him. He was in the middle of writing a report to the State Criminological Laboratory in Stockholm. A report on what was already being called the Strängnäs Incident: the disappearance of six local people. Well, six and a half – but Nordenstam tried not to think about the half.

The flickering screen seemed to be taunting him. However hard he tried, he couldn't make any sense of the disappearances. No crime had been committed, he was sure of that. This was no kidnapping, or the work of a serial killer.

So what was it?

One of the local officers had already suggested alien abductions. Nordenstam had immediately put him on filing duty. He wasn't going to have any of that talk. Ten years in the Criminal Investigation Department of the Swedish State Police Board had instilled in him a trust that was close to love in two things: empirical evidence and justice. You can't argue with empirical evidence, with the facts; in a world that was accelerating towards the millennium with more and more bizarre and motiveless crimes taking place even here in rural Sweden, Nordenstam found comfort in facts. Facts were the basis of justice. If you could prove a felon had done a thing, then he had done it, and that was that. Lack of evidence, of proof, was an irritation to Bengt Nordenstam.

But this case, which had dragged him from the city a week before his annual holiday in Greece, was different. So different from the usual saddening toll of suicides, murders, alcohol-fuelled fights, feuds, vandalism, theft and drug addiction which were becoming more and more commonplace these days. The facts were there, yes, but they didn't mean anything. Six inexplicable disappearances. And now the equally inexplicable appearance of a creature that looked as though it had hopped from the screen of the latest Hollywood special-effects showcase. Only this beast was real.

So did this evidence point to the world of the paranormal? He couldn't believe it. He wanted no part in the cult of the unexplained. That was for the craven and the credulous. And he was neither. Everything could be explained.

A nagging voice in his mind whispered: but could it?

He offered up a silent prayer: please, God, let the disappearances have a rational explanation. Let the creature be a very clever prank, a chimera made somehow by medical students from Uppsala with too much time and soft drugs on their hands. Please. He could handle that. It was, if not rational or excusable, at least explicable.

He typed a word into his laptop, but the word was nothing to do with the case.

There was a knock on the door. Nordenstam quickly deleted the word on the screen. Must be seen to be professional at all times. 'Come in.'

A young local officer opened the door and popped his head round. 'Sir, there's been an incident outside the station.'

Nordenstam sat up straight, instantly alert, trying to remember the officer's name. 'What sort of incident?'

The young officer – Karl Hansson, that was it – stuttered slightly as he answered. 'Nothing – nothing strange, sir; a disturbance of the peace. Two tourists. They say their friend's gone missing.'

Nordenstam stood up, scraping his chair across the floor. Not another disappearance. He slipped on his jacket over his shirt to hide the sweat marks under his arms, and followed Hansson along the corridor to the front desk.

There, waiting patiently, were the two men Hansson had been talking about. The one on the left was tall and gangly, clad in a loose white shirt. His face was sullen and distrustful. A student, maybe from Uppsala, down for the holidays like the Bergman girl and her unfortunate fiancé? There was something odd about him, as though he were deliberately following the fashion of twenty-odd years ago.

His companion was sporting an even stranger get-up, his clothes seemingly aping the style fashionable Stockholmers were wearing at around the turn of the century. He had the face and attitude of a film star: wide blue eyes alive with intelligence, an aquiline nose and a sensitive mouth.

Nordenstam was instantly on his guard. This had all the hallmarks of a practical joke, and Nordenstam didn't have time for that. He stepped up to the counter and immediately took control of the situation. 'Good afternoon, gentlemen. I'm Inspector Bengt Nordenstam of the Criminal Investigations Board. What can I do for you?'

'That rather depends,' said the well-groomed man in English. 'I am the Doctor and this is my friend Fitz Kreiner.'

Nordenstam raised his eyebrows. 'Doctor? Doctor what?' he said, also in English.

The 'Doctor' waved his hand in a dismissive gesture. 'Doesn't matter.' He leaned against the counter, staring straight at Nordenstam. 'Who was the young lady who recently left this station?'

Nordenstam tried once more to assert his authority. 'I think I should be asking the questions.'

'What was her name?' said the scruffy fellow. He looked quite distressed. Under the influence of something? 'Was it Samantha Jones?'

An English name. 'It was not.'

Fitz swore and looked crestfallen. The Doctor patted his shoulder.

Nordenstam exchanged a glance with Hansson. He was probably thinking the same thing. Nutters. Publicity seekers. The best tactic would be to humour them, trick them into revealing what they were really after. 'Is that the name of your missing friend?'

'Yes,' said the Doctor. 'Yes it is. She went missing in the forest.' He exchanged a glance with Fitz and Nordenstam intuitively knew that he'd made it up on the spot, said the first thing that had come into his head. Perhaps they knew more about the disappearances than they were letting on.

He motioned for Hansson to open the hatch in the desk and let them through. 'I think we'd better continue this conversation privately.'

Once they were all seated in an interview room, Nordenstam felt more comfortable, more in control. He could observe the pair more closely, assess them. The scruffy one, Fitz Kreiner, was nervous and truculent. The Doctor seemed completely at ease.

'You realise the seriousness of what you're saying? Reporting a missing person when six others have already vanished?'

'Yes, yes, yes,' said the Doctor. 'Now can you tell me about the other disappearances? Was anything strange witnessed at the scene – flashing lights, strange, erm...'

'Whirlpools in the air?' added Fitz tentatively.

Nordenstam shifted in his seat. How could they know this? 'The husband of one of the victims reported a flash, like lightning.'

The Doctor frowned. 'Unusual.'

Nordenstam felt a rush of anger. Of course it was unusual. 'I think you'd better tell me exactly who you are, and about the disappearance of Miss Jones.'

Fitz frowned. 'Are we under arrest?'

'Of course not,' Nordenstam said coolly, noting the young man's guilty tone of voice.

The Doctor told Nordenstam that Samantha Jones was an English tourist staying in Stockholm. A week ago, she'd gone on a trip to Strängnäs and went for a hike in the forest with her friend. She hadn't come back, and her friend had reported a strange glowing tunnel in the air.

'And what is your connection with Miss Jones?'

'No special connection,' said the Doctor airily. Nordenstam did not miss Fitz's reaction to this – he blinked rapidly and looked down at his lap.

He then knew that everything the Doctor had said was a lie. If anyone had gone missing, then the district police would have heard of it. 'Now come on, Doctor. You come in here, reporting the disappearance of an English tourist, and then claim to have no connection with her?' He glanced from Fitz to the Doctor. 'Is she special to one of you?'

'She's special to both of us,' said the Doctor sharply.

Fitz put his head in his hands and groaned.

Nordenstam couldn't help but smile. 'Gentlemen, it is not for me to intrude, but you must appreciate that I do need to know more about your... connection with the missing person.'

'It's not what you think,' said Fitz, rather defensively. 'She's a friend.'

'Of course. And how am I to know that you had nothing to do with her disappearance?'

Fitz sighed in exasperation. 'This is getting us nowhere.'

The Doctor leaned forward across the table between them. 'Would it smooth the way if I told you that we're investigators from UNIT, the United Nations Intelligence Taskforce?' He sat back, grinning widely.

Nordenstam had never heard of UNIT, and said so.

If this fazed the Doctor he didn't show it. 'You may not have heard of us. We don't exactly advertise our services. No recruitment drives, no adverts in cinemas, none of that. We were set up to deal exclusively with unexplained or extraterrestrial phenomena. I'm their scientific adviser and Fitz is my assistant. We were sent here specifically to investigate the disappearances.'

The unexplained. Nordenstam gritted his teeth. He clung to the facts. 'But the first disappearance happened in the small hours of this morning. How could you have possibly heard of it?'

'Miss Jones vanished a week ago,' said the Doctor. 'We've been hereabouts ever since. We tried to keep it quiet, but now that six more people have vanished we decided to come in and help the police.' The Doctor smiled, as if he'd solved everything.

If only he could, thought Nordenstam. 'So how did you get to hear about the disappearance of Miss Jones?'

The Doctor and Fitz exchanged a glance. Nordenstam watched them narrowly.

'Sam Jones wasn't really a tourist. She was – she is – a UNIT operative investigating UFO activity around this area,' said the Doctor.

Nordenstam frowned. 'I haven't heard about that.'

'You wouldn't,' said Fitz. 'We've tried to keep the whole thing quiet.'

Nordenstam shook his head. How could they expect him to believe any of this? Where was the evidence? He was beginning to get a floating feeling in his stomach, a feeling he'd learned to trust, a feeling he always got when people were trying to deceive him. 'This is the talk of fantasists. Of hoaxers!' He realised he was shouting. 'How can you expect me to believe any of what you're saying?'

The Doctor leaned across the table and Nordenstam was struck by the look in his eyes, a compelling look of absolute authority. 'Inspector, people have gone missing and you can't explain it. Before the day is out I have a very, very, very strong feeling that you're going to have to start believing things that previously you would never have even considered possible.'

Nordenstam blinked, and passed a hand in front of his face. Hot in here. He mustn't let these weirdos get to him. But who were they really? What was UNIT? There was one thing he could do – there was one thing they had to have by law, and if they didn't produce them he could lock them up and never have to look into the Doctor's eyes again. 'Have you any ID? Proof of the existence of this UNIT?'

The Doctor began delving into his pockets. Nordenstam tensed; of course, he should have searched them – but the Doctor produced nothing more threatening than a laminated pass, sliding it across the desk towards him. 'That's my UNIT pass – the picture on it is a bit out of date, I'm afraid.'

The picture was of a completely different person – a dignified-looking man with a shock of white hair.

'Get that checked,' he said, handing the pass to Hansson, utterly confident that it would be bogus. Then he would have reason to arrest them.

The Doctor called out after Hansson. 'You need to contact Brigadier Winifred Bambera, in Geneva, or her replacement.'

'Got that?' said Nordenstam, suppressing a grin. He had the upper hand again.

'I don't know why you're smirking,' said the Doctor, his face set. 'I'm deadly serious.' He leaned back, narrowing his eyes, a smile playing across his lips. 'The investigation isn't going well, is it? You have no idea what's causing the disappearances. Am I right?'

Nordenstam should have been angered by this, but the Doctor's low, hushed tones, his compelling eyes, drew him in – but not totally. 'Neither do you.'

The Doctor shook his head. 'No. I don't know. But I can make some pretty shrewd guesses.'

'And…?'

'I conclude that we're all in dire danger.'

'Really.'

Nordenstam massaged his temples with his fingers. The day had taken a wild and unexpected turn. He turned to Fitz, so that he didn't have to look at the Doctor. 'And what have you got to say?'

Fitz sniffed and shrugged. 'Nothing. Only that, if anything weird *is* going on, we're your best hope.'

Nordenstam had had enough. This was getting him nowhere.

Then Hansson opened the door without knocking. His young face showed a trace of excitement. 'Sir, I've faxed the UN. The Doctor's story checks out. There is an outfit called UNIT, and they do have a scientific adviser called the Doctor.' He handed the pass back to Nordenstam, then left the room.

Nordenstam slid the pass towards the Doctor. 'How do you explain this photograph?'

The Doctor frowned. 'How do you mean?'

Nordenstam sighed. 'Well, it's not you, is it? I think you're an impostor. Where did you get this pass from?'

The Doctor slammed his fist down on the table, rising from his chair. 'There's no time for this! You've got to trust me!'

'Sit down!' barked Nordenstam. 'Do you realise the trouble you're in? Masquerading as a UN official?'

The Doctor sat down, glowering. 'I'm not masquerading. I am the Doctor.'

'You must believe him,' said Fitz.

There was a knock at the door. 'Come in,' said Nordenstam.

It was Hansson again, with a thick buff folder. He placed it on the desk. 'The photographs, sir.'

Nordenstam's pulse quickened. At last, they were here. Pictures of the scenes of the disappearances. Perhaps if he showed them to this Doctor and his friend, they would be prompted to confess. He reached across and opened the file. Black-and-white photos spilled out over the desk.

The Doctor and Fitz hunched over the desk, examining the photographs.

One showed a wooden cabin, its front half missing, the interior revealed like a doll's house with the front removed. A shallow crater was scooped out of the earth.

Another showed a house, its side sliced away. There was a pair of legs in the middle of the room, sliced off just above the knee.

Nordenstam sighed wearily. 'Olla Wenberg. Married with three daughters.'

The Doctor's face crumpled. 'Terrible, terrible.'

'What do you think is causing this?' muttered Fitz.

The Doctor sighed. 'Could be any number of things. Luckily it's fairly localised at present. Something is going round taking chunks out of reality.'

'Like that hole I fell into.'

'Chunks out of reality,' muttered Nordenstam wearily. 'Is that your conclusion?'

The Doctor shook his head. 'I need more evidence.'

Nordenstam considered. If the Doctor really was from UNIT, really was used to dealing with the paranormal, the unexplained, then he was just what Nordenstam needed. And if he was involved with, or responsible for, the disappearances, Nordenstam didn't want to let him out of his sight.

He stood up, beckoning for the Doctor and Fitz to follow him. 'You want more evidence? Follow me.'

Fitz stared down at the dead creature, lying on a tarpaulin in the station's tiny mortuary. It was a mess, and it stank of rotting seaweed. He could make out the head: savage teeth in a circular mouth. It had a round, compact body, covered in black spines, and powerful hind legs. 'Looks like a kangaroo crossed with a cactus,' mumbled Fitz.

'Chupacabra?' said the Doctor, making tutting noises. 'No, no, no. A mutation?' His face was alive with interest, for the first time since they'd left the TARDIS. 'Where did you find our dead friend?'

'On a local farm. The farmer killed it while it was attacking his livestock.'

The Doctor bent to examine it, not the least put off by the smell. 'It's definitely alien,' said the Doctor.

'You think it could be chums with that dragonfly thing we saw in the forest?' wondered Fitz aloud.

Nordenstam looked sharply at him. 'You saw something? Another like this?'

The Doctor shook his head. 'No. An airborne creature, like a large insect.'

Nordenstam's square, lined face was creased in a mask of mixed incomprehension and bemusement, an expression Fitz was getting used to seeing on his travels with the Doctor. The 'either-you're-mad-or-I-am' look.

'Are you sure it's alien?' Nordenstam obviously wanted a rational explanation but it looked like there wasn't going to be one.

'Yes,' said the Doctor. 'Things are worse than I thought.' He grew silent, tapping his lips with his fingers.

'Well?' said Nordenstam,

The Doctor clapped his hands together. 'I think that the boundary between our dimension and another is breaking down. And I think it's being done deliberately. The disappearances, and the sudden appearance of alien creatures like this, are just the start. This has the hallmark of a full-scale alien invasion.'

Hang on, thought Fitz. That was jumping to conclusions rather too quickly. 'Can you be sure?' he said doubtfully.

The Doctor was pacing about, waving his hands in the air as if shaking drops of water from his fingertips. 'It all makes sense. What happened to the TARDIS - they tried to kill me first because they knew I could stop them!'

'But they got Sam instead.' The thought of Sam at the mercy of such creatures was too horrible to contemplate. Fitz contemplated it anyway, and felt racked with guilt. If he'd never argued with Sam. If he'd got to her room earlier. If, if, if.

The Doctor spoke, breaking into his thoughts. 'Inspector Nordenstam, I want you to take me to where this creature was found right now. We haven't got a moment to lose!'

Chapter Five
Missing People

Fitz lifted the lid of the wood bunker warily. Taking a deep breath, he threw the heavy rubber cover back so it bounced on the rust-coloured side of the farmhouse. He stepped back quickly. Nothing emerged. He peered inside.

It was bare except for a few logs, fluttering skeins of spiders' webs, and a sour, damp smell. There – a movement. But it was only a shiny black spider scuttling out of sight beneath a log, hiding from the sunlight that had invaded its dank domain.

Fitz slammed the lid back down, licking his lips. He was desperately thirsty, and dying for a smoke. The two desires warred within him. Should he go into the farmhouse for some water, or hang around here and have a quick drag?

He was on the brink of a decision when Inspector Nordenstam came round the side of the farmhouse, his face set. Nordenstam was a tall, fit-looking man in his fifties, with tanned skin, grey hair and a salt-and-pepper moustache. His suit and tie were a soft pastel grey which reflected the sunlight brightly. Fitz's heart sank to see him. It was proving to be quite an effort, keeping up the pretence of being a UNIT operative. Fitz's imagination kept throwing up unhelpful images of rainy streets, tall men in long coats waiting near railway stations, exchanging packages and talking in code. Too many spy films.

Like Nordenstam, Fitz had never heard of UNIT before today. Just another reminder of how little he still knew about the Doctor. It didn't help that Nordenstam kept up an almost ceaseless flow of questions. Fitz had parried most of these by saying that UNIT's operations were top secret. The inspector had accepted this with a raised eyebrow and a twitch of his moustache, which made Fitz suspect that Nordenstam was stringing him along, waiting for him to make a big mistake.

Nordenstam noticed Fitz and shaded his eyes. 'Found anything?'

Fitz shook his head. 'Nope. But I wasn't really expecting to.'

He had agreed to help Nordenstam and the local police search the farm, for want of anything else to do.

Nordenstam slapped the side of the farmhouse. 'Nor have I, nor any of the others.'

Fitz wished the Doctor would turn up. Since returning to the farm over an hour ago, the Doctor had been dashing off all over the place, taking soil samples, generally behaving like a manic one-man whirlwind. Good to see him keeping busy, but he was little help to Fitz right now.

'I'd rather not come across any more of those creatures, though,' said Fitz, with heartfelt relief.

Nordenstam picked up on this instantly. 'Why not? I thought you UNIT people were used to such things. Besides which, we're armed.' Nordenstam opened his jacket to reveal a jet-black pistol snug in a calfskin holster.

'Well, I'm not,' said Fitz, spreading his arms to show the lack of weapon. 'We UNIT operatives prefer to use wits and diplomacy.'

Nordenstam shook his head in obvious wonderment. 'Even against senseless beasts? Come on, let's go inside and get something to drink.'

He turned and headed into the farmhouse.

There was a sudden machine-gun clatter overhead – a helicopter. Fitz ducked instinctively, but there was no need – it was way overhead, its rotors a blur against the blue sky.

Nordenstam let out a long, sighing breath. 'They're still searching for the missing people. I just hope they're successful.'

As they reached the door of the house, it opened and a tall, blonde girl in a yellow T-shirt and shorts came out, stopping short at the sight of them.

Fitz couldn't stop himself from gaping. This must be the girl he had mistaken for Sam, but on closer inspection she was nothing like her. Taller, more muscled, her skin tanned a glossy brown. Her eyes were blue, like Sam's, though somehow different – smaller, and with fine blonde lashes which looked almost white in the sunlight. Her mouth was a lot smaller than Sam's, the lips darker and fuller. She met his stare with a cool expression of defiance.

Fitz felt the first stirrings of lust. 'Hello,' he said, putting on his best smile.

She brushed past them, carrying herself like an athlete.

She must have seen the look in his eyes. He instantly felt guilty. Fancying someone at a time like this? Still, he couldn't help it. It was human nature. His nature. 'What's her problem?'

Nordenstam's features hardened slightly. 'Her fiancé is one of the missing people. That's her "problem". And ours. We –' There was a sudden, insistent bleeping from inside his jacket, and Fitz watched as he produced a sleek, black oblong of plastic. He pressed a button – one of many on the front of the thing – and spoke into it in Swedish.

Must be a phone, realised Fitz. A phone without a cord? Well, this was the future…

Fitz watched as Nordenstam's tanned, lined face slowly broke into an expression of total astonishment. Fitz could hear the voice at the other end of the line, an excited babble. Nordenstam said something in Swedish and then put the phone away.

He looked at Fitz, his eyes wide. 'They've found something. In the forest.'

Fitz gulped. Could it be Sam? 'One of the missing people?'

Nordenstam shook his head. 'No. Nothing like that, though I wish it was. Come on – this should be your area of expertise.'

Nordenstam set off at a run towards his vehicle, a big jeeplike thing, sleek and powerful-looking. Fitz was used to cars with things sticking out of them, shiny metal radiator grilles and goggling headlights. Nordenstam's vehicle, a dark fir-green affair with matt-black radiators and bumpers, looked to Fitz so advanced that he wouldn't be surprised if it could fly.

He hauled himself up on to the passenger seat beside Nordenstam. The vehicle chugged into life and they set off along the road that ran under the timber store. Fitz craned round in his seat, hoping to catch a glimpse of the Doctor, but there was no sign of him. Where was he? Had he gone back to check on the state of the TARDIS?

The TARDIS. Perhaps that was what they had found.

'Are you all right?' said Nordenstam. 'You look a bit pale.'

'I'm fine,' answered Fitz. What if they had found the TARDIS? What would the Doctor say if Fitz managed to get the TARDIS taken away? His need for a smoke intensified.

Björn aimed the hose at the concrete pen, sluicing out the last remains of the slaughtered pigs. The police had taken away what was left of their bodies for analysis. The rest of the pigs were curiously quiet. Björn could sense their fear.

The concrete washed clear of blood, Björn laid the hose on the side of the pen and went to the tap to turn it off. The back of his thigh still hurt, he felt light-headed and his eyes ached, thanks to the whisky he'd been drinking all morning. Well, it helped him deal with things.

Björn went along the pens, stopping at each one and stroking the pigs, muttering comforting words. There would be no monsters tonight. They were safe. At least, he hoped they were safe. He picked up a young piglet, scarcely two weeks old, and held the little life in his large hands. It squealed and its trotters scraped against his shirt, so he put it back down with its mother.

He straightened up painfully, massaging his aching back. Some pains even whisky couldn't soothe. He looked down at the piglet. It had wormed its way between its litter-mates, snuggled against its mother, its wet mouth closing around a teat. So safe. What he wouldn't give, sometimes, to be in such a state of blissful ignorance. Ignorant of loss. Ignorant of how life just goes on, and on. Ignorant of the realisation that pain doesn't go away as you get older, but becomes part of you, part of your personality, and there is nothing you can do about it.

As he stood there, he became aware of a figure standing in the doorway, a tall silhouette against the oblong of bright sunlight.

How long he had been there Björn could not tell. He squinted and stepped towards the new arrival.

'Hello, I'm the Doctor,' said the newcomer, in English. He walked further inside. 'How do you do?'

Björn didn't reply. He didn't like speaking English. He was of the opinion that visitors to his country should make at least some attempt to learn the language.

The stranger wandered up and down the pens. 'I see you take good care of your livestock.'

He was one of the police investigators, the one from the UN or whatever. Hadn't they bothered him enough?

Now he was inside the pen Björn could make out his odd old-fashioned clothes, his long brown hair and pale, intelligent face. Strange get-up for a policeman. Could he be in what they called 'plain-clothes' branch? But these clothes were hardly plain: they were like a theatrical costume. Whoever this Doctor was, he was more than he seemed. 'They need to be comforted,' said Björn defensively.

The Doctor leaned over the side of a pen to look at the pigs, his face alive with interest. 'Of course they do.' To Björn's incredulity, he began making little piggy 'oink-oink' noises.

'Look,' said Björn, feeling uncomfortable in the presence of an obvious madman, as not even he, who loved his pigs, made 'oink-oink' noises. 'What do you *want*?'

The stranger stood up and faced Björn. His long, handsome face was scarred with confusion, his eyes wistful and distant. 'What do I want?'

Björn felt his temper rising. 'Yes, what do you want? You've taken the bodies away, I've told you what happened, you've got the thing that did this. What more could you possibly want?'

The Doctor didn't seem to have heard a word he was saying. He stood, staring into a dark corner of the pen, seemingly oblivious of everything. 'I want her back,' he whispered.

Björn was instantly on his guard. Those words formed the very core of his own being. He looked at the Doctor with fresh suspicion, and not a little fear. 'What did you say?'

The Doctor stepped up to Björn, reached out and grabbed him by the shoulders. He talked quickly, quietly, his voice a whisper, his eyes gleaming in the gloom, his words stabbing like a knife of ice into Björn's heart. 'You've lost someone close to you. I can sense it. It was an accident. You live in such pain, blaming and torturing yourself. You know what it's like and I think I'm going through the same thing. You see, my best friend's gone missing and I think she might be dead and –' The Doctor stepped back with a sharp intake of breath, his hand flying to his mouth. 'I'm sorry. I'm so sorry. Sometimes I just can't help myself.'

Björn was finding it difficult to breathe: there was a pain in his chest and he badly wanted to be away from this madman. 'What are you talking about?'

The Doctor apologised again. 'It's my friend, Sam. She's vanished, gone. I'm not dealing with it too well.'

Björn thought of Kerstin, sitting inside the farmhouse, refusing to be consoled about the loss of Johan. What was it the police had told him? Five other people had vanished. No one Björn was close to, but then he rarely spoke to anyone these days. And now this Doctor's friend. That would explain his odd behaviour. He didn't like to think how he had been, in the days, weeks and months after Nina's death. 'That sort of thing is never easy to deal with.'

The Doctor nodded, and just stood there, head bowed.

Björn wanted to console him, but he knew there was nothing he could say because he had been there himself. He sighed. Whatever was going on was creating ripples like a stone being thrown into a still, silent pond. And, like it or not, he was at the centre, right where the stone had landed.

But something else was bothering him. 'How do you know that I've lost someone? Did Kerstin tell you?

The Doctor frowned. 'No, no, no, she didn't tell me. I don't fully know. I get flashes, insights into people's lives.' He stepped closer to Björn, his face now animated, compassionate. 'You really should forgive yourself. You're going to live for many years yet and you shouldn't spend them consumed with regret and remorse.'

'Do you think I don't know that?' said Björn, realising that his voice was shaking. 'But I don't know how to forgive myself.'

'How did it happen?' said the Doctor.

Björn hadn't spoken about what happened to Nina for years. Amazingly, he felt he could open up to this complete stranger. Something about him made Björn trust in him totally. So he stood there in the darkness, the warm smell of the pigs in the air, and told the Doctor how Nina had died.

There wasn't much to say. A few words was all it took to convey the pointless horror of his wife's death.

'A shotgun,' Björn said, his voice dull. 'Backfired. She died instantly. My fault. Should have checked it.'

The Doctor's face had hardened into a pale mask. 'A gun?' he said, spitting the word out. Björn nodded. 'But you shot the creature,' said the Doctor slowly. 'You used the gun. That's what you told the police.'

Björn was confused again. What was he driving at?

'I – I had to kill it. It was trying to kill me, for God's sake!'

The Doctor winced. 'Of course you did. I'm sorry.'

They stood awkwardly for a moment. Björn suddenly had a feeling akin to being lost in the forest as a child, and then suddenly finding himself in a part he recognised. A feeling of mixed relief, and disappointment that the adventure of being lost was over. Shaking his head and rubbing his eyes, he composed himself. 'What *did* you want in here?'

The Doctor waved his hands in the air in a vague gesture. 'Oh, only to see where that creature was found.' He sighed. 'It doesn't matter. There aren't any more of the things. We can at least be grateful for that.'

Björn motioned for the Doctor to leave. 'I'm not used to visitors – my hospitality is a little rusty – but you can have some coffee and something to eat, if you go to the house.'

'I'd rather have tea,' said the Doctor, smiling sadly. 'Coffee gets my hearts racing.'

He turned and walked from the pen.

Left alone, Björn felt a sadness well up inside him until his face crumpled and he began to cry. He crouched down on to the floor and let the sobs come. What had the Doctor said? 'You're going to live for many years yet…' The words had chilled him, made him see the long lonely road stretching out ahead of him. And at the end? Suddenly, Björn found himself laughing, laughing at himself, seeing how absurd it was to think in this way. He suddenly grasped that he was master of his destiny, that he could shake free of the past, if only he could try.

He stood up, yawned, and walked out into the sunshine. It was odd: at his core, he knew he was still miserable, still lonely and in pain, but there was an extra lightness to his step, and things looked brighter. He didn't know what the Doctor had done to him, if anything, but he felt… different. Things weren't so bad, after all. Johan would be found, and the Doctor's friend and the others, and then they'd all go away and leave him in peace again.

He limped up the hill to the farmhouse. He smiled as he remembered that he didn't have any tea, only coffee. Ah well. The Doctor deserved the best coffee he could make.

Fitz winced, and held on more tightly to the handle on the car door as they hit another pothole. They were driving along the same track he and the Doctor had walked earlier that day. The road was very bumpy and it didn't help that Nordenstam was driving like a man possessed. The jolting and juddering had already caused Fitz to bite his tongue. Nordenstam was keeping up a staccato dialogue with another officer via the radio in the vehicle.

They entered the woods. Fitz looked out of the window, hoping to catch a glimpse of the TARDIS. But the fir trees grew too close together – it was impossible to see further than a few yards.

They bounced and bumped for a mile or so, and then stopped as a white-shirted officer waved them down. They parked next to a police van. Nordenstam undid his seatbelt and got out.

Fitz fiddled with his seatbelt, listening to Nordenstam's urgent voice. Looking out of the window, he saw that the officer was the same one they'd met in the police station earlier: Hansson. He looked practically beside himself.

By the time Fitz had extricated himself from the seat belt, Nordenstam and Hansson were already striding into the forest. Fitz ran to catch up and followed as they crashed through the undergrowth.

Presently they came to the edge of a large clearing, about the size of a tennis court. Yellow police tape had been attached to the trees at the edge of the clearing, forming a makeshift arena. White-shirted officers were searching the undergrowth beyond.

'That's it,' said Hansson, pointing at the thing in the middle of the clearing.

Nordenstam stood with his hands on his hips, beads of sweat shining on his forehead. 'What the hell is that?' he whispered.

Fitz couldn't quite make out what it was. The central mass was a bright, vibrant life-jacket-orange, an hourglass-shape with open ends, about the size of a large van. Various fleshy tentacles and tubes trailed out of the bowl-shaped ends. At first glance Fitz thought it was a giant flower or fungus. Then he noticed that radiating out from the waist of the hourglass were six long, jointed, black legs, splayed and crooked in the undergrowth.

He became aware that both Nordenstam and Hansson were looking at him expectantly.

'You're the expert,' said Nordenstam. 'Or so you would have us believe. So tell me, Mr Kreiner, what exactly is that thing?'

Fitz had absolutely no idea. Where was the Doctor when you needed him? 'I'll have to go in for a closer look.' He ducked under the police tape, and walked up to the thing. Those legs were as thick as a man's arm and ten feet long. They ended in sharp six-pointed claws. On some of the tree trunks were deep gouges, where the creature must have flailed at them. In attack? Defence? Or just dying spasms? Fitz gingerly touched one of the legs. The edge was razor sharp and he drew his hand away hastily.

The central body was fleshy, rubbery, bent and buckled out of shape. Fitz's shoes were sticking to the forest floor – there was a clear liquid everywhere. It smelled pungent, like a bouquet of flowers thrust under the nose – a sickly, sweet smell which made Fitz gag.

Having seen enough, he walked back to Nordenstam and Hansson. What was he going to say? This was surely the acid test.

'Well, what do you think?' said Nordenstam, looking at Fitz expectantly.

'It's definitely alien,' said Fitz. 'But it's not like any species I have seen before.'

Hansson's eyes were boggling. 'You mean, not of this world?'

Fitz nodded. 'Yeah,' he said casually. 'All in a day's work for us UNIT chaps.'

Nordenstam sighed, evidently disappointed in Fitz.

The sound of an engine. Fitz looked back towards the road. Nordenstam's vehicle and the police van were just about visible through the trees. Pulling up next to them was a large, white, windowless van. At first Fitz thought nothing more of this, thinking it was another police truck, until he realised Nordenstam and Hansson were staring as well. A door opened in the back and figures in bulky white suits stepped out. There were about a dozen of them and they were carrying guns.

'More police, right?' said Fitz hopefully.

Nordenstam was frowning. 'No.'

The figures were getting closer, fanning out.

They wore all-enclosing suits of a shiny white material, the heads encased in silver helmets with inverted triangular faceplates. They were rounding up Nordenstam's men, sending them back to the police truck.

Nordenstam swore. He said something in Swedish and marched up to the leader of the strange figures.

'What's he saying?' Fitz whispered to Hansson.

There were about three guns – machine guns, Fitz noted with dread – trained on Nordenstam.

Hansson's eyes were wide with fear. 'He's telling them what an outrage this is and demanding to know who the hell they are.'

Great. It was fine to be righteously outraged, but not when someone was pointing a gun at you.

Fitz ran up to where Nordenstam was standing. He hoped the guys in suits could speak English. 'Hey, wait, I'm sure there's a peaceful way we can sort this out,' he said, aware that this was exactly what the Doctor would say.

The figure confronting Nordenstam spoke, his voice amplified through a grille below the triangular faceplate. 'You must leave the area. We are the State Biohazard Protection Unit. This is the site of an accident involving classified material. Please leave the area.'

All of Nordenstam's men were now being shepherded into the police van. Hansson, looking scared, complied with their request but Nordenstam stood his ground. 'State Biohazard Protection Unit?' He folded his arms. 'Well, I'm Inspector Nordenstam of the State Criminal Investigations Department and I have never heard of you.' His voice was shaking with anger. He gestured to Fitz. 'Perhaps, Mr Kreiner, this is something to do with you.'

Fitz saw a way out. 'I think it's best if we do as they say, Inspector – could be dangerous to stay around here.'

Nordenstam was quivering with indignation. 'We leave, then – but this is not the end of the matter.'

Nordenstam shoved past the figures, who stood aside. Fitz followed, his limbs moving jerkily, anxious to be away from these impassive figures, away from the machine guns.

Nordenstam got into his vehicle and slammed the door. He waited until the police van had left, and then started the engine.

Fitz looked back into the wood. The State Biohazard Protection Unit were standing like sentinels, guns held across their chests, watching as they drove away.

They drove in silence, Nordenstam uttering the occasional curse. Fitz could hardly blame him. Mysterious disappearances, alien creatures, and now interference by the government, so it seemed. Things were getting complicated. Out of control.

He had to find the Doctor. If the dead thing in the forest was the vanguard of an alien invasion, if there was a cover-up going on, if they had any chance of finding Sam, they had better stick together. Perhaps he should get out, go back to the TARDIS, see if the Doctor was there.

Then, suddenly, something white stumbled from the woods into the road in front of them.

'Look out!' yelled Fitz, and Nordenstam swerved just in time to avoid the man in the middle of the road.

Nordenstam brought the vehicle to a hasty stop and they both leapt out.

The man, who was totally naked and streaked with dirt, was walking away from them, swaying from side to side, oblivious to everything around him.

They ran to catch up with him. It wasn't difficult. He seemed to be operating at the extremes of exhaustion. As he saw them approach he went to run, but tripped over and fell, sprawling on the road. He just lay there, face down, screaming and scrabbling at the dried mud.

Fitz bent down and touched him on the shoulders, but he writhed away, yelling incoherent words. Yeuch. He stank: the same overpowering scent as the dead thing.

The man rolled over. His face was a grimace, a knot of pain and terror. He was younger than Fitz, with blue eyes and black hair. The hair was plastered to his head and the eyes were crazed, unseeing.

Fitz felt a rising sense of panic. What could they do? He remembered Nordenstam's little cordless phone. 'Call an ambulance!'

Nordenstam shook his head. 'There's no time. We'll have to take him.'

The man's struggles ceased and he lay still, taking ragged breaths. Nordenstam crouched down beside him. 'He's in a state of shock.'

Fitz leaned back on his haunches, wiping sweat from his forehead. 'Is this one of the people who vanished?'

Nordenstam's face was grim. 'Yes.' He looked at Fitz gravely.

'And, if the ident photo is anything to go by, this is Johan Svensson. Miss Bergman's boyfriend.'

Kerstin felt as though she'd been given a second chance. Johan was alive. Alive, but still distant; drugged, tended by nurses and machines. But at least he was here. Kerstin rested her forehead against the glass window. There wasn't much of him visible. Just his closed eyes, the lids twitching every now and then; his black hair, his nose, a saline drip snaking into the right nostril. The sheets were pulled right up under his chin. His bed was surrounded by monitoring machines, their LED read-outs blinking silently.

Kerstin felt a numbness inside, broken up by occasional pangs of irrational anger. Why did they have to sedate him? She wanted to talk to him – but so did the police. They were waiting, in a room further along the corridor. Waiting to interview him, find out what had happened to him. Right now, Kerstin didn't care. Johan was back, and that was all that mattered to her.

She heard footsteps approaching and turned. A stout, white-coated doctor was walking towards her, Inspector Nordenstam beside him.

'This is Dr Lindgard,' said Nordenstam. 'He'll be taking care of Johan until he recovers.'

Dr Lindgard had a bland, flat face with a wide mouth and a slightly retroussé nose, which made him look pugnacious and uncompromising. He wore steel-rimmed glasses and his receding blond hair was neatly trimmed. He spoke in a monotonous, bored-sounding voice.

'We have carried out blood and saliva tests and will be carrying out other tests, but apart from shock, abdominal bruising, minor lacerations to the gluteus maximus… er, the buttock, there does not appear to be anything wrong with him.'

Kerstin let out a huge sigh, and felt as if a weight had been lifted from her chest.

'When will he come round?' asked Nordenstam.

'The sedatives should wear off in a few hours,' said Lindgard.

'We'll see then if he requires any more.'

Nordenstam looked at Kerstin. 'You do realise that when he comes round, if he is fit, I will need to question him?'

Kerstin nodded.

Nordenstam gazed at Johan's still form. 'And then we'll have some answers, at last.'

Kerstin felt a flash of anger. To them, Johan wasn't a person: he was a slab of meat, a statistic, a vital clue. Not a living, breathing person.

'That's all he is to you, isn't it?' she found herself saying, her voice sounding shaky and loud. 'Just something to help you solve your case.'

Nordenstam sighed. 'Miss Bergman, there are still five people missing – six, including the Doctor's friend. I'm sorry if I sound callous, but whatever Johan tells us could be vital.'

'Sorry,' said Kerstin, aware of how childish she sounded. 'It's just…'

He put a hand on her shoulder. It was heavy and warm. Kerstin was instantly reminded of her father. Emotions curdled within her and she began to cry.

Just then the doors at the end of the corridor burst open and two figures entered, walking quickly along the corridor. One of them was that Doctor guy that Björn had said was weird – weird, but harmless. The other was the shifty-looking guy who Nordenstam had said was a UN operative. The one who'd been with Nordenstam when they found Johan.

'Hello,' said the Doctor. 'I'm the Doctor and this is Fitz.' His voice was cultured, and he spoke English.

Fitz's eyes met Kerstin's. They were big and grey. She wanted to thank him for finding Johan, but the words wouldn't come.

The Doctor's face was a mask of concern, real concern, not professional interest. 'Is Johan all right?'

Dr Lindgard coughed self-importantly, then spoke in English. 'Mr Svensson is stable.'

'Good,' said the Doctor. He looked over at Kerstin. 'Do you mind if I have a quick look at him?'

Kerstin blinked. 'OK.'

Lindgard stepped in front of the door that led into the isolation ward. 'I cannot allow that.'

'I've studied under Hippocrates himself,' said the Doctor. 'Surely you can let me examine the patient.'

Lindgard frowned and gave a curt shake of the head. 'You may not.'

Nordenstam spoke up. 'I think we should allow the Doctor to examine Johan.'

'So do I,' added Fitz, but Kerstin got the impression it was just for something to say, to make his presence felt.

'As long as the patient remains in this infirmary, I am in charge,' said Lindgard.

The Doctor dodged past Lindgard, opened the door and was in the isolation ward before anyone could stop him.

Kerstin followed, her heartbeat quickening. She wanted to reach out, to touch Johan, but something made her hold back.

The Doctor straightened up as Lindgard approached. 'Just having a quick look.'

Lindgard bustled them all out of the room. Kerstin noticed the Doctor give a sly wink at Fitz.

'I think you should all leave now,' said Lindgard.

There was no way she was going to leave, not now Johan was back, and safe – if not exactly sound. Whatever happened now, she wanted to be the first to know. 'I'm staying here.'

Lindgard shrugged. 'It's up to you, but I can assure you his condition won't change for hours.'

Nordenstam looked concerned. 'Someone ought to stay with her. I could post an officer.'

Fitz and the Doctor exchanged glances. 'Number sixty-three?' said the Doctor.

'You what?' said Fitz.

The Doctor winced, and then smiled, glancing around quickly at everyone and sliding an arm around Fitz's shoulder. 'Quick conference with my fellow UNIT operative.' He drew Fitz aside.

Lindgard looked at Nordenstam over his glasses. 'This Doctor, Inspector. How did you meet him?'

Nordenstam scratched his chin. 'Turned up outside the station. He's from something called UNIT.'

'UNIT.' Lindgard smiled. 'Of course.'

Kerstin slipped away from them, towards where the Doctor and Fitz were urgently talking, so she could overhear what they were saying.

What she overheard made no sense whatsoever.

'...back to the TARDIS. See if she's recovered. And you stay with Kerstin; I'll be back here as soon as I can.'

She went back to Lindgard and Nordenstam, who were debating the authenticity of the Doctor's credentials.

Nordenstam looked deeply pained. 'How come you've heard of UNIT and I have not?'

Lindgard shrugged. 'I've worked abroad. Africa, America. They have operatives everywhere.'

Shortly the Doctor and Fitz joined them.

'I'm staying with Miss Bergman,' said Fitz.

Nordenstam passed him a mobile phone 'This is my spare. Call me if anything happens. Doctor?'

'I'm going back to the forest,' said the Doctor. 'Do, um, er, a bit of investigation.'

Nordenstam nodded. 'I'll give you a lift.'

They left.

Dr Lindgard bid them a curt but cordial good day, and he left also.

That left Fitz. He smiled at her, sitting down on one of the grey plastic chairs against the wall of the corridor. There was an awkward silence, during which he examined the mobile phone as if he had never seen one before in his life.

She could start a conversation. Ask him what this TARDIS was. Find out about his job with this UNIT. But he didn't matter to her. Just another policeman. She stood up and looked through the glass at Johan. He hadn't moved, of course. She could go back to the farm – but to stay there, listening to Björn bemoaning the invasion of his privacy? Or back to her parents? She should at least phone them. But the thought of speaking to her mother again just made her feel tired. No. Her place was here with Johan.

Fitz's voice broke the silence. 'I was there when we found him, you know.'

'I know. Thank you.'

'Don't thank me. If anything, Johan found us.' He told her what had happened, and she listened, appalled.

When he'd finished speaking, Kerstin just stood there, staring at Fitz. His grey eyes and thin nose made him look rather sardonic. Nothing like a policeman at all. 'Who are you?' she whispered. 'Who are you really?'

'Like I said,' said Fitz, his eyes darting from side to side as if seeking a means of escape, 'we are who we say we are. And believe me,' he added quickly, as though trying very hard to maintain her credulity, 'we're used to dealing with things like this.'

She decided to give him the benefit of the doubt. 'OK. So, what do you think is going on? Where has Johan been? Is he – is he going to be all right?'

He shook his head and said gently, 'I'm sorry, but I don't know.'

Kerstin slumped down into a chair opposite him. 'Well, have you got any theories, then?'

Fitz shrugged. 'I haven't got any theories.'

Kerstin sighed and ran a hand through her hair. 'OK. You're keeping your options open. You're not keeping anything from me, are you?'

He smiled, as if at a private joke. 'No.'

He obviously was and she told him so.

He began to look irritated. 'Well yes, there are some things I am not telling you but they're nothing to do with Johan. As far as what happened to him's concerned, I know about the same as you.'

Kerstin sat back. The chair was uncomfortable, cutting into her back. 'What about the creature that attacked Björn?'

He shrugged again. 'All I know is that it's alien.'

Kerstin felt a chill pass across her shoulders and down her back at the sound of the word. She hadn't really thought about this yet. Alien. She'd never seriously considered such a thing – seen films, read novels, entertained the intellectual possibility of life on other planets. But for such a thing to impinge on her ordered, sensible, healthy, sane life? 'I'm having trouble believing all this,' she whispered.

'I did at first, but you get used to it.' She looked into his eyes. They were deadly serious.

'You get used to it,' he said again.

Kerstin looked down at her hands. 'Looks like I'm going to have to.'

'Don't worry,' said Fitz. 'Once the Doctor's on the case, it's as good as solved.'

He didn't sound totally convinced himself, but Kerstin didn't say anything because she wanted it to be true.

The Doctor had a natural sense of direction where the TARDIS was concerned. A feeling for her presence. It was his home, after all, more so than any planet, any Time Lord chapter, any person. He'd been separated from the TARDIS many times, often in seemingly permanent ways. But even when she had been worlds away, or in a different time zone, he'd known she was safe.

This was different. As he plunged through the forest, he couldn't sense the TARDIS at all. The telepathic circuits weren't working. It meant that Fitz couldn't understand the local language, but that was a minor problem. If the telepathic link remained down for too long...

He turned his thoughts to his plan. While examining Johan, the Doctor had taken a blood sample using a tiny cybernetic mosquito. The product of a particularly nasty corporation, it was meant for surreptitiously taking blood samples from potential plague victims on human colony planets in the thirtieth century, so that they could be tagged, traced and eliminated if necessary. A terrible product of a terrible time. The Doctor had acquired one for himself, thinking it would come in

66

Chapter Six
Isolation

The Royal Infirmary in Eskilstuna was a calm, efficient building, two storeys tall. It had an air of self-possessed serenity, like an ocean liner. It looked so seamless and clean, as though it were not constructed from bricks, mortar, sweat and toil but had unfolded itself gently from a prefabricated envelope. Well, for all Fitz knew, it had – technology had moved on frighteningly quickly since 1963, he was seeing it all around him.

Fitz slid a packet of Camel cigarettes from his rear pocket. It had been crushed in his fall back at the farm, and the half-dozen cigarettes within had bent and split, the tobacco crumbling over his fingers. Damn. He could really do with a smoke. That was why he'd come out here. No way could he smoke in a hospital.

Fitz selected the most serviceable-looking Camel and took out his silver lighter. He flicked a flame into life, pale and ghostly in the unrelenting sun. He lit the cigarette, and took a long deep drag, feeling calmer instantly. Sod the damage it was doing to his body. He could almost hear Sam reeling off another gruesome nicotine-related statistic.

Sam.

The nicotine rush turned into a spasm of guilt. Fitz realised he hadn't thought about her for at least an hour. He should be on the case, looking for clues. He should be doing *something*, not just looking after Kerstin and waiting for the Doctor.

Maybe he hadn't been thinking about Sam because he was afraid she was dead.

A flicker of light caught his eye. He looked up to see the wide revolving door of the entrance to the hospital lobby swing round and Kerstin step out on to the paving stones. In her white shorts and yellow T-shirt, with her tanned skin and blonde hair, she was a striking vision. If circumstances were different, he might even consider – But no. He knew nothing of her. All he knew was that she was a student, and her parents lived in Stockholm; Nordenstam had told him that. A student of what, though? wondered Fitz as she walked towards him, her face averted, arms folded. Physical education, probably. Nothing arty or literary, that was for sure. He felt a little guilty – after all, she must be going through hell.

Fitz smiled at her, dropping the cigarette to the pavement and stubbing it out with the toe of his boot – an automatic reaction, which may not have been necessary, as he had no idea if Kerstin disapproved of smoking. He was still programmed for Sam.

He looked hopefully at her. 'How is he?'

Kerstin's voice was flat and weary. 'No change.'

'The doctor said the sedative wouldn't wear off for a while,' Fitz reminded her.

Kerstin let out a long breath of frustration. 'I don't think he's ever going to wake up.'

They walked around the hospital gardens for a while. There weren't any flower beds, but a lot of neatly tended shrubs and hedges, their leaves pale and brittle-looking. Fitz wished there was something he could say. Kerstin appeared to be deep in thought. She kept looking sideways at him, as if assessing him.

As they passed a bizarre piece of statuary made of corkscrews of metal and glass, Kerstin asked him, straight out of the blue, what a TARDIS was.

Ah. She must have overheard him talking to the Doctor. Fitz prepared yet another lie, sick of making things up to hide the truth, worried he would say something that would contradict his story. 'It's a code word for our base of operations.'

Kerstin shrugged. 'Another thing. At the farm, when I met you with Nordenstam, you stared at me as though you seemed to know me.'

That one was easy enough. 'Well, you look rather like Sam.'

Kerstin frowned. 'Who's Sam?'

No need to lie here. 'A friend of mine. She's gone missing. Unlike Johan, she hasn't come back yet.'

70

Kerstin turned to look at him fully, her eyes widening, searching his face. They were bright, sharp, like blue jewels against the nut-brown skin of her face. This close, Fitz could see a light dusting of freckles across her nose and under her eyes. 'Oh, I never realised. Was she your girlfriend?'

Fitz grinned at her directness. 'No. More of a friend.' He remembered Maddie, the last girl he'd been involved with, back in the late sixties. They'd had something, for a while. He briefly wondered what she was doing now, if she was even alive. Perhaps the Doctor would know.

'So you've lost someone too,' mumbled Kerstin, half to herself and half to Fitz. 'That's the way life must be, I suppose. Getting used to loss.'

Fitz opened his mouth to agree, thinking of his mother, how he still hadn't got used to losing her – but he didn't want to talk about that, not now. Didn't want to reopen that wound. So they walked on in silence, along the paving stones which led between the low hedges. Beyond the garden, the buildings of Eskilstuna stood drab and grey, crowding like onlookers at a funeral procession.

'You speak English well,' said Fitz, to break the silence.

'I spent a year in England,' said Kerstin, staring into the distance. 'That's where I met my first boyfriend.' She glanced sideways at Fitz. 'You're from England, aren't you?'

'Yes,' said Fitz, not wanting to discuss his origins in too much depth. How could he explain that he was from 1963?

Fitz noticed that Kerstin kept looking back at the hospital building, as though she expected Johan to come running out of the revolving door, arms raised ready to hug her, trailing bedsheets and frantic nurses behind him. Something positive had better happen soon, thought Fitz. They all needed cheering up, even the Doctor.

The Doctor. He'd been gone a long time, hours now. Perhaps the TARDIS was working again and the Doctor was polishing the console and brewing the tea – in which case, hooray. Or perhaps he'd gone inside and been sucked out of existence by the glowing whirlpool that had taken Sam away – in which case, total bummer, to say the least.

Either way, it was high time he found out. 'Look,' he said, 'I'd better go and find the Doctor.'

Kerstin turned to look at him, a smile playing on her face, though her eyes still held their distant look. 'You know, I'm having terrible trouble thinking of you as UN officials. You're more like… more like a pair of amateur detectives, bumbling about and getting in everyone's way.'

She had them pretty much pinned down there, thought Fitz. 'Hey, you've stumbled upon our secret modus operandi!'

She laughed, a short, brisk sound, which Fitz was glad to hear, and then her face grew serious. 'See you later?' she said.

Fitz nodded, and watched her turn and walk back into the hospital through the revolving door. He realised he was beginning to fancy her. He smiled. If he'd stayed in 1963 he'd now be old enough to be her grandfather.

He walked to a bench beside a bed of bright-yellow flowers, and took out the mobile phone Nordenstam had given him. It took him a while, but eventually he sussed out how to operate the bloody thing. If you pressed the blue MENU button a few times, a list of names came up on the little green screen: Jonsson, Nordenstam, Persson. There was a flashing cursor next to the list, and then if you pressed OK the phone would call the indicated person. Simple trial and error. He could have asked Kerstin – but how would that have looked? A UN operative, not knowing how to use a mobile telephone?

He called Nordenstam, the phone burbling in his ear.

'Nordenstam?' came a tiny voice.

'This is Fitz Kreiner.'

'What do you want? I'm rather busy.' Fitz could hear voices in the background.

'I'm looking for the Doctor – have you seen him? Do you know where he is?'

A crackling noise drowned out the first part of Nordenstam's reply. '–lutely no idea at all.'

A long-fingered hand plucked the phone from Fitz's and snapped the cover shut.

Fitz almost fell off the bench in surprise. 'Doctor! How did you get here?'

'Public transport,' said the Doctor, looking around himself as if afraid of being watched. 'Highly efficient, clean and reliable. Well, in this country at least.' He sat down on the bench next to Fitz, handed the phone back to him, and let out a long, sighing breath. 'Things are grim.'

This was hardly news to Fitz. 'How's the TARDIS?'

'She's reverted to her original form,' said the Doctor, a forlorn lilt in his voice. 'Using all her power to heal herself. And I'm locked out,' he added, through gritted teeth.

Fitz grinned, putting on an act to try to cheer the Doctor up. The Doctor's bouts of melancholia gave him the creeps. 'I'm sure there's a locksmith in the town who can knock up a spare key, Doctor.'

The Doctor shook his head. 'It's worse than being merely locked out physically. I'm locked out mentally, too. I can't reach the telepathic circuits.' His face drooped in sadness. 'If the bond is broken for too long, the TARDIS will die.'

Fitz didn't know what to say.

They sat in silence for a while, listening to the hum and rumble of the traffic, the sun beating down on them from a clear blue sky. An aeroplane threaded itself through the clouds like a needle. Fitz had a sudden moment of vertigo. Here he was, in 1999 – the future. And he had no way of relating it to anything he knew. Was Sweden in 1963 any different from Sweden in 1999? He had no idea. Everything was strange – but then it would have been if he'd come here in his own time: it was a foreign country, he was a first-time visitor. He had a sudden urge to see England, to see London. Somewhere he knew, so he could see how much it had changed. Had he lived a normal life, not involving the Doctor or Sam or the TARDIS, he would be in his mid-sixties by now. Would he have changed with the times, or would he still be living in 1963, wallowing in the Good Old Days and bemoaning all the new-fangled technology like Nordenstam's mobile phone?

That would never happen now. Fitz Kreiner would always be an outsider. Just like the Doctor. Where was home now? How could he settle anywhere now? Was the TARDIS home? Were the Doctor and Sam his family? Sam...

He put his head in his hands, suddenly feeling more alone than at any time in his life. Then the Doctor reached into his pocket, took out a little transparent cube and tossed it to Fitz.

Fitz caught it, expecting it to be cold like an ice cube, but it was warm. Inside, there was a little metal insect. 'What's that? Another alien creature?'

The Doctor shook his head. 'A sample of Johan's blood. Couldn't use the TARDIS lab to test it, obviously.'

Fitz thought of Johan, pale and drained-looking in his hospital bed. 'So, there's no way of telling if he's carrying an alien virus?'

The Doctor shook his head. 'No.'

'We'd better get back in there then, keep an eye on him.' Fitz stood up, but the Doctor remained seated. Where was his sense of urgency? 'Doctor?'

The Doctor stood up, clapping his hands together. He looked over at the hospital, a worried expression on his face, as if he were steeling himself for something. 'You're right. Mustn't let the situation get out of hand.'

They started walking towards the hospital, the Doctor talking quickly, seeming to have recovered some of his verve. 'Tell me about that creature you found in the forest.'

Fitz recalled the image of the thing, its spiderlike legs and deflated, hourglass-shaped body. He described it for the Doctor. 'What do you think it is?'

The Doctor shrugged. 'No idea. From what you say it sounds like a creature used to lower gravity, which ties in with the creature from the farm and that insect we saw in the forest. That wasn't used to Earth's gravity at all – that's why it couldn't fly properly.'

'That's three types of alien creature we've seen today, Doctor.'

'All within a fairly localised area,' said the Doctor as they went through the revolving door into the hospital lobby. 'Interesting.'

'So where are they coming from?' said Fitz.

The Doctor quickened his pace. 'From where Sam's gone, from where Johan has been.' He was almost running now, along the wide grey-tiled floor towards the wing containing the isolation ward.

'Hang on,' said Fitz. He hadn't told the Doctor about the strange white-suited figures from the State Biohazard thingummy who had arrived to take the creature away. Oh well, time for that later, he supposed.

They found Kerstin standing in the grey-tiled corridor outside the isolation ward, her hands pressed on to the glass separating her from Johan. She didn't look up as they approached.

Fitz could plainly see that Johan was exactly the same as he had been before. Still and silent, like a corpse, the only movement the slow rising and falling of the crisp white sheets across his chest as he breathed.

'Kerstin,' said the Doctor, touching the girl lightly on her shoulder. 'How are you feeling?'

She looked up at him, her eyes damp with tears, which she brushed away. She smiled at the Doctor and said, 'I'm feeling as though I'm standing on the edge of a cliff, waiting to fall.'

The Doctor nodded sympathetically.

'It's the not knowing that's the worst part.' Kerstin's voice was flat, lifeless. 'Not knowing if he's going to be all right. I know the doctors seem to think he's physically OK but his brain could be mush, he could be a vegetable, he could never wake up.'

Fitz noticed that she seemed to trust the Doctor instantly, instinctively, and felt a shameful envy for the Doctor's ability to get on with anyone straight away. It had taken ages to break the ice with Kerstin; she'd seemed to realise he was a person only when he had told her about Sam. And even that had sent her back into herself, thinking about Johan.

Now she was talking to the Doctor as if she'd known him all

her life. Fitz might as well not exist. What was it about the Doctor and blondes?

He was shushing her now, calming her. 'I can't tell you if he's going to be all right or not. I can't predict the future.' He glanced at Fitz as he said this. 'But Johan is in the best place.'

Fitz was looking at Johan as the Doctor spoke, wondering what he'd gone through. Where he'd been. If he'd seen Sam. And – hang on, was that a movement? Fitz stepped closer to the glass. He was sure he had seen a movement, the white sheets stirring, as if Johan was trying to raise his hand.

The Doctor was still talking to Kerstin. They seemed to have forgotten he was there. He opened his mouth to speak – but hang on, if he was wrong he'd only be raising Kerstin's hopes and then bringing them crashing back down again. He had to be sure. So he stood and watched Johan like a hawk, alert for any sign of movement. There – definitely this time, the sheet tenting slightly just above where Johan's right hand would be. And then Johan rolled his head, his lips moving slackly.

'Doctor!' said Fitz. 'He's coming round!'

The Doctor and Kerstin were at his side in an instant, Kerstin's eyes and mouth wide, the Doctor's brow creased in a frown of concentration.

'Are you sure?' said the Doctor, obviously not trusting Fitz's powers of observation since he mistook Kerstin for Sam earlier that day.

Fitz sighed. 'Do bears sh–'

'All right, you're sure,' said the Doctor quickly.

Then Johan opened his eyes, let out a low moan and tried to sit up. Then slumped back down again, his eyes wide and glistening, staring at the ceiling.

The Doctor opened the door to the isolation ward and hurried in, followed by Kerstin.

Where were the doctors? wondered Fitz, looking around. And the police? Had Nordenstam left anyone waiting in the room further down the corridor? He darted down to have a look. The room was empty, coffee cups on the table, a folded newspaper on a chair. Fitz realised belatedly that it was he, Fitz, whom Nordenstam was relying on. Should he call him? The mobile phone bulged uncomfortably in his trouser pocket. No. The last thing they wanted was the police bumbling around, interfering.

With a mental apology to Nordenstam, Fitz went back to the isolation ward. The Doctor was kneeling by Johan's side, whispering his name into his ear. Kerstin knelt on the other side of the bed.

Fitz hovered in the door, not sure of what to do. He watched as the Doctor passed his hand in front of Johan's blue eyes.

'He's not responding,' said the Doctor softly.

Kerstin hid her head in her hands and began to cry softly.

Then Johan spoke, his voice barely a whisper. 'Ker... Kerstin?' His eyes searched the ceiling, looking anywhere but at her.

'Johan,' said Kerstin, leaning over him. She spoke some words in Swedish, stroked his forehead.

On hearing her voice, Johan struggled to sit up, his voice rising in panic, babbling in Swedish – Fitz wished he could understand.

The Doctor leaned over him, smoothing his hair. 'Johan, what can you see?'

Johan began panting, moaning and writhing from side to side. Fitz walked around the bed, held Kerstin back. Cruel as it looked, the Doctor had to question Johan.

'Things,' said Johan, in English – responding to the Doctor. 'Horrible things. What are they? Where am I? Kerstin!'

His convulsions became too much for the Doctor and Fitz moved to help calm him down.

Then there was a voice from the doorway. 'What is going on here?'

Fitz turned to see Dr Lindgard bustling into the room, a nurse in tow.

'Please step away from the patient,' said Dr Lindgard calmly.

Johan was still thrashing around on the bed. Kerstin was holding his hand, trying to calm him.

The Doctor bent over Johan, muttering something into his ear and fishing in his waistcoat pocket. He drew out a silver pocket watch, and began swinging it before Johan's eyes.

Lindgard took a step nearer, firmly pushing Fitz out of the way. 'I said step away. The patient needs more sedative.'

'Stop calling him that!' yelled Kerstin, her face red and streaked with tears. 'His name's Johan. Got that?'

The Doctor was ignoring everyone, concentrating on Johan, swinging the watch back and forth. Incredibly, Johan was focusing on the silver object.

'This is ridiculous.' Lindgard's voice was still calm and even. 'What can he hope to achieve?' He motioned the nurse towards the bed. She was holding a small plastic syringe.

'It may be ridiculous,' said Fitz, holding the nurse back, 'but it's working. Look.'

Lindgard looked. Johan's convulsions had ceased and he was breathing normally. His eyelids had drooped closed, and he looked at peace once more.

Kerstin wiped away her tears and looked over at the Doctor. 'What did you do?'

The Doctor stood up, smiling from ear to ear and pocketing the watch. 'Simple hypnotic trance. He'll sleep peacefully for hours now.' He frowned as he caught sight of the nurse, hovering near the bed bearing her syringe. 'Far more beneficial than that muck. I'm afraid that's what may have caused his convulsions.'

'Nonsense,' snapped Lindgard.

Fitz could see that the Doctor was enjoying annoying the Swedish doctor.

'As a medical man, you'll agree that my methods, if not conventional, have had the desired effect.'

Lindgard drew himself up to his full height, and was about to say something when there was a scream from the other side of the bed.

They all turned to see Kerstin, struggling to get away from Johan, trying to prise his pale fingers away from her tanned brown forearm, where they held her in a vicelike grip. She looked terrified. Johan's eyes were still closed but his body was juddering, shivering, as though he were freezing to death.

'He's gone into reactive shock,' said Lindgard, glaring at the Doctor. 'The desired effect? I think not.'

Fitz dodged round the other side of the bed and tried to help Kerstin free herself. It was impossible.

'Doctor,' said Fitz, looking across the bed to where the Doctor and Lindgard stood. 'What's happening to him?'

The Doctor was shaking his head, his eyes wide. 'I don't know.'

Lindgard turned to the nurse and pointed to Johan. 'Sedative. Now!'

They shoved past the Doctor and rolled back the sheets. Fitz gasped. Johan's chest was simply swimming in sweat. It was running down his stomach and on to the sheets, where it spread out in a dark stain.

Ever professional, Lindgard didn't bat an eyelid at the sight. He held Johan's left arm while the nurse slid the needle into a prominent blue vein and depressed the plunger.

They both stood back, watching expectantly.

Fitz tried to prise Johan's fingers away again, but to no avail. They'd drawn blood, which ran over Kerstin's forearm to drip on the floor.

Kerstin's face was a knot of agony and Fitz could practically hear her gritting her teeth with the pain.

'It's not working,' yelled Fitz. 'It's not bloody working!'

The Doctor was staring down at Johan, his eyes wide, shaking his head.

What was wrong with him? He was usually so calm in a crisis, so confident, knowing exactly what to do. But he was just standing there.

Dr Lindgard ordered the nurse to get some morphine and she ran off, with a terrified stare at Johan's body. He was still shaking, bucking in the bed, his back arching, the perspiration dripping from him. Fitz's stomach lurched. It was pink. He was sweating blood.

Dr Lindgard was doing his best to hold him down, and even

his calm façade was beginning to crack a little.

'Somebody help him,' cried Kerstin, her voice strangled with pain.

And then Fitz saw that a large bruise was forming on the flesh of Johan's stomach. A round, purplish blotch the size of a small plate. It was swelling, slowly, like a giant blood blister. A strange gurgling was coming from Johan's throat, and flecks of blood and spittle sprayed from his mouth.

'I think we should all get out of here,' said the Doctor.

Fitz had never been so angry with him. 'We can't leave Kerstin! What do you want me to do, cut his arm off?'

'That may be necessary,' said the Doctor, looking around as if for the most appropriate surgical instrument.

'Don't be ridiculous!' said Lindgard. His white coat was speckled with blood.

And then Johan sat bolt upright in bed, opened his eyes, let out a ragged scream, and flopped back down on the bed. At the same time he released Kerstin's arm and she staggered backwards, grimacing as blood flowed freely from her wound. Fitz ripped the sleeve from his shirt and used it to make a tourniquet.

'Look!' cried the Doctor.

Lindgard stood up, and backed away from the bed.

The purple blister on Johan's stomach was now the size of an upturned bowl. Suddenly, it split open, spraying them all with a clear, viscous fluid. Fitz dragged Kerstin away from the bed and back towards the door, glancing at Johan on the way.

What he saw would stay with him forever and he froze on the spot.

Long, black legs were forcing open the sides of the deflating blister, hauling out an orange hourglass-shaped body which quivered and pulsed with life. A smell hit Fitz's senses, the sickly smell of the thing in the forest.

'Everyone out of here!' yelled the Doctor.

His words shocked Fitz into action and he half dragged the hysterical Kerstin from the isolation ward. Dr Lindgard and the nurse followed, with the Doctor last, who slammed the door closed.

They all watched as the thing squatted on Johan's shattered body. Its black legs were glistening with blood, the hourglass-shaped body quivering, a ropelike grey tube emerging from it, as if tasting the air.

'Fascinating,' said Lindgard.

'What?' said Fitz, holding Kerstin's face against his chest. 'He's dead, you callous bastard!'

Lindgard turned to look at Fitz. His eyes betrayed no emotion. 'I've developed an air of detachment over the years.' He smiled, a prissy little expression which chilled Fitz to the bone.

Inside, another blister was forming, on Johan's chest. The first creature had dragged itself to the edge of the bed, leaving a trail of blood and entrails, and Fitz heard a wet slap as it flopped to the floor. The other blister burst open and another, similar creature emerged. Smaller versions of the thing in the forest.

The Doctor banged his fists together. 'I should have known something like this would happen! Something must have laid eggs in his gut, where they would have remained undetected.'

Fitz took his breath. It had all happened so quickly. Kerstin's face was blank, streaked with tears. Fitz shuddered. She was in deep shock. He was reminded of the looks on the faces of Charles Roley's test patients back home in London in 1963, at the time he first met the Doctor and Sam. The look on the face of his mother.

Dr Lindgard tried to usher them away from the isolation ward. 'I'm afraid I'm going to have to ask you all to leave.'

The Doctor shook his head. 'Impossible. We have to capture those things, analyse them.'

Lindgard shook his head. 'That will be taken care of.'

'Doctor,' said Fitz, concerned for Kerstin. 'We've got to get her out of here.'

The Doctor looked at Kerstin. 'Yes, of course. Come on.'

They walked along the corridor, watched by Dr Lindgard.

Once outside the hospital, they sat on a bench in the brilliant sunshine. Fitz felt as if what had happened was a dream. The horror of Johan's death could not possibly have taken place in the serene Swedish summer.

But the blood all over his white shirt, the tattered cloth of the arm he'd torn off to make the tourniquet for Kerstin, the wound in Kerstin's arm were all incontrovertible proof.

Kerstin was shaking her head. 'That didn't happen. Johan is OK. He's gonna be OK.'

'What are we going to do with her?' whispered Fitz.

The Doctor seemed to consider. 'Take her back to the farm.'

'How?'

The Doctor waved a hand. 'Oh, Fitz. This is a hospital, she's not well, get them to take you in an ambulance. And get them to treat that wound first. Your makeshift bandage won't do.'

Fitz felt a surge of anger. 'Well sorry, Doctor, but I didn't see you doing much back there to help.'

The Doctor appeared to ignore this remark, and stood up, practically hopping from foot to foot. 'While you're doing that I'm going to go back in there and get a good look at those creatures.'

The Doctor set off at a run towards the hospital, and Fitz followed at a slower pace. Kerstin was holding his hand, as if she were a little girl.

Fitz swallowed. He'd suddenly realised that what had happened to Johan could have happened to Sam.

Fitz took Kerstin back to reception, where alarmed nurses took her away to get her wound treated and to give her something for shock. All Fitz had to do now was wait for her, and then an ambulance would whisk them both back to the farm.

It seemed to Fitz that he was doing a lot of waiting around today. Still, this was welcome – his hands were still shaking after what had happened in the isolation ward, and his heart was beating fast and erratically. He desperately wanted a smoke, but none of his Camels were in a decent enough condition.

The lobby was tiled in grey with white walls, with a seating area opposite a picture window. Fitz sat there for a while, trying to take his mind off things, letting his anger towards the Doctor cool off. Perhaps he shouldn't be so hard on him. The plight of the TARDIS, the loss of Sam, must be affecting him deeply.

Someone hurried in through the revolving doors, and Fitz looked up. It was Inspector Nordenstam, looking flustered.

'Inspector!' cried Fitz, standing up and waving.

Nordenstam came over, looking him up and down. 'What happened to you?'

Fitz's white silk shirt was missing a sleeve and spattered in blood. He took a deep breath. 'It's not so much what happened to me, as what's happened to Johan.'

Nordenstam frowned. 'I was just on my way here to see how he was. After you called and got cut off, I thought something might have happened.'

Damn. Perhaps he should have called Nordenstam, after the crisis. He hadn't given him a thought since...

'Um, something has happened, but it was after I called. Come on – the Doctor's with Johan's body.'

'Body?' hissed Nordenstam, gripping Fitz's arm. 'You mean he's dead?'

Fitz nodded gravely. 'You'd better come with me.'

They made their way to the isolation ward, to find the Doctor standing in the corridor, his hands in his pockets, staring through the glass. He didn't look up as they approached.

And then Fitz saw. The bed was empty. Fresh sheets had been put on and all the blood and mess had been cleaned up. Of Johan, or the creatures, there was no sign.

'Where have they taken him? To the mortuary?'

The Doctor shook his head. 'I don't know.'

'We were the only ones to see what happened,' said Fitz slowly. He was thinking of the figures in the white suits. How easy would it be for them to take Johan from the hospital? The whole thing had the ring of a conspiracy. A bloody big one. 'They must have taken him.'

'Who?' said the Doctor and Nordenstam simultaneously.

'Those guys we saw in the forest,' said Fitz, 'who said they were from the State Biohazard Protection Unit.'

'Yes, I've run a few checks on them,' said Nordenstam. 'There is no such organisation.'

Fitz explained about what had happened in the forest to the Doctor.

After he'd heard all, the Doctor's face was grim, his mouth set in a stern line. 'This is worse than I thought. Did you get a look at the faces behind the masks?'

Neither Fitz or Nordenstam had.

'Then we can't be sure they're even human,' said the Doctor. He slammed his palm against the glass window of the isolation ward. 'I hate not knowing who the enemy are.'

Chapter Seven
Siege

The hot day had melted into a cool, clear evening, the bright sunlight fading to a brooding, humid half-light. The town of Strängnäs was quiet and deserted, its narrow streets harbouring shadows and silence, as if a curfew had been imposed. No one felt like leaving their home that night. The shock of the disappearances had stunned the whole town, and the people of Strängnäs were scared. Scared of the same thing happening to them or their loved ones. Many had visited the lake, to stare in wonder at the remains of the cabin, returning to the town to debate what could have caused such a thing. Relatives and friends in Eskilstuna, Västerås, Stockholm and beyond had been telephoned. The press had got wind of things, but the media feeding frenzy of British tabloids was unknown here. Tomorrow's edition of *Aftonbladet* would carry a short article on the 'Strängnäs Incident', reporting the bare facts and listing the names of those who had vanished:

> Johan Svensson, 21, medical student
> Per Ollson, 46, bank clerk
> Svetlana Persson, 32, teacher
> Lars Petersen, 64, store owner, Harad
> Peter Jonsson, 12, schoolboy
> Bo Vikarn, 32, unemployed
> Samantha Jones, 22, English tourist

They wouldn't mention Olla Wenberg, the unfortunate person who had been 'half abducted.' Nordenstam, acting on her family's request, had managed to keep that quiet. He would be a busy man for the next few days, trying to find out more about the so-called State Biohazard Protection Unit, trying to find out what had happened to Johan's body.

He wouldn't get anywhere. The explanation of the disappearances, if it ever came, would probably be so far beyond human comprehension that a cover story would have to be deployed.

The Doctor stood outside the farmhouse, looking down at the dark mass of the forest, the lights of the small village of Harad bright in the distance. He was emptying his mind, trying to focus on the here and now, listening for subliminals in the noosphere, anything that might give him a clue.

The Doctor closed his eyes. It was so quiet here. He could hear the low voices of Fitz and Björn talking in the farmhouse kitchen. He blotted them out, trying to focus his mind. But nothing came. He opened his eyes, looking at the dusky landscape around him with sinking hearts. He hated being one step – or even more steps – behind his enemies. Whoever they were.

'Who's behind this?' he said out loud. 'Come on, show yourselves! I'm not afraid to face you. I'm not afraid!'

He heard footsteps from behind him. Heavy, shuffling, uneven. Björn. The old farmer walked to stand beside him, still limping from his leg wound. His big saggy face was slack with fatigue and the Doctor could smell alcohol on his breath. Just like Fitz, using a drug to numb the emotions, to escape.

'Come in and have some food, Doctor. And mind not to shout – you might wake Kerstin.'

The Doctor felt himself blush. 'Yes, of course. Is she still sleeping?'

Björn nodded. 'Best thing for her. Poor, poor girl.'

The moment they'd arrived at the farmhouse some hours earlier, Kerstin had gone upstairs and fallen fully clothed into a natural, deep sleep. No sedatives, no tricks with pocket watches, just normal, healing sleep.

Protecting herself, mending herself. Just like the TARDIS.

The Doctor smiled at Björn, deciding to take up his offer of food. After the strain of the day, he was feeling quite peckish. 'I think I will come in now.'

Fitz had changed out of his ruined silk shirt and was now wearing one of Björn's, a blue-and-black-checked lumberjack thing. It felt thick and as heavy as a jacket in the humid evening. For once, however, Fitz was past caring how he looked. There were more important things to worry about.

An empty plate sat on the trestle table in front of him. He'd polished off a pile of cold meat, cheese, hard-boiled eggs, salad, some fish stuff and whisky, and now felt as fat as a house, and very tired. The events of the preceding day kept going round in his head: the disappearance of Sam, the strange insect, the hole, the thing in the forest, Johan. All connected in some way. The Doctor seemed convinced there was some sort of alien invasion under way, but Fitz doubted that. He was beginning to doubt a lot of what the Doctor was saying, even beginning to doubt the Doctor himself.

Fitz yawned, and decided it was time to hit the hay. Which, if there were no spare beds, could be a literal description of the sleeping arrangements. As he stood up, the Doctor and Björn came in. Both of them were smiling, which Fitz thought was a bit off, considering all that had happened.

Björn sat down opposite Fitz and took the whisky bottle, pouring a generous measure.

'Ah, Fitz,' said the Doctor. 'How are you set for a spot of midnight breaking and entering?'

Fitz rolled his eyes. 'You may as well ask me to sprout wings and fly.'

'That won't be necessary.' The Doctor rubbed his hands together. 'We're going back to the hospital. I'm pretty sure they've hidden Johan somewhere.'

Fitz groaned. 'Doctor, there's no way I'm going back there now.'

The Doctor frowned. 'Why?'

Fitz's anger boiled over. 'Because I'm rather fagged out. It's so easy for you. You're the guy with two hearts, who never farts. Never swears, smokes, drinks, or even sweats. Well, I'm sorry, Doctor, I can't even begin to come up to your ideal. I'm only bloody human!'

The Doctor raised his hands and made shushing noises. 'Sorry, sorry, sorry!'

'There's nothing we can do,' said Fitz. 'Look, I'm going to get some sleep. We'll all be fresher in the morning and then we can talk.'

The Doctor nodded.

Then Fitz noticed someone standing in the door. Kerstin, still in her white shorts, though she'd put on a black T-shirt to replace the yellow one, which had been stained with Johan's blood. Her left arm was bandaged and her face was puffy. 'What were you talking about?'

Fitz shrugged. 'Just things.'

Kerstin walked up to the table. 'Don't lie to me. I heard you talking about going back to the hospital, to find Johan.'

The Doctor smiled blandly. 'It was just an idea.'

'I'm with you,' she said.

'Oh, bugger,' muttered Fitz.

'What's your problem?' said Kerstin. 'I thought you were a UN operative.'

'Well,' said Fitz.

'Um,' said the Doctor.

'Shh!' said Björn.

They all looked at him. He was clutching the whisky bottle, and his eyes were wide. 'There's something outside.'

Just as he finished speaking Fitz could hear it. A scrabbling at the wooden exterior. As though something was trying to get in.

'Just an escaped pig, isn't it?' said Fitz, hoping fervently that it was.

Björn shook his head.

The scrabbling was coming from all around them, and something leapt at the kitchen window. Fitz caught a glimpse of a round maw with sharp white teeth and spiny, green flesh.

'We're surrounded!' cried Fitz. 'What the hell are we gonna do?'

The Doctor looked around the room, waving his hand. 'Under siege, there's only one thing we can do – barricade ourselves in and try to hold out.'

Kerstin's eyes were wide and she was walking towards the window, as if in a trance.

She'd be easy meat, thought Fitz. Ripped to pieces in seconds. *This could have happened to Sam, too.*

'Kerstin,' said Fitz, putting his hands on her shoulders. He couldn't believe he was taking charge here. 'Listen to me. Go upstairs and shut yourself into your room.'

She didn't move or speak, just stared at him with a glassy expression.

He shook her more roughly. 'Now!' He shoved her out of the kitchen and watched her half stumble, half run up the stairs. He heard the bedroom door slam and then, to his right, from the sitting room, there came the sudden, startling sound of breaking glass.

Fitz darted across the hall and slammed the living-room door closed, just as something small and powerful hammered into it from the other side, splintering the white-painted wood. He scurried back into the kitchen, shutting the door behind him.

Björn was just sitting at the trestle table, staring into the middle distance. 'They've come back,' he whispered. 'For me.'

The Doctor had found Björn's double-barrelled shotgun, propped up in a corner, but he wasn't bloody doing anything with it, just staring at it. 'Doctor! Pick up the gun!' yelled Fitz.

The Doctor put both hands to his head. 'I – I can't!'

Then something began butting at the outside of the door. The thing had obviously got out of the living room. To his horror, Fitz saw the kitchen door slowly start to open, and heard the scrabble of claws on carpet as the creature prepared for another run-up.

Fitz hurled himself at the door, slamming it closed just as the creature impacted from the other side. It was like getting a breeze block in the shoulder and Fitz yelled in pain. He had to use all his strength to keep the door shut. 'It's bloody strong!' he shouted.

The Doctor had picked up the gun, was aiming it at the door, grimacing. Fitz was painfully aware that he was in the way; if the Doctor pulled the trigger...

Björn was still sitting, hands clasped around the whisky bottle. 'Björn – get over here!' The old farmer stood up and came over, walking as though he were in a dream. 'Help me hold this door!'

Björn shook his head, blinking, as if to bring himself round. 'Better if we shove this in front of it,' he said, slapping the side of the large refrigerator next to the door.

'Brilliant!' cried Fitz, amazed and surprised. 'Doctor, quick, lend a hand!'

To Fitz's relief, the Doctor leaned the shotgun against the sink. He helped Björn manhandle the heavy refrigerator in front of the door, bottles and jars clanking inside. Fitz stepped adroitly back as it slid into place. It covered all of the door except for a six-inch strip down one side. As they watched the wood splintered and a green-scaled claw shot through, pawing the air.

The three of them retreated to the middle of the room. Fitz picked up the shotgun. It was heavier than it looked. The Doctor's face was pale. 'I'm sorry, Fitz.' Fitz suddenly felt more scared than ever. The Doctor was apologising to *him*?

Björn was cowering back against the sink, eyes fixed on the claw, which was busy widening its horizontal gap.

Fitz thought of Kerstin, hiding upstairs, and swore silently. If the things could get in through the living room, they could run up the stairs, make short work of the door, and –

The window behind Björn burst open and one of the creatures fell through. Björn stepped to one side and it skittered on to the floor. Fitz got a rushed impression of powerful hind legs, toadlike green flesh covered in black spines, and a gaping round maw lined with teeth. Yelling, he swung the shotgun round and blasted the creature at point-blank range.

The noise was deafening, setting Fitz's ears ringing. The blast filled the kitchen with acrid smoke which made them all cough violently. Through smoky tears, Fitz could see more of the things, piling through the window.

'The back door!' yelled the Doctor.

They ran to the back door, which led on to a concrete porch. It was crawling with the creatures. There was no way past them. Though they had no eyes, the things seemed to notice them and prepared to leap, their circular fanged mouths gaping.

They all piled back into the smoke-filled kitchen, slamming the door behind them.

Fitz whirled round, covering the creatures in the kitchen with the shotgun. One of them had injured itself on the broken glass, leaking green blood from a gash on its flank. The others were tearing and slashing at the stricken beast with their hind claws. The injured creature was making a horrendous wailing noise, like a baby.

They skirted round the fighting creatures.

The one in the hallway had destroyed the strip of door, and was trying to shove its blunt head through, snarling in frustration.

The only way out of the kitchen was past the creature.

Fitz lifted the shotgun and aimed the barrel right down the creature's throat, feeling sick.

He pulled the trigger and there was an almighty bang, another cloud of acrid smoke and the creature was gone, blasted into fragments in the hall.

'Upstairs, it's our only chance,' said Fitz, his voice sounding dull in his ringing ears.

They hauled the refrigerator – its side blackened – out of the way, piled into the hall and dashed up the stairs, Fitz first, followed by the Doctor.

They dodged into the nearest room and slammed the door behind them. Fitz glanced around the room; double bed, wardrobe, chest of drawers, no sign of Kerstin. She must be in the room opposite, on the other side of the landing. Fitz hoped she was all right.

'Where's Björn?' gasped the Doctor.

Kerstin huddled in the corner of the spare room, closing her eyes and floating back to the last moment of sanity in her life, the last time she remembered feeling safe. Swimming in the lake, just last night, not even twenty-four hours ago. The sound of a gunshot from downstairs made her heart leap in her chest, and brought her back to her senses.

She listened, desperately wishing she knew what was going on. Were the others still alive? Had the creatures got them?

Another gunshot rang through the house. She heard footsteps on the stairs, clambering quickly, and then Björn's bedroom door slam closed. Then a scrabbling on the stairs.

She backed away from the door, and found herself beside the window. She peered out. The things were hopping about outside, leaping over fences, converging on the house, making an unearthly hissing, rattling noise. Kerstin stumbled back from the window in a daze, bumping against the bed and sitting down hard.

Then she became aware of another noise, a low rumbling which reverberated inside her skull. The noise of engines. She got up and went to the window again.

Driving at speed along the road from the forest were three large white trucks. They weren't like any vehicles she had ever seen: low and windowless, with big chunky wheels, and a cab that looked like something from a space shuttle. They passed out of her field of vision, following the road that led to the barns and the timber store. What were they? Were they here to rescue them? Or had they set the things loose?

Björn felt himself being dragged backwards down the stairs. He could feel their teeth in his legs, sharp hooks digging in. As he reached the bottom of the stairs, they climbed up his body and started ripping at his chest and throat. He screamed, his vision blurring, misting red, and he tried to shove the creatures away but it was no use and numbness began to envelop him, a delicious numbness and all he had to do was give in. His last thought was that the Doctor had said he would live a long while yet. He was wrong. Wrong.

One last shudder of pain, then numbness, then nothing.

Fitz heard Björn's screams, and felt even more sick. Sick and scared that it was going to happen to him. Ripped apart by alien creatures, Sam still missing. Everything had gone wrong. For the first time, he wished he'd never seen the TARDIS or the Doctor.

The Doctor's face was pale, as pale as Johan's had been, and he was shaking his head. 'He wasn't meant to die like that.'

Fitz frowned. 'What do you mean? How was he meant to die?'

The Doctor's eyes were wide with fright. 'Peacefully, in ten years' time after drinking too much whisky.'

'How the hell do you know that?'

'I get flashes of people's futures. Sometimes. But in this case I was wrong.' The Doctor's face twisted in anguish. 'It's the TARDIS, Fitz. I didn't realise how much I needed her. Without her I'm... incomplete.'

Then the window shattered and one of the creatures shot through, its circular mouth drooling and gaping.

They piled out of the room, and hammered on the door opposite. To Fitz's relief, Kerstin opened the door and they went inside. The Doctor shut the door and leaned against it, panting.

From the other side came the sound of sharp claws scrabbling against wood.

Kerstin's face was pale and drawn. 'Where's Björn? I – I heard a scream.'

'He's dead,' said Fitz.

Kerstin sat down on the edge of the bed

They needed help. The police. Nordenstam. Fitz took the mobile phone from his pocket. He stabbed at the buttons. The words LO BATT appeared on the screen. What did *that* mean? He put it to his ear. No sound. He tossed it to the floor.

Outside, Fitz caught a glimpse of shambling white figures.

They were carrying long, strange-looking guns. As Fitz watched, one of the men brought his weapon to bear on a crowd of creatures. A jet of flame billowed out from the end, setting them alight. There was a terrible screeching, black figures twisting and hopping as they burned.

'It's the ones I told you about,' he said. 'The State Biohazard Protection Unit.' He was trying to open the window – quite a drop, but what choice did they have? – but the bloody thing was stuck. He managed to heave it open when a gout of flame blasted up the side of the farmhouse. Fitz ducked, feeling a wave of heat wash over him. He leaned out of the window, just as one of the suited figures lined up to fire at the farmhouse again. 'Stop that for God's sake!' he yelled as loud as he could. 'There are people in here.'

The flame-thrower was lowered – he'd been heard.

'Have you noticed something?' said the Doctor.

'Yes, several things,' said Fitz hotly.

'No no no,' said the Doctor. 'Listen!'

Fitz listened. He could hear the dry belch of the flame-throwers, the sound of engines, excited metallic shouts from outside. And from beyond the door to the room – nothing. The creatures had stopped scrabbling at the door.

'Are they gone?' asked Kerstin.

'I don't know,' said the Doctor, walking over to the door. 'Shall we see?'

'Doctor, no!' shouted Fitz – but it was too late. The Doctor had opened the door.

Fitz braced himself, shielding Kerstin with his body.

But nothing leapt through the doorway – and, lying on the landing, Fitz could see one of the creatures, lying on its side, its hind legs moving weakly.

They peered down the stairs.

The creatures were strewn on the staircase, their legs moving feebly, their round maws slack and dribbling.

'They're dying,' said the Doctor. 'Now I wonder why.'

'Who cares?' said Fitz.

They walked down the stairs, picking their way past the dying beasts.

Björn's body was in the hall but Fitz looked quickly away, as it appeared that the beasts had torn him in half.

'Someone will have to answer for this,' muttered the Doctor.

They stepped outside. The creatures were lying around in heaps, dead or dying. The white-suited figures were burning them, making funeral pyres. The roar and hiss and crackle of the flames filled the air. The stench of burning flesh was sickening.

Two of the suited figures noticed them, and motioned them away from the farmhouse. They stood back as the figures squirted something over the side of the house and then applied their flame-throwers.

The side of the building went up in a yellow bloom of flame.

Kerstin broke free from the Doctor, screaming, demanding to know what was going on.

'I don't like the look of this,' said the Doctor.

The two white-suited figures approached them slowly.

'They did save our lives,' said Fitz hopefully. Perhaps these were the good guys.

The Doctor was hiding behind him, mouth close to his ear. 'I could recall a well-known saying involving a certain kitchen utensil and a hot orangey thing rather like that one over there but I fear that would be rather otiose,' he babbled.

Fitz stepped back, so that he and the Doctor stood side by side. 'Kerstin, get away from here,' said Fitz.

She moved back, to stand behind them.

'Doctor, talk us out of this,' hissed Fitz. 'Do something!'

The Doctor looked dazed, but he stepped forward, motioning for Fitz to step back. He did so, grabbing Kerstin.

'Good evening!' said the Doctor, spreading his arms out wide in welcome.

The two figures didn't move.

The Doctor seemed to be recovering his old bravado. 'Thank you for rescuing us. I am the Doctor, and you are?'

The figure on the right reached up with a gloved hand and

95

lifted up his triangular faceplate. It took Fitz a second or two to recognise the bland, wide-mouthed face inside, but when he did he shouted in anger.

It was Lindgard.

'Well, this is nice,' said the Doctor.

Kerstin hurled herself at Lindgard. 'What have you done with Johan?' she screamed.

The other suited figure caught her and shoved her back towards Fitz. She collapsed to the ground, sobbing.

'What's all this for, Lindgard?' said the Doctor, walking right up to him.

Lindgard's face was bathed in sweat, and his eyes were wide, gleaming in the flickering firelight. 'You have a knack, Doctor, for turning up at the right place at the wrong time.' He raised a gloved hand. In it was the deadly shape of a pistol.

Fitz's heart gave a jolt.

The Doctor cocked his head on one side. 'You've been sent to capture me, haven't you? You won't shoot me.'

Lindgard shrugged. 'Won't I?'

The pistol jerked silently in his hand and the Doctor clutched his chest, a look of surprise on his face. 'Run, Fitz,' he croaked.

But the Doctor was falling backwards, and Fitz stooped to hold him. His body felt slack, heavy. What had they shot him with? Fitz felt totally powerless.

'Run!' said the Doctor. It sounded as if he was putting his last energies into the word.

Fitz felt the world spin away from him for a second, images flashing before his eyes: Björn with the whisky, then lying dead; Sam flying away down that impossible whirlpool; Kerstin, screaming in pain as Johan's fingers dug into her arm; the Doctor, sipping tea in Strängnäs only that morning and now lying at Fitz's feet.

Fitz stood up, swaying.

Lindgard observed him, an amused look on his face. 'Well, you heard him. Run!' He raised the pistol.

Suddenly Kerstin leapt up, brandishing a log. Fitz had no idea where she'd got it from, but she hurled it right at the two figures. Lindgard stepped back, losing his footing as it connected with his chest.

Fitz grabbed Kerstin's arm and they ran. He dared not look back to see if Lindgard was giving chase.

Kerstin dragged him round the back of the farmhouse, crouching down by the wood bunker. Above them, the building blazed. Fitz could feel the heat on his face, like a blast from some huge oven, hear the crackle and pop and roar of flames.

Lindgard and his mob would find them soon. They couldn't stay here.

'Into the forest,' said Kerstin.

Fitz ran, Kerstin ahead of him, hopping over feebly moving, dying creatures. She opened the gate. The field stretched out ahead of them, the dark line of forest some distance away. Could they make it?

He looked back, half expecting to see the tall figure of the Doctor running pell-mell after them. Instead he saw two white-suited figures run round the side of the blazing building and point something at them.

Without looking back further, Fitz ran. Something whizzed past his ear and he staggered. But they reached the forest in one piece, and once inside, in the warm, aromatic darkness, he felt safer; but he still kept running, stumbling through the undergrowth, just about keeping pace with Kerstin.

He looked back over his shoulder. The burning farmhouse was just an intermittent orange flickering through the trees now.

He had no idea where they were heading. Away from the fire, that was the best thing. Away from the fire and away from the Doctor – *they'd shot him, he could be dead.*

They ran into the dark forest, and behind them the farmhouse burned, the flames long and yellow in the pale night, flickering into the starless sky.

Book Two
Hope

Chapter Eight
Under/Above the Sky-Sea

Pain, before everything. Before she realised who she was, before she opened her eyes, there was pain. Distant at first, as if her whole body were numb. Then it sharpened to specific points, each one clamouring for attention: head, knees, elbows. She was lying on her front, on a slope, her head pointing downward, face pressed against something rough, like stone. She could feel it under her bare arms as well. She had the strangest idea that she had fallen from a great height. But, if she had, surely she would be dead, her body smashed and broken. But she clearly remembered now, falling as slowly as a leaf from a tree.

And then everything came back. She was *Sam Jones* and she was really pissed off with Fitz. After two years apart, they'd ended up arguing. Arguing about the Doctor. Fitz had stormed out. Then a strange whirlpool of light had swallowed her, taken her from the TARDIS.

Taken her – where?

She tried to move, awakening other pains, in her knees, her toes, her elbows, her chest, her face. She couldn't breathe properly, and her heart felt as though it were tripping over itself trying to keep up with her racing mind. She opened her eyes, but she couldn't see anything except a blurry image of pale-pink things against blackness. Was she blind? Her throat tightened in panic. *Please, please don't let me be blind.* She stared at the pink things, but they refused to resolve into anything recognisable. The image was all wrong, as if she were wearing someone else's glasses. She blinked, moved her hands to rub her eyes. The pale-pink things moved correspondingly, and a stinging pain registered in her palms. Ah. So that was what they were. Her hands.

She sat up, rubbing her eyes gingerly. Her body was racked

with the most excruciating pins and needles, and, though she was breathing more easily, she still felt a tightness in her chest, recalling a childhood bout of asthma. She still had an inhaler, somewhere, in case of a recurrence, but that was in the TARDIS, and the TARDIS was –

Was *where* exactly?

She remembered sitting on her bed, staring into the whirlpool, clinging on, watching familiar objects twirling away down its throat. She remembered the sudden lunge when it had grabbed her, like that feeling you get in a lift, magnified a hundredfold. She remembered falling, the bed spinning away from her, its sheets billowing like cartoon ghosts. She remembered a sense of great speed, glowing walls of spiralling light whipping by like a million Catherine wheels. Dizzying, sickening. She must have blacked out.

Had it taken Fitz and the Doctor too? 'Doctor!' she cried. Her voice echoed, as if she were in an empty cathedral. 'Doctor, are you there?'

She listened to the echoes of her voice fade away slowly, surprised by its loudness. Stupid – now anything nasty that might be lurking nearby knew she was here. She crouched tensely for a while, looking around, grimacing, ready for flight, wondering how she could run if she couldn't see properly.

Perhaps the whirlpool had destroyed the TARDIS, and she'd managed to escape somehow. Or maybe she was still in the TARDIS, in some long-forgotten area. Gradually the pins and needles shrank away to a dull ache. And things were getting clearer, sharper. Soon, she was able to see everything clearly.

She was sitting halfway down a slope of black rock – rough, porous, spongelike. It had chafed her face and arms, hence the pain. The slope ran down into a valley, and the other side of the valley rose up and up, in gentle waves, to meet –

The sky?

Sam's jaw dropped.

It wasn't like any sky she'd ever seen. It was a pink swirling mass, ever-changing, glowing and pulsing, like the biggest, grooviest lava lamp ever made. As she stared, it began to resemble a sea, which meant, she realised with a dizzying sense of dislocation, that she was looking down.

She shook her head. Up was up and down was down, whatever optical tricks this place played on her. She turned round, scuffing her jeans on the rock, her movements feeling strange and dreamlike. Perhaps this was a dream. But the pain in her hands and on her forehead was all too real.

Everything was bathed in a pink neonlike glow. There was a low background sound, a moaning, like the wind in a storm, which she supposed was being made by the strange 'sky'. The air was clammy, with a hint of something flowery.

So, she wasn't inside the TARDIS, unless it had somehow been transformed into something really weird. She stood up carefully, gently touching her forehead. There was a little blood, a slight graze.

She took a step forward and rose into the air, her feet pedalling to reach the ground. She yelled out, her stomach turning over as she sailed up and up, over the bottom of the valley to land gracelessly on the other side, bumping her knees and elbows on the spongelike rock.

Low gravity. Well, now she knew how she had survived her fall.

She set off carefully back down the slope. Here and there were scattered some of the things from her room – books, pages torn; CDs, strewn like forgotten Frisbees; the sheets from her bed and even the bed itself. The chessboard.

Fitz?

No sign of him or the Doctor, or any form of life.

She neared the bottom of the valley, and slowed down, aiming to land in the middle. She did, stumbling a little. The valley floor was covered in crumbled-off bits of black rock, like little lumps of coal. She set off along the bottom of the valley, which curved slightly to the left. In the low gravity, she could move quite quickly, but even so the valley seemed to go on for ever. At one point, she looked up to see that the 'sky' met a shore of bluish stuff like burnished metal.

Her brain boggled again. Now the 'sky' looked even more like a swirling pink sea. Which meant she was somehow walking upside down above it. She crouched down, fighting a wave of nausea. Taking a deep breath, she looked up. The blue shore curved down until it met the walls of the valley, the black and blue rock fusing in a disturbingly organic-looking web. Ahead, darkness. She was staring into a vast, wide tunnel where the light of the – oh, what to call it? sky-sea – did not reach. She could just make out stalactites, stalagmites and weird twisted spurs of rock. It looked as inviting as the business end of a Dalek gun.

She had an idea.

She ran up the side of the valley, until she was right underneath the sky-sea. Her perception adjusted itself, so she now felt she was standing beside the sky-sea, the bottom of the valley arching above her like a vast vaulted ceiling.

Up close, the glow of the sky-sea was intense, and she could hear a strange sighing as it lapped against the blue shore. She reached out tentatively. It wasn't radiating any heat, but she was loath to dip her fingers in. It could be anything. She picked up a black pebble and tossed it into the pink mass. It vanished soundlessly, with no telltale hiss. So it wasn't some sort of burning, corrosive acid, then.

She took out a tissue from her jeans pocket and dunked it quickly into the sky-sea. It emerged exactly the same, not even wet. Tentatively, biting her lip, Sam dipped a finger into the stuff.

She couldn't feel anything. It was though she'd dipped her hand into nothing, into pure light. She put her whole hand in and swooshed it around, creating swirling white patterns in the surface. Then she took her hand out and scrutinised it closely. No change.

Sam leaned backward on her haunches. She'd hoped to gather some of the stuff, use it to light her way. Oh well. She loped back down the valley, and, taking a deep breath, ventured into the tunnel. She squinted, trying to make out the shapes in the gloom. There was a sort of humped mass ahead. Had it moved just then, or was it a trick of the light? Swallowing, she walked deeper in. After a while, she could see an orange glow from up ahead. Fire? Presently, she emerged into another cavern, carpeted with tiny orange crystals which glowed with an inner light. The cavern floor sloped up in a steep bowl shape to meet a twisted landscape of arches, tunnels and buttresses, soaring way above her head. Behind the arches came the glow of another sky-sea, this one neon-blue.

Sam stared. It looked forbidding, unwelcoming. There was no sign of life. And the arches and tunnels offered at least twenty different routes. Sam chose a tunnel at random, her trainers crunching on the fiery crystals. She had no idea where she was going, but at least she was going *somewhere*.

Fitz ran through the forest, his breath coming in ragged gasps, the smoke he'd inhaled making him cough and splutter. He felt so unfit. There was a stitch in his side which sang with pain each time he breathed in. He could just hear Sam now, telling him that if he had never smoked he'd be able to run without wheezing like a faulty TARDIS.

Ahead, Kerstin stumbled through the ferns and bushes. She was sobbing, a high keening sound tearing from her throat with every breath. They were making so much noise between them that he was surprised they hadn't been found.

Fitz stopped and leaned against a tree to get his breath back. 'Kerstin!' he gasped. 'Slow down.'

Kerstin came back to him. Her eyes were wild, unfocused. 'I've had enough, I've had enough.'

The pain in his side was easing now. 'Look, so have I,' he snapped.

Kerstin blinked and frowned, wiping tears and snot away from her face with the back of her hand. She seemed embarrassed by her tears.

'We've both been through a lot,' he said more gently. 'But we've got to think. We've got to find out what's going on.'

The silence all around them was spooking Fitz, as if the whole forest were listening in. Above, he could see dark-blue shards of sky through the branches.

Kerstin's face was pale in the gloom. 'They burnt the farm. They'll do anything. They'll kill us!'

Fitz didn't respond. It was probably true. What the hell should they do now? Go back to the TARDIS? Fitz remembered Sam telling him that there was a spare key above the P in the POLICE BOX sign – but the Doctor had said the TARDIS had reverted to its original form so presumably there was no way in, even if the spare key was still there.

'We have to go back,' said Fitz.

Kerstin visibly tensed up. 'No.' She waved a hand in the air. 'We'll go to the town, to the police – they'll sort everything out.'

'Look,' said Fitz. 'We've got to go back for the Doctor. He might not be dead, and he's the only person who could sort out what's going on. And he's my passport home.'

Kerstin put her hands on her hips and stepped closer to Fitz. 'Right. I've had enough of this man-of-mystery stuff. Who are you? Who are you really working for?'

She was shouting, her voice echoing loudly through the forest, and Fitz shushed her frantically. 'All right, all right! You may as well know the truth.' Fitz took a deep breath, wondering what to tell her first. 'Well, for a start, we don't work for anybody. And the Doctor – well, he's not like us. He's a thousand years old and not even from this planet. The TARDIS is his ship. It travels in time, which is how come I'm here. I'm from 1963.' He gestured to the forest around them. 'This is my future.'

Kerstin was staring at him as if he was mad. 'Your future?'

'Yep,' said Fitz. 'Not too different, really,' he added lamely.

Kerstin's eyes had grown distant. 'A *time* machine?' She shook her head. 'I don't know *what* to believe any more.'

A noise in the distance alerted Fitz and he motioned for her to be quiet.

There was someone in the forest, heading straight for them.

'Quick, over here,' whispered Fitz.

They hid in bushes as three white-suited figures walked past.

When they were a safe distance away Fitz let out a long breath of relief.

Then an idea popped into his mind. He almost wished it hadn't. 'We'll follow them,' he whispered.

'You're mad,' said Kerstin. 'We go to the police.'

'This is bigger than the police,' argued Fitz. 'Those bastards are operating outside the law. If you go to the police you'll only come up against some cover-up. They'll say the fire at the farm was an accident. Even that Björn did it himself for insurance purposes, and got caught in the flames.'

Kerstin looked pensive. 'Then who are they? The government?'

'The only way to find out is to follow them.'

Kerstin slumped against the trunk of a tree. Fitz watched her anxiously, realising that he was acting towards her as if she were Sam. Tough, capable Sam, who could take anything in her stride. Almost anything. But could Kerstin take any more?

'Fitz?' said Kerstin, her voice tinged with fear.

'Yes?'

Her face was set, resolute, and he could tell that she was thinking about Johan. 'All right. We follow them. Find out what's really going on.'

A feeling of relief washed over Fitz, until he realised that he'd been half hoping for her to say no.

Still, they were committed now.

Together, they crept through the forest.

The Doctor sat up suddenly. He gasped as a stinging pain radiated from a spot on his chest, from where he'd been shot. He could feel the drug in his bloodstream – a dragging, dulling impurity. Some sort of tranquilliser. His body was working overtime to get rid of it. There was a nasty taste in his mouth and his skull felt several sizes too small for his brain.

He stood up, looking around. The room was large, airy, tastefully decorated. There was a pastel-pink three-piece suite arranged in front of a large stone fireplace. Underfoot, sanded pine floorboards. A fresh, artificial tang laced the air, and the slow whine of an air-conditioning unit was the only sound. There was no visible door. No window. So. However plush, this was a prison cell. Under different circumstances, the Doctor would have admired the items of minimalist art – reproductions, of course – adorning the walls.

But not while he was locked up.

He hated being locked up. Hated it. *Hated it.* Hated. It.

He tried to calm himself, his breathing becoming ragged and wheezy. His respiratory bypass system was contracting, as it often did in times of stress, or when it thought he was going to be knocked out. So perhaps he should let the panic out, externalise it. But was he being watched? If so, by whom?

Questions whirled inside his head. He had to be seen to be calm, unflappable, a force to be reckoned with. Never let the enemy see your vulnerable side. Hands shaking, the Doctor wandered around the room, feeling in every corner, peering behind every picture. He even tried to lift up one of the chairs, only to find that it was fixed to the floor. What he was looking for he couldn't exactly say. A hidden microphone or camera, a secret door, anything.

He thought of Fitz and Kerstin. He hoped they had run, quickly, and in a sensible direction. Maybe they had been captured like himself. He hoped they were safe. To lose one companion was bad enough, but to lose them all, *and* the TARDIS... that smacked of carelessness.

The Doctor squeezed his eyes shut. Calm, calm, calm, Doctor. You've been in worse scrapes than this.

The Doctor opened his eyes, rubbed them and resumed his search. The fireplace was false, its flue blocked off. That left the mirror on the far side of the room. It ran the whole length of one wall and he knew somehow that it was a two-way mirror, that he was being watched.

He stood before the mirror, hands on hips, arranging his features in a way he hoped would be imposing and threatening. 'I demand to know why you have brought me here and what you have done with my companions!'

Silence.

A sliver of doubt; perhaps there was no one behind the mirror. Perhaps they were all too busy, and had dumped him here to deal with later. The Doctor swallowed, his mouth dry with panic. He fought the emotion down, curdling it into anger. How dare they treat him like this?

Anger. Good. In its most positive form it was an energy, and it was about time he turned it to good use.

But it was no good without something to vent it upon. Turning round on his heel, the Doctor scowled at the plush sofa, and with a roar of rage gave it a hefty kick in the pillows.

Sam had lost track of time. She'd been walking and climbing and floating through her strange new environment for what seemed like days. Her main aim was to find the surface, get out in the open air, but she was beginning to lose hope. She was tired, hungry, and her arms and legs were aching. She hoped this was from the effects of low gravity. She had no way of knowing what radiation her body was soaking up.

The planet – if it was a planet – seemed to consist of a series of interconnected caverns, all with a sky-sea providing illumination at wildly different angles. These sky-seas varied in colour. Some were pink, others blue, others a burning yellow like the sun. Sam wondered if they were some bizarre form of life.

Life. There wasn't much of it around. It was as though the place were deserted, abandoned; it had an air of neglect. She saw the odd insectoid thing – an elongated black dragonfly with four orange wings and a round, gaping mouth – but, apart from that, nothing.

She had got the hang of the strange gravity, though it took some getting used to. There really was no 'up' or 'down' here, not in any conventional sense. Gravity seemed to be strongest on the edges of the caverns, and weakest in the middle. A thrown pebble would sail away from her outstretched hand, its velocity decreasing visibly, until it came to a standstill somewhere near the middle of the cavern. So, some sort of rule of surface tension seemed to prevail, but she was blowed if she could work it out. What it meant in practical terms was that, wherever you were standing, your personal 'up' would be 'down' for someone standing at a point opposite you on the far side of the cavern.

Mental.

Sam coped with it on a cavern-by-cavern basis. If there was a sky-sea below her eyeline, then that direction was 'down'. If the sky-sea was above her then it became more sky than sea and that direction was 'up'. If the sky-sea was opposite her, in the far wall of the cavern, then she just had to walk around for a bit until she could fit it into some kind of perspective.

At length she found herself clambering over a lip of the ubiquitous black rock, a pink sky-sea flowing and churning far behind her. She'd been attracted to this lip of rock because above it was a narrow crack, through which poured what appeared to be daylight. Earth daylight.

She climbed through the crack into a cavern which took her breath away.

A slope of white sand ran down towards a beach which seemed to stretch on for ever. Massive pillars of rock rose like stacks of dominoes from the white sand. Through the middle of the cavern ran a cylindrical sky-sea, golden bright like the sun. It hurt to look at it, and its further ends were lost to distance.

The whole place was bathed in its golden glow and Sam's heart surged in her breast. It was one of the most beautiful sights she had ever seen.

She climbed over the ridge and ran down the slope, her feet scuffing white clouds into the golden air.

It was a slope only in appearance, of course. In this low gravity she felt almost weightless, and, as she'd discovered, up and down were entirely subjective. Looking back, she saw that she had climbed through a crack in the side of a cliff of grey rock. It looked as though something had made the hole. Something intelligent.

If she squinted, she could just about convince herself that she was on a Cornish beach, in blazing sunshine. She walked across the sand, and, as she passed one of the columns of black rock, she became aware of a sound. She thought she was hallucinating at first, but she could definitely hear it. The sound of children laughing, splashing water. Playing.

She crept round the side of the column, and saw two small figures beside a pool of liquid which sparkled and dazzled, reflecting the sky-sea. She gasped. For an instant, she'd taken them for human children, but now she could see that they were alien. For a start, their skin was pale green, the colour of apples. They were small, about three feet high. Their limbs were thin and sticklike, and they had webbed feet. They were clothed in pale-blue leaflike garments, and their heads were elongated, with small red mouths from which flicked black tongues, and the occasional excited hoot. Their heads were covered in a mass of feathery yellow 'hair' from beneath which peered perfectly round blue eyes. The overall impression was of a frog crossed with a fairy-tale pixie.

They were capering, their movements perfectly at ease in the low gravity, tossing pebbles across the pool and shrieking with unmistakable laughter as a black appendage flailed about, trying to catch the pebbles, scattering bright splashes of liquid which rose and fell languidly. It was a scene of such normal childish merriment that Sam felt irresistibly drawn to the small creatures.

But something held her back. She knew that appearances could be deceptive. Perhaps this was one of those crazy places where the ugly things were good and the cute things were evil.

But what choice did she have? She could go on walking for hours, or even days, and not come across any other signs of life. She'd eventually die of fatigue or thirst. Was that stuff water? She licked her dry lips and her stomach rumbled. Would she be able to eat the same things as these creatures? An image of the Doctor preparing one of his recipes in the TARDIS kitchens flickered into her mind.

She crouched down, keeping close to the pillar of black rock, intending to creep up slowly on the alien children. The shoulder of her T-shirt caught on a spur of the spongelike rock. She reached up to dislodge it and some of the rock crumbled away, falling soundlessly to the white sand.

She held her breath, watching the children. They had seen her, and now they were staring straight at her. One of them was holding a pebble, which it threw into the pond. It fell with a plop. The black appendage slipped below the surface.

No point in concealing herself now. Time for first contact. She emerged from hiding, putting on her best smile. 'Hello,' she said. 'I'm Sam Jones. Don't suppose you know any decent sandwich bars?'

Their reaction was instantaneous. They ran up to her, dancing around her, their voices high and squeaky. Sam felt their tiny hands on her jeans, tugging at her Mansun T-shirt.

Sam couldn't help but laugh. She stooped down, and one of them leapt on her back. It weighed next to nothing. The other capered before her, babbling. Then the one on her back gave a squeak, leapt down and scuttled off with its companion.

Sam followed them. They had run around the far side of another of the pillars. She didn't want to lose them – they were the first sign of intelligent life.

Then two figures stepped from behind the pillar of rock, and Sam stopped in her tracks.

They were as tall as Sam, and similar to the 'children,' the same green skin and blue eyes. Their hair was paler, almost white, and they wore a darker, more intricate type of clothing with ropelike leggings. The one on the left was dressed predominantly in red, the other in a mixture of purples and blacks. They stood, barring her way, arms hanging loosely by their sides.

'Hello,' said Sam, getting ready to run. 'Do you know when high tide is?'

The creatures exchanged glances, and then lunged in unison, grabbing her, their movements surprisingly swift. They pushed her across the sand towards a thing which looked like a giant lilypad.

The children peeped over the edge, staring at Sam.

She clambered on to the thing, and was shoved to the back, where a leaflike seat awaited her. She sank into its soft embrace, and tendrils emerged, whipping around her body, holding her tightly in place. She struggled briefly, but that only made them grip tighter, so she stopped.

The 'adults' were busying themselves at the front of the vehicle, adjusting stemlike controls. She felt a movement from beneath and they began to rise into the air.

'Who are you? Where is this place?'

But they weren't listening to her, as they took off over the beach and headed up into the golden sky.

The children were staring at her with round goggle eyes.

Perhaps it was the children. Perhaps they thought she was going to hurt them. 'Look, let me go, I wasn't going to harm your children.'

The one in red turned to her. His voice was fluting, almost musical, and he waved his hands in smooth, flowing gestures.

But she couldn't understand a word he was saying. Of course. Separated from the TARDIS, she wouldn't have the luxury of universal translation.

That might be a problem.

The creature stopped hooting, and turned back to the controls of the flyer.

Sam peered over the edge. They were borne aloft by the motion of flippers arranged around the edge of this giant 'lilypad'. Crazy. Would only work in this low gravity, she supposed. They were flying high in the cavern now, far above the 'beach'. Here and there, glittering pools shone brightly against the white sand. It was getting brighter all around, and Sam realised with a jolt of shock that they were heading straight towards the sky-sea.

Chapter Nine
Beneath the Twilight Forest

Professor Jennifer Nagle walked briskly along the dull concrete-floored corridor, allowing herself a big grin of satisfaction. It had been the first time she'd smiled for days. She just couldn't believe her luck. The Doctor, here, right at the time of crisis. It was just like all those stories the UNIT guys told. Mysterious things would start happening – aliens emerging from sewers or people being transformed into the slaves of some despotic computer – and then the Doctor would appear, in one of his many guises, solving the problem in a display of dazzling brilliance.

That was what she needed right now. The Doctor's brilliance.

She'd been studying theoretical physics at Princeton University back in the 1970s, when Earth had seemed to come under attack from an alien or home-grown menace every other week. And yet this was kept secret from the entire world. After she got her PhD she did a little digging around and soon discovered the existence of UNIT. A United Nations setup dedicated to combating alien menaces, hiding behind a skilfully constructed mask of disinformation. There was a huge cover-up going on, and she desperately wanted in. She craved the thrill of walking among the common people and *knowing*. Of being elite.

One day, in her rented apartment, she'd had a visitor. A well-dressed English man in his fifties, who told her all she wanted to know about UNIT and offered her the ultimatum of either joining or waving goodbye to her career for ever.

She remembered even now the way her scientific zeal ('curiosity' was way too lame a word) had blossomed. She had said yes right away. She just wanted to know. Know everything. She wanted to discover new worlds and new processes and be rewarded for doing so.

That was twenty years ago. Joining UNIT had been the best thing she had ever done. She'd been based in the US at first, rising to Professor of Theoretical Physics at Princeton. After that, her attachment to UNIT had taken her all over the world. And now, thanks to her hard work and one incredibly lucky discovery, she was deeper in, involved in research kept secret even from most of UNIT.

Professor Nagle quickened her pace. She had to get to the Doctor before Major Wolstencroft did, before he was 'interrogated'. She reached a door, outside which a UNIT soldier stood, rifle held across his broad chest, barring the way. He had a youthful face, close-cropped hair and pale-blue eyes. English, like most of Wolstencroft's men, and fiercely loyal.

She resented the presence of so many troops, but, after the events of the last few days, it looked like they'd need them.

'Private Schofield, isn't it?'

The soldier nodded, eyes fixed on a spot on the wall opposite.

She sighed. 'Well, aren't you going to let me in?'

'Pass, please.'

She waved a hand irritably. 'You know who I am, so let me in.'

'Yes, ma'am.' There was the trace of a smile on his face.

A pointless show, a reminder that Wolstencroft had stepped up security several hundred notches.

Private Schofield stood aside and Nagle entered the observation room. It was a small, boxlike space with three swivel chairs behind a monitoring unit. A two-way mirror spanned the far wall.

Two men looked up as she entered. The one on the left was Captain Daniel Rogers, Wolstencroft's right-hand man – an OK guy despite that. And next to him, Dr Boris Lindgard, the Swedish expert on extraterrestrial life. Lindgard was one of the few people in the base – apart from the soldiers – who had actually been outside. Nagle hadn't ventured outside for almost two years now. Lindgard was good – almost too good; a cold, calm professional. He'd been able to infiltrate the hospital with ease – with a little help from HQ, of course. He'd brought in the creatures from the forest, the body of Johan Svensson, and now this. The Doctor. The god from the box, who would save her reputation.

Through the two-way mirror Nagle could see the debriefing/detention room. Sitting on the sofa was a man with wavy golden-brown hair and an intelligent, long, sensitive face. He was wearing an expression of studied boredom, with just a hint of tension in the set of his shoulders and around his eyes.

She'd not seen this incarnation before. He was by far the best-looking, and the best-dressed: dark-green velvet frock coat, patterned waistcoat and a white wing-collar shirt with a cravat neatly tucked into the waistcoat. A smooth, unruffled, timeless look. Much better than – hold on now. How could she be sure this handsome stranger was the Doctor? 'Are you sure that's him?' she said, slipping into the chair next to Lindgard.

'Oh, yes,' said Lindgard. 'That is certainly the Doctor.' He spoke English well, along with a dozen other languages, some of them alien. A key factor in his selection for the job of man on the outside.

'This one's been turning up ever since 1997,' added Captain Rogers. He had close-cropped red hair and a thoughtful, freckled face. He laughed, showing perfect white teeth. 'That's the trouble with the good old Doc – always a few versions of him knocking about.'

Lindgard shot him a withering look. 'The captain is quite correct. The man in there is the eighth incarnation of the Doctor. I myself have also encountered the seventh.' He looked at the Doctor, a smile playing over his thin lips. 'Believe me, this one is far easier to deal with. Far more predictable.'

This was good news. 'As long as you're sure.'

'Believe me, it is him,' said Lindgard, a trace of impatience creeping into his voice. He smiled coldly. 'And now that I've got him for you, what do you want to do with him?'

Captain Rogers coughed. 'Well, the major will want to interview him. As a matter of security.'

Lindgard blew out through his lips. 'I don't think we have time for that.'

117

'We certainly don't,' said Nagle with feeling. 'I think it's time Major Wolstencroft realised who's in charge.' She leaned past Lindgard and addressed Captain Rogers. 'You guys are just here to protect us and keep outside eyes from prying, got that? Leave all the important stuff to us.'

Captain Rogers blushed visibly, but his eyes were defiant. 'We'll see,' he said tightly, and left the observation room.

Lindgard raised his eyebrows. 'One day you'll provoke them too far.'

Nagle shrugged. 'Yeah, but what can they do? We're their paymasters, after all.'

She reached out and pressed a switch on the desk in front of her.

The Doctor sat on the sofa, a cushion in his lap. He stroked it absently, as if it were a cat.

'Sorry for booting you like that,' he mumbled. 'Had to let it out somehow and you see you're a mere inanimate object. Though I've met many life forms which look like inanimate objects.' He was talking to himself to keep the panic down, until either something happened or he thought of a means of escape. 'The Ogri, for a start. Look like monoliths. Or is it megaliths?'

Suddenly a voice came from a hidden speaker, and the Doctor jumped to his feet, the cushion falling forgotten to the floor. It was a calm, professional-sounding, female voice, with an American accent the Doctor placed in Seattle or probably New York. 'Do not panic. You are safe. I am Professor Jennifer Nagle, Chief Scientist of this installation.'

Good, thought the Doctor – at least I'm speaking to someone in charge. 'Then you can doubtless tell me why you have brought me here against my will?'

There was a pause. Then: 'We have brought you here because we believe you can help us.'

They were very close to the sky-sea now. It was blinding, like staring into the sun, and Sam had to sit, eyes tight shut, so that her world turned red and black. She could hear the two creatures hooting instructions to each other.

'You're not gonna fly into that thing, are you?' she yelled, knowing they couldn't understand her, but unable to keep the panic down any longer. The pink sky-sea had been safe enough but this one looked hot, as hot as the sun. She opened her mouth to scream, struggling against her bonds, convinced that she was about to be burnt to a crisp.

But it didn't happen.

Everything got brighter and brighter – and then went back to normal.

Sam opened her eyes.

They were inside the sky-sea, travelling along it. It was like being inside a golden tunnel, stretching ahead into the distance. The stuff of the sky-sea wasn't wet, it exerted no pressure, and she could breathe normally. 'This is too weird,' she breathed, relieved nonetheless.

The creatures ignored her, standing impassively at the prow of their leaf-vehicle, while the children oohed and aahed.

The Doctor would love this, thought Sam. It seemed to be three things: a sky that wasn't a sky, a sea that wasn't wet – and which gave light – and a sun that you could travel inside, without getting burnt instantly to nothing.

At length, they emerged from the tunnel of light into a wider area of sky-sea. They broke the surface to emerge into a vast cylindrical cavern, whose walls expanded and flowered into a trumpet shape. As they rose up, Sam could see hundreds of brown domelike dwellings dotted about on the walls, and just make out dots of green, where the froglike creatures moved.

There was something above them, some sort of structure. As they grew nearer Sam realised how big it was – easily as big as a city. It hung from the ceiling of the cavern, an onion-shaped ball with spiralling towers and minarets, all formed from a dark-green material, shining with lights.

The leaflike flyer drew closer and closer to one particular tower, towards an opening. They flew inside, into a wide long hall, filled with a milling crowd of the creatures.

Ah. The crowd were above them, seemingly standing on the ceiling, and they were flying up to them –

Sam's mind boggled, and she made a quick adjustment.

And she now saw that the crowd were standing on the floor of the amphitheatre. The air was thick with their cries. They all seemed to be in a great rush about something, and this mood passed to the pilots of the leaf-vehicle, whose hootings had become to sound rather stressed. The children cowered in a corner, their round blue eyes shining in the golden light which streamed in from the sky-sea miles below – erm, above, or whatever.

Their flyer settled down and Red and Purple disembarked. The two young creatures ran off into the crowd, soon to be lost out of sight amid the bustle. Sam was alarmed to see that the adults did not seem to notice or care about this.

A crowd had gathered around Sam. She felt as if she were at a slave auction. Perhaps that was what this was all about. Green faces and blue eyes peered at her from all directions. Sam shook off their probing hands. 'Hey, get off.' After a while they began to lose interest and drift away.

Her original captors led Sam across the arena to the other side, shoving through the crowd. The sense of panic was palpable, and contagious. Sam felt light-headed with hunger and exhaustion.

Red pulled her towards what looked like a giant finned aubergine, which she presumed was another sort of low-gravity dirigible. Other hands grabbed her, shoving her inside, into a leaf-seat next to some spindly creatures which resembled giant praying mantises. Tendrils emerged from under the seat, binding her firmly. She sighed, settling back, resigned for the moment. Despite the restraints, it was actually quite comfy.

She looked at the creature next to her. It was a pale-bluish colour, its six legs covered in thin silver bristles which kept tickling Sam now and then. Its head was flat, ovoid, with black compound eyes at the edge, and mandibles hidden underneath near the jointed neck. It chittered at her and rubbed its forelegs together, making a noise which set Sam's teeth on edge.

One of the froglike creatures was walking up and down a central aisle, handing out chunks of a brown fungus-like stuff. The Mantises ate it hungrily, and Sam saw some of the frog-things tuck in, too. Sam took a piece, wondering briefly if it would be poison, but she was tired and hungry, so she ate. It tasted remarkably good, like a floury fruit with a hint of cinnamon.

Soon they were airborne, above the crowd. She looked out of the slitlike window to her left. Below, the creatures were silent, staring up at the dirigible. It was an eerie sight – a sea of alien faces, lifted up towards her, their yellow-white hair contrasting with their green faces and varying pastel shades of their costumes.

The dirigible sailed out of a wide opening in the side of the amphitheatre. Above – or below – the sky-sea glowed at the bottom – or top – of the cylindrical cavern, looking for all the world like a sun. The dirigible plunged down and down, back towards it, and Sam had to shield her eyes from its glare.

She chewed her last mouthful of food, trying to put together what was going on. Where was she? Who were these creatures and what were they afraid of? And, most importantly, what were they going to do with her?

Fitz and Kerstin had followed the three men to a small clearing, and they now hid at the edge in the cover of the trees. Moonlight threw everything into sharp relief – the wooden cabin in the centre of the clearing, the white-suited figures approaching it, opening the door and stepping inside.

Kerstin shifted restlessly. 'This just gets weirder,' she said. 'What would they want in there?'

Fitz glanced at her. Her face still held a strained look, especially round the eyes. 'Depends what's in there. What is it, something to do with the farm?'

Kerstin shrugged. 'I don't know. I only come here on holiday.'

Fitz stood up, stepping into the clearing.

A hand on his shoulder. 'What are you doing?' said Kerstin in a panicky whisper.

'They've been in there for ages. I'm just going to have a peep inside.'

Fitz left the safety of the trees and walked over to the cabin. It looked neat and compact, its wooden walls painted the usual rust-red. He walked around it, discovering a grimy window on the far side. Holding his breath, Fitz peered through. In the gloom he could just make out the far wall, and a blocky shape in the middle. As his eyes adjusted he saw it was a table. Of the three men there was no sign.

He walked back round to the door, giving the handle a tug. It was locked. He knocked, heart hammering in his chest, ready for flight.

But there was no answer. It was as if the men had vanished, as if the cabin was some sort of TARDIS.

He heard Kerstin run across the clearing and turned to her.

'Do you want to bring them back out?' she hissed.

'There's no one in there,' said Fitz.

Kerstin stared at the door as if she expected it to burst open at any moment. 'Well, where did they go?'

'That's what I want to find out. Now help me bust this door open.'

It took several attempts, but between them they forced open the door by repeated kicking that Fitz feared would attract unwelcome attention. But at last, after a hefty kick from Fitz, the door crashed open.

Fitz went in first, hoping Kerstin wouldn't notice how scared he was. The cabin was bare, and Fitz relaxed.

'No danger here,' he said, turning round to her and smiling widely.

The interior was dusty and dim, with a few shelves and a workbench at one end, a chair and table in the centre. There was no other exit apart from the door.

Kerstin followed, her trainers making no sound on the wooden floor. 'What now?'

She looked as if she was about to suggest going to the police again – which, Fitz realised, was the sensible thing to do. 'Find out where they went,' he said lamely.

Kerstin walked around the shack. 'This is a dead end,' she muttered.

Fitz walked up to the workbench. There was a vice clamped to the side of it, and Fitz idly toyed with the handle. As he did so the floor gave a jolt beneath them. Fitz gave a yelp of surprise and grabbed on to the workbench, exchanging a panicky look with Kerstin.

Then he noticed that at the bottom of the walls was a lengthening strip of concrete. It took him a moment to figure out what was going on. The floor of the shack was descending. The whole thing was a lift.

'Well, now we know how they got out,' called Fitz above the noise of the engine. He watched fearfully as they descended into the shaft, its concrete walls streaked with oil, the ceiling of the shack receding above them. The table and chair were juddering about with the motion, Kerstin trying to still them.

At length the far wall gave way on to an open corridor, brick-walled, concrete-floored and lit by dim bulbs hanging from a concave ceiling.

They stepped out of the lift. Fitz's heart was thumping in his chest and one look at Kerstin told him that she was feeling the same. 'Don't suppose Björn knew about any of this,' said Fitz.

Kerstin smiled thinly. 'Suppose not.'

Fitz sighed. Anything was possible. This passage probably led to the cavern of some exiled alien dictator, or the underground base of an alien advance force.

And they were walking right into it. What the hell was he doing?

They went a little way along the corridor. It smelled of oil and cement and neglect. Fitz expected to bump into the white-suited chaps at any moment, but the place was deserted. Presently they came to a metal door, covered in peeling green paint. It was ajar and he gave it a gentle push. It swung open to reveal a large area which looked like the changing rooms of a football club. There was a row of showers at the far end, lockers and benches. Slung on to hooks on the wall near the door were half a dozen of the white biohazard suits, the silver helmets stowed on a shelf above them. The perfect disguise.

'Come on,' he said to Kerstin. 'Put one of these on.'

Kerstin's eyes widened. 'Are you mad?'

Fitz took one of the suits down and handed it to her. 'Totally and irretrievably.'

The Mantises had started chittering and struggling to escape the moment they'd left the golden sky-sea. Sam looked out of the slit-window to see that they were now floating through the middle of a cavern with a floor of undulating red rock dotted with stalagmites. Jagged stalactites hung down from a low ceiling. It was like flying inside the mouth of a giant monster. The whole place was lit by a distant pink sky-sea.

The flyer spiralled down towards the far end of the cavern, away from the sky-sea. Sam frowned. There was something there. A blackness which was hard to look at. It seemed to draw her mind out through her eyes.

As they grew nearer, the Mantises became more and more agitated.

She felt a gentle bump as they landed in a shallow bowl of dusty red rock near some stalagmites which towered twice the height of their dirigible. Beyond them, dense, impenetrable blackness.

One of the frog-things appeared before her, bearing a trident as tall as itself. The tendrils binding her fell limp and retracted. Other frog-things herded the Mantises from their seats and out through a hatch in the side of the dirigible.

The eyes of the frog-thing before her were wide, their lids almost invisible white lines against the pale-green skull. Its mouth was gaping and Sam noticed with a slight sense of disgust that it was drooling, thick strands of saliva running out of its round red mouth and on to its brown leaflike garments.

She was hauled roughly out of her seat and pushed down a ramp on to the dusty cavern floor amid the Mantises, which were now screeching in abject terror. Sam grimaced in anger. They were manhandling her as though she were a sack of spuds. And she wasn't going to take it any more.

She made to clamber to her feet, ready to fight the creatures off and make a run for it, but the bloody Mantises were clawing at her jeans, their spiky limbs drawing her down with them.

Unable to resist, she was herded towards the row of stalagmites which loomed before the blackness. Two of the frog-things were drooling over the glassy red rock, thick mucus pouring from their mouths in streams.

Sam was lifted up and taken to one of the stalagmites. They pressed her against the side that faced the black wall. She wriggled, but her back, legs and neck were becoming stuck to the rock, her feet a whole metre above the dusty ground. She felt them grab her arms and dribble all over them, sticking them to the side of the stalagmite. She saw that they were doing the same to the Mantises, which had kept up their unearthly screeching.

The frog-things let go, and Sam struggled but she couldn't move her arms or her legs, or even her head. The mucus had hardened and held her as fast as superglue.

And before her the strange blackness. It had the quality of a swarm of flies, its edges indistinct and blurry, and it was spreading over the rocks, advancing towards her.

'Hey!' yelled Sam, her voice rising in fear. 'Let me go!'

The frog-things had prostrated themselves in front of the blackness, all six of them, their arms and heads raised towards it, a slow moaning wail rising from their throats.

She suddenly realised what was happening. This was a sacrifice. They were going to sacrifice her, and themselves, to this unknowable blackness.

She struggled anew, but it was no use.

All she could do was watch, her only movement her terrified thumping heart, as the blackness closed in on her.

Chapter Ten
A Means to an End

Professor Nagle observed the Doctor's reaction through the two-way mirror. It was interesting. He had jumped up when she'd first spoken, his look of surprise changing to a scowl of righteous anger. When she'd asked for his help his long, handsome face had adopted an expression of almost comical surprise.

'Help you?' came his voice through a speaker on the monitoring desk. '*Help* you?' He stepped right up to the glass. He really was a looker, and his strange clothes only went to accentuate his good looks. The way his hair curled above his forehead so naturally would have looked like an affectation on anyone else. The refined, epicurean set of his mouth, those intense eyes.

He was ranting on now about being shot and imprisoned. Nagle exchanged a grin with Lindgard. She enjoyed being in this position of power. They could see the Doctor, but he couldn't see them.

She leaned forward and pressed the button that activated the mike. 'Doctor, your attitude isn't helping either of us. If you calm down, I'll explain everything.'

She heard Lindgard catch his breath. 'Is that wise?'

She switched the mike off. 'Probably not. But we've come as far as we can. The Doctor really is our last hope.'

Lindgard frowned. 'If you're sure. But you really will annoy Major Wolstencroft.'

Nagle grinned. 'So what?'

'OK,' said Lindgard, smiling back at her. There was no warmth in his expression. 'Play it your way.'

'I will.' She turned back to the Doctor. He really was no use to her in there. 'Doctor, I'm going to come in through a door to the

127

left of the fireplace. Please stand well back, with your arms by your sides.'

The Doctor did as he was told and stood beside the sofa, a feeling of expectation and relief surging through him. At last, freedom of sorts, though he supposed they weren't going to let him go just like that. This Professor Nagle certainly sounded civilised, though he didn't let his guard drop for a second.

Sure enough, a door opened to the left of the fireplace. The Doctor mentally kicked himself for not noticing it before. Through the door came a petite woman in a crisp white lab coat, her shoes tapping on the floorboards. She was smiling, showing perfect white teeth.

The Doctor didn't smile back. Instead he walked right up to her. He was a good head taller. 'You know, I loathe pastel colour schemes. Bland. Boring. Soul-sapping.'

Her smile wavered, but only slightly. She had a pale, long face, and wore round glasses. Her brown hair was tied back in a ponytail. Streaks of grey put her age somewhere in the mid-forties. 'Hey, I'm sorry about all this,' she said, waving a dismissive hand at the soft furnishings. 'It's our interview room.'

'I know a euphemism when I hear one,' said the Doctor. 'Why am I being kept here?'

The woman shrugged. 'We had a bit of clearing up to do. At the farm. We had to put you somewhere.' She was observing him closely, as if he were an interesting though slightly disturbing painting. 'You *are* the Doctor?'

The Doctor folded his arms. 'I am indeed. The definitive article.'

She smiled and extended a hand. 'I'm Professor Jennifer Nagle.'

The Doctor took her hand. Her eyes were sharp and green. Her glasses magnified them, something the Doctor always found slightly unsettling.

The Doctor opened his mouth, closed it again. What to ask first? Probably best to start with the basics. 'I have some questions I want answered. Now. Such as, what exactly is this place? What are you doing here and what have you done with my friends?'

Nagle looked surprised. 'Friends?'

'Back at the farm,' said the Doctor. 'There were two people with me. A young man called Fitz and a young lady called Kerstin. I didn't see what happened to them after your cronies shot me.'

'Ah,' said Nagle, glancing back through the two-way mirror. 'I guess they must have gotten away. No one else was brought down here.'

'Down here?' said the Doctor. He'd guessed from the air pressure that they were some distance underground. And he'd only been unconscious for about an hour, so they must still be in Sweden. 'So we're beneath the forest?'

'Yes,' said Nagle. 'This is a former nuclear shelter we purchased from the Swedish government.' Her smile was beginning to waver and signs of agitation were showing in her face. 'Doctor, I must know if you are going to help us. There's not much time.'

'I can't help you if I don't know what's going on!'

'OK,' said Nagle. 'Follow me.' She turned and walked out of the plush prison cell.

The Doctor followed, eager to be out of confinement. She led him into a monitoring room, in which a fair-haired man with a retroussé nose sat behind a desk.

The Doctor recognised him at once. 'Dr Lindgard, I presume,' he said coldly.

Lindgard stared back, his face blank. 'I see you have recovered, Doctor. I am glad.'

The Doctor rubbed his chest. The pain was still throbbing like a wasp sting. 'If you wanted my help, you should have asked me. There was no need to shoot me!'

Lindgard blinked. 'We couldn't be sure you would agree to help.'

The Doctor whirled round to Nagle. 'Oh, so we're up to something dodgy down here!' he cried. 'No doubt you're responsible for the disappearances, and the appearance of those creatures which attacked the farm. And the disappearance of Johan's body!'

Lindgard and Nagle were staring at him. He realised he had been shouting. 'Well?'

Lindgard shifted in his seat. 'Mr Svensson's body was a biological hazard. We have it here under observation.'

'And the creatures which hatched from him? I'd like a closer look at them.'

'All in good time,' said Nagle.

'I take it you are not the State Biohazard Protection Unit.'

Lindgard smiled thinly. 'That was just a cover for our operation here.'

The Doctor was getting tired of Lindgard's supercilious manner. 'Well, don't keep me in suspense – who are you?'

Nagle's face was serious, her green eyes wide behind her glasses. 'You may have heard of us before. We're a section of C19.'

'Ah.' C19. The part of the British government that funded the UK arm of UNIT. In return, they took possession of all the alien technology UNIT left behind. And they did dangerous, unethical things with it. 'So why are you, an American, and you –' he pointed at Lindgard – 'a Swede, working for the British government?'

'Exploiting alien technology for the furtherance of humanity,' said Nagle, her eyes gleaming with evangelical zeal. 'Nationality doesn't come into it. I worked for UNIT for years, before C19 requisitioned me for this job. The same with Boris.'

The Doctor narrowed his eyes at Nagle. 'How exactly does abducting innocent people and causing plagues of vicious aliens contribute to the furtherance of humanity?'

Nagle and Lindgard exchanged a look.

Nagle took off her glasses and started cleaning them with a cloth. 'There were teething problems...'

'And that's why you need my help. Well let's not stand here talking – take me to this wondrous whizgig.'

Nagle shook her head slowly. 'I'm disappointed in you, Doctor.

Your attitude leaves a lot to be desired. Here, in this base, we have something that could make the world a better place for everyone. I would expect you to have a little respect for that.'

She turned and walked out of the room, her heels clicking briskly on the floor, leaving the Doctor speechless.

The Doctor caught up with Nagle in the corridor.

'Your little speech didn't impress me, you know,' he whispered into her ear as he kept pace with her. 'People have died. Nothing, no project, however beneficial to the mass of humanity, is worth that sacrifice. The end never justifies the means.'

Nagle didn't slow her pace or turn to look at him. 'I'm disappointed in you for having such a restricted world-view.'

'And I'm very disappointed in you!' said the Doctor hotly. 'Can't make an omelette without breaking a few eggs, eh? Well this had better be the tastiest, most fantastic omelette ever cooked for me to even consider thinking about the mere possibility of condoning your actions!'

She smiled at the overblown metaphor, but only very slightly.

'Tell me one thing – why have your base here, in Sweden?' asked the Doctor.

Nagle shrugged. 'It's a neutral country, nobody ever bothers us.' She gave him a wry look. 'Not even visitors from outer space. All those alien invasion attempts in the seventies and eighties, Doctor – none of them came anywhere near Sweden.'

'Until now,' muttered the Doctor darkly.

She led him along a corridor which curved slightly to the left, and ended in an imposing double door.

Nagle turned to the Doctor, pride evident in her smile. 'This is the centre of our operations.' She entered a code on the keypad to the left of the door with deft fingers, not too deft for the Doctor to be unable to note down the code. That sort of thing was bound to come in useful before the day was out.

The doors slid open with a hiss of hydraulics and the Doctor followed Nagle into a large, gleaming white control room. His hearts lifted at the sight – he'd been in more control rooms, nerve centres, headquarters and whatnots than he dared to count. Doubtless within minutes he'd be told what the problem was, have it fixed and have Sam, Fitz and the TARDIS back, all in time for tea. Oh, the boundless optimism of this incarnation, he reflected as he followed Nagle into the room.

The room was a semicircle, with banks of monitoring instruments lining the curved section. The Doctor walked along an aisle between two rows of desks.

'Here it is,' said Professor Nagle, pointing towards the far end of the room. 'The heart of the project. The TC Warp Generator.'

The far end of the room, the flat side, was dominated by a large, gleaming silver apparatus supported on a square trellis. From each corner of the square, silver prongs lanced in towards the centre. There was a control desk on a dais in the middle of the room. The Doctor walked up to this, frowning. The control desk consisted of a QWERTY keyboard, a computer screen and a bank of monitoring equipment. The mainframe computers were probably housed in a room beneath, away from the generator, he guessed. He noticed that there were a few soldiers stationed here and there, which was a bit disconcerting. They were in UNIT uniforms, however, and technically the good guys.

He turned to Nagle, who was still smiling broadly. 'Very pretty,' he said. 'But what's it for?'

'A means to an end. It's a Telecongruency Warp Generator,' said Professor Nagle proudly.

The Doctor frowned. 'I see.' That in itself wasn't enough to breach the TARDIS. And telecongruency warp drives were way beyond the reach of current Earth technology. 'All your own work?' he asked, a sarcastic edge to his voice.

Professor Nagle was staring at the generator. 'It's an incredible breakthrough, made after years of studying captured alien vessels.' Nagle pointed at the area where the silver prongs converged. 'Its focal point actually exists simultaneously in two places – here in the generator chamber, and at a spatial location selected by computer.'

The Doctor nodded. 'So that when you walk through the focal point, you are instantly transported to another location.'

'Yes, yes.' Nagle turned to look at him. There was a disturbing light in her eyes. 'Don't you see what this means? Instant transportation, of anything! Space exploration would be a cinch – it would make the Mars landings look like a trip to the drugstore. And we could also use it to send supplies to impoverished areas. Distance, any distance, will be no object any more. The list of applications is without limit!'

The Doctor rounded on her. 'And so is its potential for misuse. Have you even considered what this thing would really be used for? It's a perfect delivery system for weapons. Imagine if it fell into the wrong hands!'

Nagle stared at the generator. 'I'll never let that happen. The TC Warp is mine.'

'With the current state of information and communication technology it won't be yours for long. How long before its details are on the Internet? How long before someone else builds one? Warfare would become precise, devastating and instantaneous. Nowhere would be safe.'

Nagle was shaking her head. 'C19 are pretty good at keeping secrets.'

'I wouldn't be surprised if C19 themselves want it developed as a weapon.'

Nagle looked shocked. 'Ridiculous! I'm head of this project team, I'm in control.'

The Doctor laughed. 'Typical. The human race needs to grow up before it has access to technology like this. You realise I'm only going to help you if you agree that this whole operation must be shut down.'

Nagle's face was white. He seemed to have woken her up to her folly.

But then she smiled wearily. 'That's the problem, Doctor. We can't shut it down.'

Sam Jones stared into the abyss, and the abyss stared back into her.

A noise like the buzzing of a swarm of flies tickled and tugged at her mind. It mesmerised her, as though she were drugged.

She watched almost distractedly as the frog-thing nearest the blackness began to scream. Its outstretched hands were engulfed and it pitched forward, the blackness fizzing around it like static. She tried to look away but couldn't, the dried mucus tugging at her hair.

Suddenly, the frog-thing was enveloped completely, its dying scream abruptly cut off. She couldn't even close her eyes, mesmerised, as the next one shuffled forward. It vanished like its fellow, into fizzing blackness. The others did the same, actually going towards the blackness, giving themselves to it. It was horrible. Why? Why were they doing this?

The last frog-thing vanished. Now Sam was alone with the Mantises, which were making the most awful screeching, a sound that seemed to scour the inside of her head. She could barely hang on to who she was, crucified on the glassy stalactite, about to be consumed by something she did not understand, in a world she did not understand. She kept quiet because she didn't want to die screaming and would not utter a word however much the blackness hurt her. Perhaps it was like tar and it would burn her flesh away. Perhaps it was alive, perhaps it really *was* a horde of tiny, vicious black insects which would devour her. Whichever it was, she was dead.

The black wall was only feet away now and she could observe the way it was creeping, crawling, encroaching over the glassy red rock of the cavern. Its leading edge was smoky, indistinct, and the rock in its path seemed to change, blur, like paint mixing with water. It was as though it actually became the blackness. So, perhaps she wasn't going to die. Perhaps the blackness wanted to transform her, wanted her to become part of itself. She'd become part of a gestalt being, a universal overmind.

Perhaps.

Or perhaps it was just like one of the sky-seas in this fantastic place, which looked so full of light and fire and turmoil, but were as harmless as a breath of springtime air.

Or maybe…

As she stared into the blackness, she felt a glimmer of recognition. As if some part of her knew what it was, some race memory, some atavistic part of her mind.

Perhaps…

Perhaps it was the way home.

True, it looked nothing like the maelstrom that had invaded the TARDIS but once the idea had formed in Sam's mind she couldn't shake it.

The blackness was the way home way home way home –

Then why were these creatures so scared of it? Why sacrifice themselves?

It completely filled Sam's vision now. She couldn't move her head and however far she rolled her eyes she couldn't see even a square inch of red rock. Only blackness.

And then something cold touched her bare arms. Touched and gripped. She let out a scream of sheer surprise, her vow of silence forgotten. Something wet trickled down her arms, and she felt a slurping dampness on her neck, as if someone were giving her a very sloppy love bite. She strained at her glass-solid bonds only to find that she could move her head. Hey – and her arms. And legs! She gave a whoop of surprise as she slid to the bottom of the stalagmite, landing on her bum with her legs splayed out, her trainers mere inches from the fizzing, hissing blackness, which stretched curtain-like across the whole width of the cavern. She watched hypnotised as the rock in the path of the blackness turned to syrupy smoke.

Sam shook her head, rubbed her eyes and scrambled to her feet, desperate to know who – or what – had rescued her. She was confronted with the sight of one of the frog creatures, wiping mucus from its mouth. It grabbed her and yanked her to her feet. She sailed into the air to land beyond the row of stalagmites.

Looking back, she saw the blackness envelop the Mantises, their shrieks abruptly cut off, leaving silence.

Sam turned away, sickened. Her rescuer was standing, staring at the black wall, mouth gaping. He was like the other frog-things she had encountered, only thinner, with spindly limbs. He wore a tunic of yellow leaves, and brown leggings which left his webbed feet bare. He seemed to be in awe of the blackness.

'Thanks for saving me,' she said.

The creature jumped, as if he hadn't realised Sam was there. He turned his face towards her. It was long, and the yellow hair was shorter than the others she had encountered.

'Can you understand me?' she said, hoping against hope.

But the creature just extended a hand, gesturing her away from the blackness.

They walked across the floor of the cavern, towards the shimmering pink sky-sea at the opposite end. It was swirling and churning like a whirlpool, almost as if aware of the blackness that would consume it within a matter of minutes. Before the sky-sea was parked a green podlike dirigible, about the size of a London bus.

The frog-thing, used to the low gravity, was way ahead of her, while she was fearful of going too fast in case she injured herself on the rocks. She landed inexpertly beside him, steadying herself against the warm pliant flesh of the dirigible.

She turned back and stared across the cavern. The blackness was advancing rapidly now. Soon it would be upon them, if they didn't move.

Her rescuer beckoned to her, and ducked inside the dirigible. With a last look back, Sam followed, climbing through an oval opening which was flanked by membranous green flaps. This led into a narrow podlike cabin, with leaflike seats growing out of the sides. On the curved, ribbed ceiling hung pear-shaped lamps, containing what Sam supposed was bits of green sky-sea. They lent the interior a comforting glow.

Sam sat down on one of the leaf-seats, which moulded itself to her shape. She was glad to find that, this time, no tendrils snaked out to hold her. Her rescuer vanished along the narrow cabin towards the front of the dirigible. She felt tired and hungry. *Alive.*

Behind her, there was a narrow slit which ran the whole length of the cabin, and Sam peered through this to see outside. As she did so she felt the floor move beneath her and the leaves of her seat take a tighter hold on her legs. They were taking off. They headed straight for the pink sky-sea, plunging straight into the glowing pinkness. This time, she knew what to expect. Its swirling beauty soothed her – it was like being inside the bloodstream of a giant creature. For all she knew, it *was* the bloodstream of some giant creature. Her eyelids drooped. So many questions.

A movement behind her. She turned. There was her rescuer, holding out a bowl of some yellowish substance.

Sam took the bowl. What was it? She sniffed. It didn't smell of anything.

She looked up at the creature. He nodded, pointing at the bowl, then his mouth.

What the hell. She was ravenous, so she tucked in. It tasted a bit like butterscotch, only more bitter.

She became so involved in her meal that she forgot all about the creature. When she looked up, he was staring at her, his head cocked to one side and then another, his bright-blue eyes reflecting the green glow of the lamps.

Her meal finished, Sam handed the bowl back to her rescuer. His three fingers were long and slender, ending in pearl-white claws. Purple veins stood out below the leaf-green skin.

Now her mouth felt dry, as if the food had soaked up all her saliva. Her rescuer offered her a vessel the size of an egg-cup, containing a dark-green liquid. She drank gratefully. It was odd-tasting, like medicine, the fumes hitting the back of her throat. She choked, gagged, and her head swam, eyes watering. Had she been poisoned? A sharp pain, like a headache, and then that sudden falling feeling you get on the edge of sleep. She felt something twist in her mind, and then all pain was gone.

And then she heard a voice inside her head.

Do not be alarmed.

Sam gasped. The voice was a dry whisper that seemed to

come from somewhere behind her eyes.

Merely an… infusion. To aid mindspeak.

So, they were telepathic. Or at least this one was. Sam composed herself. Now that she could communicate, there were many thing she wanted to know.

'How did you rescue me?'

Our salivary glands produce enzymes, which we can alter to suit our purposes. To fasten. To unfasten. To dissolve our food.

The creature licked his lips with a dark-purple tongue.

Sam forced a smile. 'That's nice.'

He extended a hand towards her.

My name is Itharquell.

Sam took the hand. It was dry, rubbery. 'I'm Sam. Sam Jones. Thanks for rescuing me.'

Itharquell blinked.

I fear I have only postponed your death.

Sam gulped. 'What do you mean?'

We are all going to be consumed by the Blight. There is no stopping it. Soon our Dominion and everything living within will be destroyed.

Chapter Eleven
Shutdown

The Doctor looked narrowly at Professor Nagle. He had a bad feeling about this. 'What do you mean, you can't shut it down?'

'What I said.' Nagle sat down in front of the desk indicating for the Doctor to do the same. 'The theory is, you set where you want the Zeta Node to be using the locator program I devised. When you activate the generator, it sends a teleengruency beam between the nodes and you should be able to walk through Alpha and be transported instantly to Zeta. I initially set the Zeta Node on the moon, the idea being to send a robotic probe through first. But when I activated, the readings went off the scale. The Zeta Node couldn't be located.'

'Hmm,' said the Doctor, sitting in the swivel chair next to Nagle, gazing thoughtfully at the silver prongs of the generator. The solution could be simple. 'A glitch in your program?'

Nagle glared at him, obviously resenting his questioning of her expertise. 'That was the first thing we checked. There were no errors in the program. The fault seems to be external – as though something grabbed the teleengruency beam and yanked it halfway across space.'

'So, you don't know where the Zeta Node is.' Things were beginning to fall into place. The Zeta Node had obviously ended up on some distant alien world. That was where all the strange creatures were coming from. But how did that explain the abductions, and the violation of the TARDIS? The effect of a teleengruency warp was limited to the two nodes. Unless…
'Oh, no.'

Nagle looked at him sharply, her green eyes wide behind her glasses. 'What is it?'

'Nothing. I hope.' He had to be sure. 'Anyway, did you send your probe through?'

'Yes we did,' said Nagle. 'And what it brought back, well, wow.'

'Well, what?'

Nagle typed in a string of commands. One of the monitors flickered into life, showing an image of a rocky, crater-pocked surface, picked out in flickering blue. The image was grainy, and the picture flickered badly. The probe moved along the surface for a while, until something scuttled in front of the lens – and then the image cut out, to be replaced by swirling static.

The Doctor watched in silence as the thirty-second sequence repeated itself three times. 'Turn it off.'

'We sent through more probes, but they were all destroyed. And then something came through.'

'What?'

Nagle switched off the monitor. 'It was a savage, uncontrollable carnivore. Fortunately, it couldn't get out of the generator chamber. After a while it died, apparently from natural causes. It's down in the lab; you can have a look at it later.'

'No need,' said the Doctor. 'I've had a close encounter with those things. Which leads me to ask, how did those things get to the farm? I have a nasty theory which I hope you're going to refute.'

'Well, after that creature came through, we had to close down. So I shut off the power to the generator and closed the nodes.' Nagle took off her glasses, and began to clean them again. 'But that wasn't the end of it. The abductions happened after that. And the attack on the farm.' Her face creased into a frown. 'I just don't understand it.'

'Unfortunately, I do,' said the Doctor. 'It's as I feared. Your little telecongruency warp has created a wormhole between the two nodes, operating independently of the generator.'

Nagle almost dropped her glasses. Recovering, she managed to slip them on, her eyes wide in disbelief. 'A *wormhole*? As in Einstein-Rosen bridge?'

'Yes, if you like,' said the Doctor, looking over at the generator. 'A tunnel connecting two places in space-time.'

'I know what a wormhole is, Doctor. But naturally occurring

wormholes are supposed to be tiny, existing only at the quantum level, for very brief periods of time.'

'Some races use them to navigate their way around the universe,' said the Doctor. 'Some even use them for time travel, because to a wormhole space and time are the same.'

'But… but how can it exist? What's holding it open?' She gave a little snort of disbelief. 'Cosmic string?'

'No,' said the Doctor. 'I don't know. Some sort of energy? Must be something to do with what's at the other end.' He tapped at the keyboard.

Nagle looked anxious. 'What are you doing?'

'Calculating the size of the wormhole.' Figures danced across the screen, and as he read them the Doctor's hearts sank. 'Well, I congratulate you, Professor.'

'I must admit,' said Nagle, her voice hushed with pride, 'creating a wormhole, even by accident, is a massive advance –'

The Doctor cut her short. 'Advance, my pants! By fiddling about with alien technology, you've raised a dragon you cannot feed!'

Nagle frowned. 'What?'

'Professor Nagle, you have inadvertently created a dimensional anomaly which could destroy the Earth.'

Fitz walked along the corridor, trying to hide his fear, Kerstin beside him, presumably doing the same. He didn't know – he couldn't see her face behind the faceplate. The suits were light and surprisingly cool, but the helmet was confining, though the triangular faceplate allowed a fairly wide field of vision. There was a strange chemical smell which was beginning to get on his nerves, and his breathing sounded loud in the confines of the helmet.

They'd walked along the curving brick-walled corridor for quite a time, without meeting a soul. On the inner wall at intervals were green doors with numbers stencilled upon them. All were locked, except one or two, which were empty. From the look of it, Fitz reckoned that this corridor was little used.

The brick was old and crumbling, spider webs thick with dust stringing down from the ceiling. Not all of the bulbs were working, which made it very dark and creepy.

'This is fun, isn't it?' he said to Kerstin.

'No,' said Kerstin uncomprehendingly, her voice muffled by her helmet.

Fitz bit his tongue. What a stupid thing to say! Bugger it, he was taking her for Sam again. Kerstin was still obviously too stunned by Johan's death to want to respond to humour. Fitz recalled the time after his mother's death. For a while, humour had seemed meaningless, and people, with their quirks and mannerisms that he could usually feel so superior to, were just annoying – a noise to be shut out.

That must be how Kerstin was feeling now. A wonder she was here, walking with him into the heart of danger, rather than going away somewhere quiet to grieve as he had done. Perhaps she was so numb that she no longer cared what happened to her.

They walked on in silence.

The corridor ended abruptly in a white-painted bulkhead, two steel double doors set into the wall. Lift doors. There was an arrow illuminated in a metal panel between the doors, indicating only the up direction.

Fitz reached out to press the button, and hesitated. 'Kerstin,' he said, 'take off your helmet a minute.'

She did do, taking deep breaths – her suit must have the same chemical tang as his. 'What is it?' she said, pouting slightly.

'I don't know what I'm getting us into,' said Fitz. 'The people behind this place obviously have something to do with what happened to Johan, so if you want to go back to the forest and wait –'

She cut him off in mid-sentence. 'No. I'm coming with you. I want to find out what's going on.'

'Are you sure? Even though we might get shot or – or worse?' Was *he* sure? What the hell was he even doing here?

Her blue eyes glittered. 'Yes!' She reached out and pressed the lift button. The doors on the left opened almost instantly and they stepped inside.

The interior of the lift was carpeted and mirrored, but one of the mirrored panels was cracked and the carpet was faded, scuffed and torn. Fitz was faced with a row of buttons. The B button, the lowermost one, was lit, and above that were four other floors.

'Which one, which one?' muttered Fitz.

Kerstin reached out and pressed 2. She managed a brief smile. 'My lucky number.'

The lift seemed to travel for quite a distance, back up towards the forest. Fitz imagined the dark mass of trees and vegetation, silent and brooding, the perfect cover.

Suddenly the lift stopped with an efficient 'ping' and the doors slid open, to reveal another corridor, this one brightly lit, with white-painted walls. It curved in two directions away from them.

'Left or right?' said Fitz, letting Kerstin choose. Why not? Her guess was as good as his. And it was probably important for her that she felt she was in control.

'Left,' said Kerstin.

They stepped out and moved along the corridor. 'Put your helmet back on,' whispered Fitz, motioning to Kerstin as he slid his back on.

They'd walked only a few yards along the corridor when a short man in a white lab coat hurried round the corner. He caught sight of Fitz and Kerstin.

'What are you doing here?'

Fitz's mouth went dry and he felt Kerstin tense beside him.

It was Dr Lindgard.

Professor Nagle watched as the Doctor sat at the computer, occasionally tapping at the keyboard, raising his eyebrows as data scrolled down the screen. She was still reeling from what he had told her.

'This is no normal wormhole,' he said. 'It's a veritable

Ouroboros. It has random-shooting branches which fork out from the main mass. One of those must have invaded the TARDIS.' He glared up at her. 'Are you beginning to realise the enormity of your folly?'

She was still finding it hard to believe. Creating a *wormhole*? It was way beyond anything she'd planned. 'Yes,' she lied. 'I am. That's why I need your help.'

The Doctor shook his head. 'You know, I should really be intolerably angry with you, and your blind scientific fumbling. But I may as well be angry with the whole human race. Its curiosity is commendable but it never actually learns what to do with the things it discovers. And alien technology in the hands of humans – a lethal combination.'

Enough with the lectures, thought Nagle. 'But will you help me?' she said, trying to keep her voice calm.

The Doctor's face darkened. 'I have no choice. If I don't help, if I leave things as they are, then the wormhole could grow to tremendous size, and consume the Earth. And on a personal note –' he glanced over at the generator – 'Sam's at the other end, alive, I very much hope.'

Nagle shrugged, feeling a glow of satisfaction flood through her. For whatever reason, the Doctor was going to help. 'What's your diagnosis, Doctor?'

'Well it's pretty obvious to me what's happened,' said the Doctor. 'The telecongruency beam got caught up in something, probably a black hole. The laws of physics go a bit doolally when singularities are involved. There must have been some energy trade-off, and a wormhole was formed between the two nodes of the telecongruency beam.'

None of this made any sense to Nagle. She half suspected he was making it up. 'So, how can we shut down the wormhole?'

The Doctor's face clouded. 'Somebody has to go through it. Find out what's at the other end.'

This was madness. 'It's too dangerous, Doctor. What happened to the probes –'

The Doctor waved his hands in the air, suddenly angry. 'Oh,

socks to the probes! This whole thing has gone too far and it ends now. I'm going through.'

Nagle bit her lip. If they activated the node, who knew what would come through. 'You know it might be a one-way trip.'

The Doctor set his mouth in a grim line. 'I have no choice.' He stuck a finger in his mouth and frowned. 'Now, which button switches this thing on?'

As Nagle opened her mouth to speak she noticed all the soldiers in the control room suddenly crash to attention. She groaned. 'Oh, hell.'

She turned to look towards the entrance to the control room, her heart turning to lead. Major Wolstencroft, in full uniform, was walking down the entrance ramp, Captain Rogers at his side.

Major Gareth Wolstencroft was a tall, broad-shouldered man, with the handsome, chiselled face of the classic military leader. His bald head, which he shaved daily, gave his face a pugnacious look. His eyes were small and dark, his mouth wide and unsmiling. He had an aura of power about him, a charisma of control. Everyone reacted to his presence, sitting up straighter, coughing nervously, fiddling with pens. Everyone except the Doctor, who was still bent over the generator control desk.

Nagle got up from her chair and approached Wolstencroft. 'Major. To what do I owe this pleasure?'

He shot a look at Nagle, which rooted her to the spot. It was absolute controlled fury.

Nagle gritted her teeth. Whatever he was going to say or do, she was still in control of this operation. She was a senior C19 scientist, he was just a UNIT soldier. A major, but still only a soldier. She forced herself to smile at him.

'Professor Nagle, don't try to ingratiate yourself with me,' he said in his clipped, cultured voice. 'There has been a serious breach of security.'

The creatures at the farm. 'We'll make up a cover story – it's worked before.'

'People have died,' snapped Wolstencroft. 'It's too late. Nothing you say or do will change my mind about the status of this operation.'

Nagle swallowed. She knew what that meant. It was the end.

'I – I –' she began, but Wolstencroft wasn't listening.

'Who is that man?' he said, pointing with a gloved finger over to where the Doctor was poring over the controls to the generator.

Captain Rogers coughed. 'That's the Doctor, sir.'

Wolstencroft's eyes widened and he raised his eyebrows, his smooth forehead wrinkling. 'Oh yes,' he said. 'The Doctor. What's he doing here?'

Nagle decided it was about time she regained some ground. 'He's working with me on the generator.'

Wolstencroft smiled, but there was no humour in the expression. 'Not for much longer.'

She couldn't blame him, she supposed. As head of security, he had a duty to protect people. But, goddammit, now the Doctor was here she was so close to a breakthrough.

She watched Wolstencroft approach the Doctor. 'You there! Stand away from that desk.'

The Doctor turned, his face dreamy and abstracted. 'Oh, hello,' he said upon seeing Wolstencroft. 'I was just –'

'You were just about to stand away from the control desk,' said Wolstencroft in a voice of ice.

Out of the corner of her eye, Nagle saw the UNIT soldiers cock their rifles. This was madness. The Doctor was on *their side*.

The Doctor stood away from the control desk. 'Umm, why are you all pointing guns at me?' he said plaintively. 'I'm the man who can save the day, you know!'

Wolstencroft's eyes narrowed. 'I know all about you, Doctor. Every time you turn up, chaos ensues. You're not going to save the day, because I am.' He stepped back from them, raising his voice to address everyone in the control centre. 'As of now, this operation is over. We are moving out in –' he glanced at his wristwatch – 'thirty minutes.'

Nagle stepped up to the major. 'You don't understand! You can't shut it down.'

Wolstencroft ordered Rogers to restrain her. 'I can and I am. We're moving out.'

'Doctor, tell him!' said Nagle.

The Doctor opened his mouth to speak but found himself in the grip of two burly UNIT soldiers. 'What?'

'Put him in the cell again. I don't want him getting in the way.'

The Doctor was dragged away. 'You fool,' he cried. 'She's right! You can't shut it down!'

But they weren't listening. They were obeying orders. Stupid, ill-thought-out orders, but there was nothing the Doctor could do about that.

Nagle watched as the Doctor was dragged away.

'That was a stupid thing to do,' she hissed, hating Wolstencroft as much as she had ever done. 'He was going to help us!'

Wolstencroft bore down on her. 'The matter is closed, Professor. This operation is of no concern to you any more.'

He walked over to a comms desk at the side of the room.

Fitz willed Kerstin to be calm as Dr Lindgard looked them up and down. He opened his mouth to speak when a voice blared from a small speaker on the wall.

'This is Major Wolstencroft. There has been a major breach of security and this operation is compromised. Therefore, as of now, this operation is closed down until further notice. All C19 personnel are to evacuate and travel to Stockholm for a debriefing. A skeleton crew will remain in this base to monitor the equipment. All specimens are to be destroyed.'

Lindgard listened to the message, his mouth dropping open. When the message ended, he sighed and shrugged. 'Ah well, I was expecting something like this.' He pointed at Kerstin and Fitz. 'You two – come with me. We might be able to salvage something.'

He turned and marched along the corridor. Fitz began to follow, but Kerstin just stood there.

'Come on,' said Fitz. 'We don't have much choice!'

They followed Lindgard past the lifts and along a wide white corridor lined with doors. These doors were steel, and they had hefty locking mechanisms and hydraulic hinges.

One door was standing open, and Lindgard motioned Fitz and Kerstin inside. They found themselves inside a laboratory. Lab benches ran along the middle, glass cabinets on the walls. Over the far side was a bank of equipment which looked vaguely medical. The place was a bustle of activity, people in white lab suits mingling with people in uniforms.

To the left, behind a glass partition, was a series of – was it beds? No, it looked more like mortuary slabs. And on one of those slabs was a figure shrouded in a plastic sheet.

A cold sensation of dread washed over Fitz. He looked around for Kerstin but she was already walking stiffly across the room, oblivious to the bustle around her, shoving people aside.

Fitz stepped quickly after her, hoping against hope that the body on the slab wasn't the Doctor or Sam.

Kerstin's gloved hands were pressed on the glass – mirroring her posture in the hospital yesterday – her helmet resting against it in a gesture of resignation.

Fitz stood by her, not knowing what to do, staring at the body on the slab. It was Johan, his short dark hair immediately recognisable. His body, through the plastic sheeting, was snow-white, dotted with the purple blooms of bruises. There was frost on his face and on the hairs of his legs.

Fitz heard a low moan from Kerstin and she sagged against the glass. Fitz caught her, supporting her. He glanced over his shoulder. Damn – people had noticed. Time for a clever and nifty lie. Trouble was, he couldn't think of one. 'She's feeling a little faint. I'll take her outside.'

Luckily, Lindgard was at the other end of the room, so Fitz bustled Kerstin across to the door, hoping that no one could hear her low sobbing. Fortunately everyone seemed to be busy packing things up. Fitz noticed dazedly that in the middle of the room were what looked like fish tanks containing the orange starfish-like things that had hatched from Johan. Anger washed over him, mixed with incomprehension. What were they doing here? Breeding the things?

Back out in the corridor, Fitz turned to Kerstin. He had no idea if she could hear him, but he didn't dare remove her helmet in case anyone followed them. 'We're getting out of here,' he said. 'Back to the woods, and to the police. This is way too big for us to deal with on our own.'

Kerstin's voice was husky with grief. 'If only we'd gone to them in the first place.'

'We wouldn't have found this place, would have no evidence,' argued Fitz. 'If only I had a camera.'

Kerstin took off her helmet. Her expression scared him. It was blank, the eyebrows raised slightly, the mouth slack.

'Put it back on!' hissed Fitz, looking back over his shoulder. 'Don't you want to get out of here?'

Kerstin shrugged.

Footsteps, behind them.

He grabbed her helmet and slid it back over her head. She did nothing to resist.

The footsteps came closer and Fitz turned round. His heart leapt into his throat. The footsteps belonged to two soldiers and their prisoner, marching along the corridor.

The prisoner was the Doctor.

Chapter Twelve
Of Blight, Bane and Ruin

The dirigible sailed or flew deeper into the sky-sea, a bright-green blister against the swirling pinkness. Inside, Sam sat in her leaflike seat, staring out of the slit-window. She'd just had a chat with Itharquell, and she felt tired, overwhelmed with new information.

Itharquell was of the dominant sentient race, the T'hiili. They called this place the Dominion, which implied some degree of control over their environment, lost apparently with the coming of the black, encroaching Blight.

Itharquell was quite proud of his dirigible, and had taken great pleasure in telling Sam all about it. He had grown it himself from a seed, fashioning its genetic code so that it grew into a comfortable, controllable vehicle. Its nearest Terran equivalent would probably be an airship, but, in the low gravity of the Dominion, much less propulsive power was needed. Inflatable sacs controlled their altitude, and velocity was controlled by pores on the skin of the dirigible sucking in air which was expelled through tubes at the rear. The whole thing was controlled by the manipulation of a rudimentary brain which floated in the centre of a spherical chamber in the nose of the dirigible. It looked like a large cauliflower, connected to the bowl-shaped floor by a gnarled trunk. Sam had felt slightly queasy, watching Itharquell manipulate the stems and shoots that protruded from the grey knobbly mass. He had assured her the dirigible could feel no pain.

Itharquell came in from the control chamber and sat down opposite her.

'Who's flying this thing?'

Itharquell stroked his pale yellow hair.

The dirigible will scream if anything happens.

'Nice,' said Sam. 'Um, I've been meaning to ask you: why did you rescue me and not the other T'hiili?'

They didn't want to be rescued. Had I tried, I would have fallen to the Blight, too.

Sam remembered the T'hiili, prostrating themselves before the Blight. Suicide. Why?

Before she could ask, Itharquell's voice whispered in her mind.

I rescued you because I am curious. I have not seen a creature like you in any cavern of the Dominion, or any sky-sea. You are similar to T'hiili in many ways – same number of limbs and sensory organs, similar digestive system as far as I can tell. You confirm a theory I have about the Dominion.

She learned that Itharquell was a cataloguer of races. Other T'hiili found his inquiring and analytical mind rather disturbing. The T'hiili were, on the whole, a simple, superstitious race, and thinkers like Itharquell were rare. Most of the T'hiili believed, for example, that the Dominion was the calcified body of the first T'hiili Queen, and that the sky-seas were made up of the spirits of dead T'hiili. Itharquell, virtually alone among his race, thought this was nonsense, and it was his life's ambition to disprove it. His theory was that somewhere within the Dominion lived other advanced life forms, similar to the T'hiili. And the presence of Sam seemed to have proved his hypothesis.

Sam pointed out the flaw in this. 'I hate to blow a nice theory out of the water, but I'm not actually from the Dominion.'

There is nothing outside the Dominion. You must come from a distant, undiscovered cavern.

'Cavern?' Sam frowned. He must mean 'planet'. 'I'm from the planet Earth,' she said. 'You know, Terra? In the Sol system? The Milky Way?'

He pouted, a strange expression, his lips forming the shape of a flower.

What is a planet?

Sam felt exasperated. 'You know, outer space? Stars?'

Further blank looks.

So she wasn't inside an asteroid or a planet. She was somewhere else entirely. A separate universe, made of rock? Was that possible? No, they *must* be inside a huge planet, and Itharquell, even though he was a thinker, simply had not realised it yet. But she decided not to argue the point any more – there was something else she needed to know, something more urgent.

'Itharquell, you said the Blight was going to destroy the Dominion. How do you know?'

I do not know. But it shows no sign of relenting. Soon it will consume all.

Sam was thinking furiously. Perhaps it had something to do with how she'd got here.

Something else was bothering her. 'Why are the T'hiili throwing themselves into it?'

They think they can appease the Blight with sacrifice. I disagreed, and had to leave the Nest.

Sam was stunned. Mass suicide, the extinction of an entire race? It was hard to comprehend. Sam's philosophy had always been, *if there's life there's hope.* 'Surely,' she said, 'there must be a way of stopping the Blight.'

It is beyond even my comprehension. Nothing that goes in ever comes back out. And it is growing like a cancer, eating its way through the Dominion. In a way, I almost agree with the majority. There is no hope. Even if the Blight could be stopped, we as a race are all doomed.

Sam frowned. 'Why is that?'

One of the early patches of Blight appeared inside the Queen's chamber. The Queen is – was – unable to move, so she was consumed. And with no Queen, we cannot reproduce.

'Hang on,' said Sam. 'Are you're saying there are no male and female T'hiili?'

Itharquell stroked his blond feathery hair.

Those terms have no meaning. There are T'hiili, and T'vorha – warriors who tend the Queen and guard us against attack – and the Queen, who rules us and produces our young.

Sam remembered the T'hiili children. They must have been the last born.

Some say that before she died the old Queen produced a last batch of eggs. Inside one of them would be a new, young Queen. I have been searching for her for days and days. Now I think, what's the use? Even if I do find her, and fertilise her, we are all going to die soon anyway.

Itharquell's calm fatalism was beginning to get on Sam's nerves. 'Tell me more about the Queen. Just how do you fertilise her?'

Itharquell extruded something from his mouth, a slender white tube with a flower-like opening at the end.

As I said, our salivary glands can be adapted for many purposes.

He retracted the tube and cocked his head on one side, a characteristic gesture Sam was beginning to recognise.

How do your kind reproduce?

'Well,' began Sam. 'There are two genders – male and female. They get together and, erm, the male impregnates the female with his seed.'

Itharquell sat back, mouth open in disbelief.

You mean, half your race are Queens?

Sam stifled a giggle. 'Well, if you put it like that.'

And which are you – male or female?

'I'm a woman. All female.'

Then you are a Queen of your race, an egg-layer, O most powerful Sam!

'It's not like that where I come from,' said Sam quickly. 'We're equal, male and female.'

A sudden screaming noise made Sam jump. She followed Itharquell to the control chamber. On the far side of the chamber was an oval screen. It showed a view of the sky-sea, and something black, nebulous, spreading like ink through water, smoky tendrils reaching towards them.

Itharquell floated over to the brain. The blackness was advancing rapidly, filling the whole screen.

The Blight.

Sam stepped into the control chamber, floating over beside Itharquell. 'Don't just stand there: take evasive action or something!' yelled Sam.

His autumnal voice whispered inside her mind.

We may as well accept it.

'Whatever you believe, I came from outside the Dominion. That means there's a way out. That means there's something to hope for and I'm not bloody well giving up!' She grabbed two stemlike extrusions and gave them a twist. The chamber lurched around her and she careered into Itharquell.

His voice whispered in her mind:

Are you sure there is a way out?

'Yes!' But was there? There was no guarantee that the whirlpool thing that had brought her here would appear again, but the Doctor would almost certainly be looking for her. 'I have friends who will be searching for me. They'll find a way. All we have to do is avoid the Blight.'

After an agonising pause, Itharquell nodded, and grabbed the control stems.

Sam watched the screen, fascinated. The Blight seemed to be spreading more quickly through the sky-sea. It was billowing towards them like a thundercloud. Perhaps a sky-sea was easier to consume than rock. Itharquell was silent beside her, the only sound the faint hissing of his breath. Perhaps he was right, and there was no escape.

At least then she would find out what it was. Whether it was a way home, or certain death.

But at last they seemed to be putting some distance between themselves and the Blight.

Presently, they emerged into a cavern of bluish rock, with tunnels leading off in various directions. Itharquell became agitated upon seeing where they were.

'What is it?' asked Sam. 'We've escaped the Blight, haven't we?

All we have to do is keep running…' Her voice tailed off. She didn't want to finish the sentence. Keep running until there was nowhere left to run.

Itharquell had taken the dirigible close to the cavern wall, dangerously close, Sam thought, and was skirting around to the mouth of the nearest tunnel.

'What is it?' hissed Sam.

We have just entered a Ruin nest.

Sam looked at the screen. In the centre of the cavern, arranged in a rough spindle-like formation, were hundreds of creatures, like giant spiders, with orange hourglass-shaped bodies.

'What are they?'

They are our greatest enemy. They lay their eggs within our bodies. And, with the Dominion shrinking, we are being forced into greater confrontations with them.

Sam was beginning to realise why the T'hiili were favouring suicide as a way out.

They were at the tunnel mouth now and Itharquell swung a sharp left. Soon they were barrelling away down a tunnel that hardly seemed wide enough to accommodate them.

'Any other nasties lurking around you might want to tell me about?'

There are also the Bane – savage predators, mindless things, who exist merely to feed.

Sam shuddered. 'Well, I haven't seen any of those.'

Neither have I, for days.

'Maybe they've all sacrificed themselves to the Blight,' said Sam.

The Ruin and the Bane are primitive creatures, with a strong instinct for survival. Only the T'hiili, cursed with intelligence, would decide on a course of self-destruction.

'Then maybe they found a way out,' said Sam.

Then, suddenly, the dirigible shuddered, as if a great weight had fallen against it.

Sam and Itharquell clung to each other as the dirigible shuddered around them. Itharquell twisted a stem and the screen showed a rear view, blue tunnel walls whizzing past. And crawling along the ridged green back of the dirigible was a six-legged orange-bodied Ruin, tentacles thrashing. It was punching holes in the back of the dirigible, sawing its way through the pithy skin with its legs. Another appeared, and then another, crawling along the back of the dirigible.

Itharquell began hooting in panic.

'Try to shake them off,' urged Sam. 'You know, smash them against the roof of the cavern.'

The controls aren't responding. The Ruin must have severed the spinal cord. It would have been better if we had given ourselves up to the Blight.

'Rubbish,' said Sam, her insides turning to ice nonetheless. There was a crash from behind them, and Sam turned to see a thick spiderlike leg break through the ceiling, questing about, a six-spiked 'hand' at the end of it clenching and unclenching with a snapping sound.

At that point they burst from the tunnel, and almost instantly plunged into a golden-yellow sky-sea. Its light poured in through the screen.

Behind them, another leg broke through, and another, sawing away frantically.

Itharquell raised his hands in a gesture of despair. He pressed a control and a section of wall irised open in front of them. Golden light poured through. Without hesitation, Itharquell leapt out.

Sam stood on the threshold, looking down. Logic dictated that, if she stepped out of the dirigible, she would fall for ever. But logic could bugger off. Taking a deep breath, she leapt into space.

Sam gasped as the golden sky-sea enveloped her. It was like that feeling you get when you sink into a hot bath, that almost sexual frisson which makes you gulp and gasp in pleasure.

She hung there for a second, and then flexed her arms experimentally. Surprisingly, she moved quite a way. Below her, she saw Itharquell – *swimming? flying? like a fish? a bird?* –

falling down and down until he was a dot.

She looked back. And gasped.

Three Ruin were tearing the dirigible apart, placing the pieces daintily in their bell-shaped bodies, cilia waving about in obvious pleasure. They seemed not to notice her. But it wouldn't be long before they had consumed the entire dirigible. What was it Itharquell said the things did? Laid their eggs inside you?'

'Sorry guys,' Sam whispered to herself. 'That's not the way Sam Jones is gonna go.' And, jerking her arms and legs in a swimming motion, Sam set off in the direction Itharquell had taken.

Chapter Thirteen
So Fast, So Numb

Fitz stood aside, letting the soldiers past. The Doctor hadn't even noticed him. Gesturing to Kerstin, he followed. The soldiers took the Doctor off left into a corridor which looked less well cared for than the rest. The walls were of bare breeze block, the concrete floor dusty. Pale light came from circular lamps fixed to the walls.

The soldiers stopped outside a metal door, the Doctor held firmly between them. Fitz tensed. Should he risk rushing them? No – there were two of them, and they were probably very fit and highly trained. As he deliberated, the soldiers opened the door and disappeared inside with the Doctor. The door closed behind them with a hefty thump.

Fitz tried the door; the metal handle would not budge. Then it began to open and he jumped back, bumping into Kerstin. He saw an open door further down the corridor, on the opposite side, and grabbed her, almost dragging her along the corridor. They ducked inside, Fitz closing the door behind them. They seemed to be in some sort of storeroom, lined with cluttered metal shelving.

Kerstin removed her helmet and tossed it into a corner. She still had that chilling dead expression, as if nothing mattered to her. 'I'm not wearing that thing any more,' she said dully. 'Let them catch us.'

Fitz also removed his helmet, glad to be free from its confinement for a while. 'Kerstin, don't give up!'

Kerstin put her head in her hands and burst into tears, rocking back and forth on her haunches. She muttered something in Swedish.

It was too late. She had given up. She was in no state to cope with anything. What she needed was a dose of tranquillisers, a few days in bed, and time to come to terms with her loss. None of which Fitz could provide. All he had was words, and he knew from personal experience how useless they could be. Kerstin had to go through her grief, and there was nothing he could really do to help. All he could do was drag her through this and hope they both got out the other side in one piece.

Fitz swallowed hard. He had to rescue the Doctor. Act the hero again. He wasn't cut out for this sort of thing at all. What if he was captured? Or shot? What if he only made things worse for the Doctor? Fitz pushed such thoughts to the back of his mind. Once the Doctor was free, he'd sort everything out, right? Right... He remembered the Doctor in the farmhouse, after Björn had died. He'd seemed weird, not all there. What had he said? Without the TARDIS he was incomplete?

He sighed, and went over to Kerstin, sitting down beside her and putting an arm around her shoulders. The human contact made him feel a little better but probably did nothing for her. Her face was blotched and red, her eyes gleaming with tears.

'Look, I've got to try to rescue the Doctor,' he murmured, looking around at the shelves for anything he could use as a weapon, but there was nothing.

Kerstin gave no sign of hearing him. He hated to leave her like this, but he had no choice. He stood up, put his helmet on and opened the door.

To his left, the corridor was empty. To his right, footsteps.

He ducked back into the store room, holding the door to. From outside, the footsteps became louder. Fitz frowned. These weren't the clump of soldiers' boots, but the tap-tap-tap of stiletto heels. He heard the door opposite click open.

Fitz emerged into the corridor, not sure what to do. Someone had gone into the room. A nurse maybe? Someone with food for the Doctor? The door was ajar, and closing slowly. In a few seconds it would slam locked shut again. He nipped down the corridor and caught the door just before it closed, slipping inside.

The room he found himself in was small and boxlike, dimly lit by a soft yellow lamp in the rear wall. Its main feature was a picture window which ran the whole length of the room. In front of this sat a woman in a lab coat, staring through the window into a tastefully furnished lounge. There was the Doctor, sitting on the sofa, nursing a pink cushion. Fitz's heart gave a surge of joy at the sight. Then he realised that the woman had swivelled her chair round to stare at him.

She had long dark hair tied back in a ponytail, and her face was serious, pale. She wore round glasses. 'Who the hell are you?' she said; her voice had an American accent.

Fitz froze to the spot, racking his brain for a lie that would explain why he was here. He had no idea who this woman was, what role she was playing in whatever was going on here, what reason for his presence would satisfy her.

Fitz waved a gloved hand. 'I'm, er, I've come to check on the prisoner.'

Her mouth hardened in a tight line, and she stood up. She wasn't very tall, but her eyes were hard as stone. 'Can't you guys leave him alone for five minutes?'

Fitz backed away from her.

She gestured to the Doctor, who was now lying on the sofa. 'Can't you see he's had enough of all this bullshit?'

Fitz could. The Doctor looked washed out, miserable. 'Yes, you're right.'

The woman prodded Fitz in the chest. 'So go away and leave us.'

Despite her sharp fingernails, and sharper tongue, this woman posed no great threat. Fitz whipped his helmet off and flashed her his most disarming smile. 'Hello. I'm a friend of the Doctor's and therefore at least as interested in his welfare as you are.'

The woman looked stunned for a moment. She opened her mouth to speak, then closed it again. 'Hey, you're not one of Wolstencroft's men. Or anyone else I know.' She was backing towards the desk.

Any number of those buttons could call for help, so Fitz dodged round her, placing himself between her and the desk.

'I've come to get the Doctor out of here,' he said, trying to sound as determined as possible. 'And you're going to help me.'

She folded her arms. 'Look, just exactly who are you?'

Fitz sighed. There was no point in lying. 'I'm Fitz Kreiner. Like I said, I'm a friend of the Doctor's.'

Realisation dawned in her eyes. 'He mentioned someone called Fitz.'

'Yes, he would,' said Fitz, agitatedly. 'Look, are you going to help me set him free?'

She laughed. 'Yeah, right. This place is under martial law now. Freeing the Doctor is about the best way to get shot.'

'All right, I'll do it myself.' Fitz turned to the interior door, trying the handle. It was locked. He went to the desk.

The woman sighed. 'I guess you're not going to go away. It's the yellow button to the left of the monitor.'

Fitz pressed the button.

'I'm Professor Jennifer Nagle,' said the woman, walking over to the interior door. 'Excuse my manners but I don't get out much these days.'

She opened the door and gestured Fitz through.

The Doctor stood up, a look of amazement on his face, and then to Fitz's considerable surprise he bounded over, grabbed his head and planted a kiss squarely on his lips. 'Oh, Fitz! Fitz, Fitz, Fitz! I'm so glad you're alive!'

Fitz staggered back, overwhelmed. 'Glad to see you too,' he murmured, feeling himself blushing under Professor Nagle's stare of amazement and mirth. 'Now, would someone mind telling me what the hell is going on here?'

The Doctor's face was suddenly serious again. It was as if the sun had gone behind a thundercloud. 'Dangerous experiments with the fabric of reality,' he said, glaring at Nagle, who stared back defiantly.

'That's fine, then,' said Fitz, none the wiser.

The Doctor raised his eyebrows. 'This woman is responsible for what happened to the TARDIS and Sam.'

'Hey now, hang on there,' said Nagle, raising her hands and

backing away from both of them.

Fitz scowled at her. 'How is she responsible?'

The Doctor spoke quickly, the words tumbling over each other. 'She's inadvertently created a large and unstable wormhole which has attached itself to an extradimensional anomaly causing spatial and hyperspatial distortion –'

Fitz held up a hand. 'All right! All right!'

The Doctor stopped speaking and looked at Fitz sheepishly.

'All I want to know is – is Sam alive and can we get her back?'

The Doctor pulled a face. 'I don't know,' he said simply. 'But I'm going to try. Come on.'

Professor Nagle was still wearing a wide-eyed expression of fright.

'Don't worry, we won't hurt you,' said the Doctor as he walked past her.

True enough, thought Fitz, following the Doctor out into the corridor, his mind cartwheeling to catch up with events. Oddly he felt no anger towards Professor Nagle. She didn't seem evil. Whatever had happened in the TARDIS was obviously an accident.

Then he thought of Kerstin. Professor Nagle was responsible for the death of Johan. He had to keep that from her.

'Doctor,' he said, tapping his shoulder.

The Doctor turned round, a cross expression on his face. 'Yes?'

'Um, I've got someone else with me.'

Kerstin was nowhere. She was nothing. To stop herself from screaming, to stop her heart from dragging in her chest like a dead thing, she imagined herself at the bottom of the lake, where no light could reach her, where the pressure of the water kept everything away from her. An endless darkness.

She remembered another lake, back when she was a child, where her mother was teaching her to swim. She remembered the feeling of elation when she floated away from her mother's hands. I can do it, I can swim, I don't need anyone to support me.

163

Now she was sinking. And there was no one there to catch her. This was good. She didn't want anyone to catch her. She wanted to fall and fall until she hit the bottom.

She wanted to die.

To die?

She opened her eyes, and stared at the wall in front of her. Her head felt fuzzy, as if she had a bad cold. Now she had let out the pain, she felt calmer, and could analyse her feelings. Did she really want to die? Did the death of Johan matter so much?

Yes it did matter. She could still see those – those things breaking out of his flesh, the blood, the unutterable agony on his face as he died. And then in the mortuary – the body she had loved, the body that had loved her, taken apart like some fleshly machine, something that had never held life or love or swum in the lake with her at midnight.

She looked around, realising for the first time that Fitz had gone. Fitz. She didn't quite know what to make of him. He seemed concerned in the usual useless male way. But all this talk of time machines? Could it be true? She almost laughed out loud; it was too ridiculous, too far-fetched.

Too much to hope for. Because if Fitz was telling the truth, if the Doctor did have a time machine, he could take her back, to before. To when Johan was alive.

They could be together again. Could she save him? Was that possible?

She stood up, unzipping her encounter suit and climbing out of it. She inspected herself: grazed knees from the flight through the forest, and mud on her shorts and trainers. She didn't want to think what a mess her face looked and didn't really care.

She walked slowly around the room, looking at the items on the shelves without interest. The door banged open and Fitz appeared, still in his crumpled white encounter suit. The Doctor stood behind him, as did a woman in a white lab coat, with her arms folded.

Fitz seemed to be more relaxed now that the Doctor was there. 'I – um – are you all right now?' he said lamely.

Kerstin ignored the banality of the question and tried to smile, the muscles of her face aching and her eyes feeling swollen. 'As all right as I'll ever be.'

The Doctor pushed past Fitz. His eyes were full of compassion, and devoid of fear. Despite everything, Kerstin felt a wave of calmness wash over her.

'Kerstin,' said the Doctor. 'I know you have been through a lot, but I promise you it will all be over soon. Everything will be all right.'

He spoke quickly, in a cultured, lilting voice. Although his words were banal, she found herself believing him. 'Just get me out of here,' she whispered.

He smiled sadly. 'I promise you, you'll get out of here.'

She stared into his eyes, large and blue and full of the sadness of wisdom, and something changed within her. She suddenly believed all that Fitz had said – but out of Fitz's mouth, looking into Fitz's shifty eyes, it had all seemed a crazy fantasy. Now, looking into the Doctor's eyes, she knew that this was a man who travelled in time, who fought monsters – both alien and human – and usually won.

He could take her back. Kerstin's head swam. He could take her back. He could make it all right again. At all costs, she had to stick with the Doctor.

'We haven't got time for this,' said the woman, and the spell was broken.

'Come on, Doctor,' said Fitz.

The next few minutes were a blur. She followed the Doctor, Fitz and the woman in the lab coat along the white corridor and past the lifts. Fitz was no longer wearing his helmet, and his face was pale and sweaty. Soldiers and white-suited scientists bustled past, ignoring them.

Kerstin yearned for explanations, but she told herself to be patient. She was rushing headlong into the heart of the mystery, and soon she would know everything. She felt a surge of excitement – which was brought crashing down as the image of Johan's white body popped back into her mind with devastating force.

Knowing everything – anything – wasn't worth it.

Presently they came to a large double door. The Doctor tapped in a code on a keypad next to the doors and they opened.

Kerstin followed them into a large semicircular room. There was no one else there and their footsteps echoed loudly on the tiled floor. At the far end was a strange metallic apparatus, four huge gleaming prongs of metal converging, a giant silver cross. X marks the spot.

Kerstin felt as if she were walking on air.

The Doctor and the woman walked up to a desk in front of a glass wall which partitioned off the strange device, sitting down in swivel chairs before it.

Fitz was standing next to her, looking around in wonder. He caught her eye and grinned sadly. 'Well, this looks like the centre of things.'

'What is that?' asked Kerstin, pointing at the gleaming cross. 'Who is that woman?'

'Professor Jennifer Nagle,' said Fitz, scratching his chin. 'And as for that thing, I don't know. But the Doctor mentioned something about a wormhole, whatever that is.'

'Don't you know what a wormhole is?' said Kerstin, incredulous. Her knowledge of science wasn't great, but she read some of the popular science magazines. 'I thought you said you travelled in time!'

Fitz avoided her eye. 'Well, I am still rather new to all this.'

A wormhole was a tunnel through space and time connecting two places. Snatching people from their beds and sending them to an alien world where they get infected with alien viruses and –

Kerstin felt herself slipping down again. Into the lake. Drowning. Everything out of control. A dizzying moment; how did she get here, with these people? Fitz, leaning against a desk, watching the Doctor and Professor Nagle, intent at a computer screen in front of the glass partition. This room, everything white. The walls, the chairs, the desks, all white. Clinical.

Sterilised. It had the look and the smell of something secret and evil. The shining X at the far end of the room, the thing that had taken Johan from her. How long had it been here, underneath the forest? How many summers had she gone swimming in the lake with Johan, while the architects of his death lurked below? Had they meant to take Johan? Was this a weapon?

She walked up to the Doctor and Professor Nagle. Ignoring the woman, she addressed the Doctor. 'This thing killed Johan,' she said. 'You know that, don't you?'

The Doctor didn't look up, but he nodded.

'She's responsible for this,' she whispered.

Nagle looked up. 'It was an accident,' she said. 'I'm sorry if –'

Kerstin lunged at Professor Nagle, pinning her against the desk, screaming, screaming, wordless rage pouring from her throat. She had her hands round Nagle's throat. The American woman wasn't very strong and Kerstin squeezed harder, wanting to kill her, wipe out her life as she had wiped out Johan's life.

And then she felt strong arms around her waist, dragging her backwards. She didn't let go of Nagle, who was making a funny gurgling sound and her face was turning red.

And then Kerstin felt a sharp pain at the back of her head, a flash of light and then darkness.

Captain Rogers stood over Kerstin's prone body, breathing heavily, his gun in his hand.

The Doctor's eyes were like chips of ice. 'You didn't have to do that,' said the Doctor. He then turned to tend Professor Nagle, who was gasping and rubbing her throat.

It had all happened so quickly, thought Fitz. One moment Kerstin had been chatting to the Doctor and Nagle, the next moment she'd dived forward, her face contorted in fury. He'd tried to drag her away. He hadn't heard Captain Rogers come into the room.

He bent down to Kerstin. She was out cold. Fortunately Rogers had only fetched her a glancing blow with the butt of his pistol

– there was a small cut, a little blood. If he'd cracked her skull, caused a brain haemorrhage…

'She'll be all right,' said Rogers awkwardly.

Fitz glared up at him. 'If you'd had a clear aim you would have shot her, wouldn't you?'

Rogers coughed and reholstered his gun. 'She was attacking the professor.'

'I don't blame her,' said Fitz, fighting down his anger.

'I want that bitch arrested,' croaked Nagle, rubbing her throat.

This was too much for Fitz. He shot to his feet, bunching his fists. 'You're responsible for the death of her boyfriend. And others. And Sam!' He was shouting. The Doctor was just sitting there, staring at Fitz.

Nagle stuck her chin out. 'As I said, it was an accident. I never meant for anyone to die.'

'An accident!' spat Fitz.

The Doctor stood up, put his hands on Fitz's shoulders. 'Fitz, Fitz, this isn't helping. There's a time to be angry and it's not now.'

Fitz ground his teeth. The Doctor was right. He was always bloody right. He remembered the last thing Sam had said to him. *He's a hero and he never, never, never does anything wrong.* Well, he, Fitz, wasn't a hero. And he sometimes did the wrong thing. So what? 'All right, OK.'

The Doctor nodded, and whispered, 'I've got work to do. Make sure Kerstin's OK and keep your eye on Captain Rogers.'

The Doctor sat back down at the control desk next to Professor Nagle.

Rogers was standing nearby, eyes narrowed.

Fitz beckoned to him. 'Come on, help me get her into a chair.'

Between them Fitz and Captain Rogers carried Kerstin to a seat on the other side of the room. Her head was lolling against her chest and Fitz leaned her back against the wall, making sure she could breathe properly. Then he noticed that Rogers had slipped away, back to the Doctor and Nagle. Fitz followed, his eyes on the soldier's gun. Damn. He should have disarmed him when he had the chance.

'What exactly are you up to?' said Rogers. 'You know that we're evacuating.'

Nagle glanced up at him. 'Has everyone gone?'

Rogers shrugged. 'Not everyone. It's going to take time to dismantle everything. Lindgard's still here somewhere. As is the major, of course.'

'Ah,' said the Doctor.

Nagle returned her attention to the keyboard.

Rogers frowned. 'You're not planning on switching that thing on, are you?'

'No,' said Nagle.

'Yes,' said the Doctor at the same time.

Captain Rogers went for his gun. It was the chance Fitz had been waiting for. As he reached inside his jacket, Fitz grabbed his arm and spun him around, pinning him back against a desk. The Doctor sprang up to help, and between them they disarmed Rogers.

The Doctor handed Fitz the gun, a look of distaste curling his lips.

Fitz pointed the gun at Rogers.

The soldier's eyes were wide. 'This is madness. You know what'll happen if you activate that thing?'

'No,' said the Doctor. 'But we can't leave it alone. Someone has to go through.'

Captain Rogers shook his head. 'Professor Nagle, you cannot allow this! This base is under military command.'

Fitz heard Nagle's hoarse voice. 'So what. We're trying to save the planet.'

Fitz kept the gun steady, aiming at Captain Rogers's chest, at the middle button, bright against the green fabric of his jacket. He kept his eyes locked on the soldier's. They were dark brown, with large pupils. Fitz hoped he looked menacing enough, hoped he looked like the sort of person who would shoot first and ask questions later.

But what Captain Rogers said and did next gave the lie to that.

'This is totally preposterous,' said Captain Rogers, his jaw firm, resolute. 'I'm going to get the major and you, sonny, are going to have to shoot me to stop me.'

With that he turned on his heel and marched stiffly out of the room.

Fitz stood, the gun useless in his hands. He just couldn't shoot somebody in cold blood. There had been Ed Hill, of course. But he had been just about to destroy the world. Rogers was just doing his job.

Still aiming the gun, he shouted to the Doctor. 'He's getting away! What shall I do?'

The Doctor's face was dreamy, abstracted, totally absorbed in the computer screen before him. 'Oh let him go, he doesn't matter. This is far more important.'

Chapter Fourteen
Hating the Alien

Sam had been swimming or flying for what seemed like ages, but there was no sign of Itharquell. There seemed to be no end to this golden sky-sea – it was as if she moved through in an endless realm of golden light. She had no idea how much time had elapsed since she'd arrived in the Dominion – she hadn't been wearing her watch when she was taken from the TARDIS – but she felt hungry and light-headed. And tired again. Maybe this place was brimming with ambient radiation which was slowly but surely killing her. She remembered Janus Prime, with its strange glowing sands, and the radiation that had almost claimed her life. Well, at least that had been a planet. This place was... well, what was it exactly? A whole separate universe of rock, as Itharquell seemed to think? No, it had to be a planet, so vast that the inhabitants had never seen the surface.

Here and there floated clumps of rock, covered in rubbery tubelike growths, and she could mark her progress against these. She rested for a while, sitting on one of the lumps of rock, the surface of which was covered in a dense purple moss.

She glanced down, and screamed, leaping from the rock, hardly able to believe what she had just seen.

A face, a human face.

She moved around the thing she'd been sitting on. It had once been human. Its body was covered in purple growths, the only recognisable parts the face and left shoulder. Grimacing, she moved in for a closer look, praying it wasn't the Doctor or Fitz. But it was a youngish man, with blond hair.

How long had he been here? What was that purple stuff? She panicked, inspecting her skin. What if it started to grow on her?

She had to get out of here.

She kicked off from the rock, peering ahead. Nothing but an

endless honey-golden glow, streaked with currents of white and amber.

Then, before her, she saw the gold of the sky-sea darkening to ochre. She knew that this was where it met a cavern. Perhaps that was where Itharquell had gone. She moved towards it. Now she felt as if the surface was above her, and she was rising up to meet it. She couldn't see clearly through – there could be anything on the other side so she slowed her pace, until it got closer, closer, and then she popped her head above the surface.

As she did so, something buzzed past her face, wings flailing, and she put her hands up to protect herself, kicking her legs. The movement propelled her out of the sky-sea, spinning away into the cavern. Out of control, she spiralled down, her vision flashing gold, then blue, as the sky-sea and the cavern spun about her, the floor rushing up to meet her.

As she fell, she caught glimpses of furious activity on the far side of the cavern, and heard terrifying screeching and howling. The unmistakable clangour of battle.

Sam landed with a soft bump. She was in a cavern of powder-blue sand. Even the walls and roof were sand, held in place by the strange surface-tension gravity of the Dominion. Behind her, the golden sky-sea swirled like a vat of treacle for miles in either direction, meeting the roof of the cavern some hundreds of feet above her.

The ever-present flowery smell was even stronger here and it made Sam sneeze. On the other side of the valley, the ground rose up to a vast, black wall of rock, which was splintered like a broken mirror. At first Sam thought it was a patch of Blight, but it was still and shiny, reflecting the gold of the sky-sea opposite. It reared up hundreds of feet, a black shining cliff face. Before it were scattered angular shards of black rock, as if something had burst through from the other side and sent them scattering down the slope.

And, in the air above her, a battle raged.

There were at least a hundred Ruin, arranged in a ribbon formation in front of the black cliff, their orange bodies closed up into flower-like bulbs, propelling themselves across the cavern to lash out with their spider legs at hordes of winged green creatures. These occupied a flock of dirigibles near the ceiling of the cavern, from which they leapt and soared, pale wings carrying them into the fray, firing bolts from stubby harpoon-like weapons. Sam frowned. They looked like T'hiili, but they were somehow different. They had wings, to start with, and even from this distance they looked more substantial and sturdy than Itharquell.

Perhaps they were the warriors – T'vorha – that he had mentioned. The combatants were too far away to notice Sam, so she could watch in relative safety, work out what this battle was about.

It seemed that the T'vorha – if that was what they were – were trying to break through the cordon of Ruin to get to the black wall beyond. They weren't having much luck. The blue sand of the cavern was littered with their bodies, the wings crushed and folded beneath them. Some had landed on the shards of black glass, grotesquely impaled. A few tangled and deflated Ruin bodies lay here and there, but nowhere near as many as their opponents.

Something buzzed above Sam's head and she ducked down behind a dune, looking upward fearfully. She breathed out in relief when she saw that it wasn't a Ruin, but a strange, insectoid thing like an elongated dragonfly with a trumpet mouth and four wings. Now she came to look, there were quite a few of the things flitting about. This was the highest concentration of life forms she'd ever seen in the Dominion. What was so special about this cavern?

Sam felt, not for the first time, that she had more questions than answers.

Major Gareth Wolstencroft sat in his office behind his mahogany desk, looking at the wood-panelled walls, the photographs of his early days in UNIT. In the desert in Kebiria. In the Welsh valleys. Fighting monsters.

He wouldn't miss this place at all.

He hated being underground, and two years stationed in this base was more than enough for him. No place for a soldier. This place was perfect for C19 of course – allowing them complete secrecy to carry out their experiments.

Well, that would all end now. There had been too many deaths. On the green leather of the desk in front of him was a full report indicting Professor Nagle of gross misconduct. It would go to UNIT headquarters in Geneva, and to the head of C19 in Whitehall. This pleased him: he'd never liked C19. The report would show them the dire consequences of mucking about with alien technology.

Wolstencroft believed passionately in UNIT. They were a vital force. Earth had to be protected. It had always rankled that C19 were their paymasters. As far as he was concerned, any alien technology found or left over should be destroyed. Far too dangerous. His views were widely known, even at ministerial level. And the events here in Sweden would give force to them.

He hadn't wanted to come to Sweden to start with. It had sounded a humdrum job: provide security for Professor Nagle and her team. But his superiors had made it quite clear: his views were not shared by others, and he was becoming a bit of an embarrassment. So they'd farmed him out here. He smiled. They'd shot themselves in the foot there. He had enough evidence to force C19 into a severe audit.

One fly in the ointment. The Doctor.

Wolstencroft shuddered. The Doctor had been indirectly responsible for the deaths of his men on several occasions. Over the years, Wolstencroft had come to the conclusion that the Doctor wasn't on their side at all. He was an alien, after all, and Wolstencroft knew that you couldn't trust aliens. He may look human on the surface, but, beneath, Wolstencroft was sure that the Doctor had his own agenda. It seemed to include activating the generator, for God's sake. And that would only let more creatures through, cause more chaos.

There was a knock on the door.

'Enter,' he said, hiding the report on his desk under some other papers. Just in case it was Professor Nagle.

But it was Captain Rogers, and he looked unusually excited. He came up to the desk and saluted. 'Sir!'

Wolstencroft smiled at Rogers. Always so formal, yet always reliable. 'At ease, man. Now what is it?'

'It's the generator room, sir. I think you'd better come and see for yourself.'

The Doctor and Nagle sat side by side at the control desk. The screen was showing an intricate revolving pattern. Behind the glass partition, the silver prongs of the generator were starting to shimmer, like reflections in water. The Doctor and Nagle seemed unconcerned, even excited, but Fitz was getting a bad feeling about this. If the wormhole could invade the TARDIS there was no telling what it could do.

'It'll take a while to power up,' said Professor Nagle. She sighed. 'I don't think there's any hope of closing the wormhole. My generator's had it.'

'Oh, there's every hope,' said the Doctor. 'If I can shut the wormhole down, then the generator will function perfectly once more.'

'Great,' said Nagle.

'But I won't allow it,' said the Doctor.

'What do you mean, you won't allow it? What gives you the right?' said Nagle, aggrieved. 'This is my project.' She held up a hand, stalling the Doctor. 'I know it could be used for warfare. But you can't uninvent something. Nuclear weapons exist, enough to blow up the planet ten times over, yet we're still here.'

'Not if I can't close the wormhole,' muttered the Doctor.

Nagle was defiant. 'Even if you shut this one down, I've got notes. Even if you destroy them, I could still start from scratch. Perfect the generator. I believe in the TC Warp, Doctor. You're gonna have to kill me to stop me continuing my research.'

She had a point, thought Fitz. Instant transportation would

solve a lot of the planet's problems.

The Doctor's face clouded. 'It won't come to that.'

'The Doctor is trying to help,' said Fitz, stepping between them. 'I think you'd better let him, and argue the toss later.'

'Look,' said the Doctor, ignoring Fitz. 'It's founded on alien technology, and you simply haven't got the knowledge to operate it properly. Even if you kept it exclusive to C19, there would always be the danger of accidentally creating another wormhole. So, I simply cannot allow it.'

Nagle swore. 'Then I'm not sure I want you to help any more.'

'Anyway, it's academic,' said the Doctor, standing up and pointing at the generator. 'It's almost ready.'

The shimmering prongs had stabilised, and there were points of light at their tips, as bright as burning magnesium. Fitz shielded his eyes.

'How do I get into the chamber?' asked the Doctor.

'There's a door at the far end. You'll need this key,' said Professor Nagle, passing a slim card to the Doctor.

'Right,' said the Doctor, taking the card from Nagle. 'As soon as I am inside the generator chamber, activate the node.'

'Stop right there!'

The voice echoed all around the generator room. They all turned to see, framed in the doorway, the uniformed figure of Major Wolstencroft. He was aiming an automatic pistol right at the Doctor's head. Beside him, Captain Rogers stood, aiming a pistol at Fitz.

Not again, thought Fitz.

'Make one move to open the node,' said Wolstencroft calmly, 'and I'll shoot.'

Major Wolstencroft walked down the short flight of steps into the generator room, his right arm steady, aiming directly at the Doctor. He didn't want to shoot – if he, a UNIT officer, killed the Doctor, what would happen to him? Court martial, leading to dismissal, at the very least. But he had to protect Earth.

Wolstencroft frowned. There were two civilians in the

generator room – a young blonde girl, Swedish by the look of her, slumped in a chair on the far right. A dark-haired chap in an encounter suit, next to Professor Nagle at the control desk. And to the left, the Doctor, on his way to the entrance to the generator chamber. A wide range of targets. He had the Doctor covered; the captain had the others covered.

Behind them all, the generator was shimmering, points of light glowing at the ends of the silver needles. He had been right. The Doctor was going to activate it.

Nagle was staring at him unflinchingly. He felt a glow of satisfaction. This was mutiny. She'd be kicked out of C19 and stripped of her professorship.

'If you're going to shoot the Doctor you'll have to shoot me as well,' said the dark-haired man. His words meant nothing – Wolstencroft could tell at a glance that he was the type to go scurrying for cover as soon as shots were fired.

'Major, we have to let the Doctor go through the wormhole,' said Professor Nagle. Her voice was shaking. 'It's the only way to find out what's going wrong.'

Wolstencroft snorted. 'Absolute rubbish! The only way is to blow up this entire installation and bury the thing.'

'Oh, please!' cried the Doctor, throwing his hands above his head, his face a dark scowl. 'Do I always have to come up against the gross stupidity and tunnel vision of the military?'

His histrionics distracted Wolstencroft momentarily, and he caught a flash of movement out of the corner of his eye, and turned to see Professor Nagle leaning over the keyboard.

'Stand away from that computer!' he roared.

He heard the clack of keystrokes and she turned to face him, unsmiling, defiant. 'Go on, shoot me,' she said. 'It's all you know. But it's too late now. Look at the generator.'

Between the prongs, something was forming.

As Sam watched, the centre of the black wall, where all the cracks converged, began to glow with a white light. The light pulsed and spread until it formed a whirlpool in the black rock, a tunnel of white light which was instantly familiar to Sam.

The thing that had invaded the TARDIS and brought her here. This must be the way home. It had to be.

But how to get across the cavern without being noticed?

As she watched, two of the Ruin darted towards the whirlpool, their legs spread out so they looked like vast wheels. They disappeared in a flash of light.

Sam had to try to get through.

She ran down to the bottom of the valley, taking great leaps and strides, until she was directly underneath the battle. The Ruin were clustered around the whirlpool, but no more of them were going through. It was as if they were waiting for something. Waiting for the others to come back?

Now she was nearer she could see that the green-skinned things were indeed T'hiili, but they were more heavily built, and wore a leatherlike armour. The biggest difference was their wings; pale green, mothlike, and too small for flight in normal gravity, but perfect for the Dominion. They all seemed to have retreated to the ledge. What were they doing?

Then all of a sudden, dozens of them launched themselves at the Ruin. The movement was slow and graceful in the low gravity.

The battle exploded again above Sam with tremendous ferocity.

She had to try to get to the whirlpool. It was the way home.

She leapt up, shouting. 'Get me through and I'll save you all!'

The whirlpool was far above her, and unlike the Ruin and winged T'hiili she couldn't fly. She stood, watching, as the Ruin flailed at the attacking T'hiili. Limbs were shorn clear of green bodies, wings were shredded.

There was nothing she could do.

She went back across the cavern towards the sky-sea, taking one last look before she plunged in. The whirlpool was still open, the Ruin holding their position. What she needed was a dirigible, then she could fly into the whirlpool.

She turned to face the curtain of sky-sea. She stepped into it, shuddering as her whole body tingled. She could still feel the floor of the cavern beneath her feet, but as she walked further into the golden void it fell away, and she was floating again. She moved her arms and legs, and set off in a random direction.

And then she saw something heading through the sky-sea towards her, something dark and bullet-shaped, blunt and finned like a shark.

Fitz stared into the barrel of Wolstencroft's revolver and closed his eyes. Oh hell, he was going to die. Shot in the head. The thought turned his stomach. Would it hurt? Would there be a flash of pain and then nothing?

Suddenly there was a sound which Fitz felt rather than heard, a solid bass *whoomph*, and he opened his eyes, heart hammering.

Wolstencroft had dropped his weapon and was staring open-mouthed at something behind Fitz.

He turned.

There, where the generator had been, was a gigantic, swirling whirlpool, golden and white, just like the one that had snatched Sam from the TARDIS.

Fitz watched as the Doctor walked into the generator chamber, as casually as if he were getting on a bus.

And then the monsters came through the node.

There were two of them. Their hourglass-shaped bodies were bright orange, and they had six thick black legs, about ten feet long. Tentacles and cilia whipped and lashed from the open ends of the main body.

Christ, they were just like the dead thing he and Nordenstam had found in the forest, only very much alive. He thought of Nordenstam, wondered what he was doing now, what he would say in his report.

The Doctor ducked as the legs flailed above him. One of the creatures shot out of the whirlpool and cannoned into the glass partition, shattering it instantly. Fitz instinctively ducked as splinters of glass showered down around him.

Looking up, he saw that the creature impaled on three-foot-

179

long spikes of glass was dying, its black legs twitching.

But the other one was still alive, and it was stumbling out of the generator chamber, supporting itself on its six legs. Unbelievably, the Doctor was unhurt.

Wolstencroft and Rogers were firing at the surviving creature. It lashed out at them, its limbs moving so fast that Fitz could barely see them.

Fitz circled round. A hand gripped his arm. It was Kerstin, her eyes wide with fear.

'Everyone out of here!' yelled the Doctor.

He ran with Nagle to the door. Wolstencroft and Rogers, followed.

But the creature was between Fitz and Kerstin and the metal doors, which were sliding closed. The last face he saw before the door closed was the Doctor's, calling to him. 'Get out of there, Fitz!'

All very well, but how?

The creature bore down on them, its tentacles lashing. It looked like a bizarre cross between a spider, a plant and a sea creature. Fitz knew that the edges of its legs were razor-sharp. It could kill them with one swift flick of its legs.

There was only one thing to do. The Doctor had wanted to go through the wormhole – now it looked like Fitz had no choice.

Typical.

He turned, stepping over the edge of the broken partition, taking Kerstin with him. He took a step towards the node, and then found himself flying into the air, and into the glowing heart of the whirlpool. Kerstin still clung to him, screaming.

As the light closed around them, Fitz knew there was no point in pretending to be brave now. Because he was screaming too.

Book Three
Destiny

Chapter Fifteen
Moss Elixir

Professor Nagle stood outside the generator room. Her hands were shaking and she felt sick. Those things…

From behind the steel double door came a muffled thumping and clattering. It sounded like the surviving creature was wrecking the generator.

The Doctor was pacing up and down in front of the door, breathing heavily, his face pale and drawn. Every now and then he'd glance towards the door, wincing.

Fitz and Kerstin.

Professor Nagle tried not to think about what those things could be doing to them.

Wolstencroft was issuing a string of orders to Captain Rogers. These included rounding up every soldier left in the base in order to finish off the creature.

'There's no time for that,' snapped the Doctor. He went to key in the entry code.

Wolstencroft stopped him. 'We wait for backup.'

The Doctor pointed at the two doors, his whole arm trembling like a tautened wire. 'Two innocent people are in great danger! We have to try to save them!'

Nagle went up to the Doctor. 'Doctor, it's too late to do anything for them now. And anyway, they could have gone through the –'

The Doctor held up a hand. 'Yes, yes, yes, the wormhole. Even more reason to open the doors!'

Shouts and footsteps from along the corridor. A squad of about twenty UNIT troops marched up, clad in hi-tech combat gear, their faces hidden by helmets and masks. They crashed to attention and saluted. The Doctor and Nagle found themselves barged out of the way.

'Typical,' tutted Nagle. 'Now they've got something to fight they think it's all over.'

Wolstencroft shouted an order and the soldiers fanned out, aiming their machine guns at the door. Nagle and the Doctor were left staring at a wall of black-uniformed backs.

Wolstencroft addressed his men. 'If anything's moving in there, open fire.'

The Doctor put a hand to his forehead and groaned. 'Anything *not human*, for Rassilon's sake.'

Nagle grabbed his sleeve. 'I think we'd better stand back.' She pulled him back along the corridor, a vague escape plan taking shape. She could go back to her room, retrieve her notes and get out of here. But she had to see what had happened to the generator. Where was Lindgard? Probably still skulking in the lab. She knew that he wouldn't want to destroy his specimens.

She watched as the soldiers filed through the opening doors, the Doctor following on their heels. Once inside, she took in the damage with thumping heart. 'It's ruined,' she whispered, 'it's all ruined.' Equipment lay smashed, desks overturned, chairs scattered. Over the far side, the glass partition was broken, its jagged edge like a line on a graph. One of the aliens was impaled on a spike of glass, clearly dead, its body deflated, grey cilia drooping from the ends.

Behind it, the prongs of the generator itself seemed intact, but the shimmering whirlpool of the node was gone. The UNIT guys were picking their way through the debris, checking and double-checking. The other creature lay slumped in a corner, its legs curled in upon itself like a giant dead spider. Two soldiers were prodding it with their rifles. The stench was overpowering.

No Fitz or Kerstin. It was obvious what had happened. She thought of what happened to the probes, to Johan, and swallowed, a sick taste souring her throat. She looked over at the Doctor. His face was relaxed, almost vacant-looking. Calculating, assessing.

She walked over to him. 'Doctor?'

He glanced down at her, but his eyes were elsewhere. 'Nothing to be scared of,' he muttered absent-mindedly, patting her arm.

She sighed. 'I'm not scared, Doctor. Pissed off, yes, a little freaked out, maybe. But not scared.'

The muscles around his eyes twitched, a tiny change of expression. 'No sorrow? Not even a little bit?'

She opened her mouth, about to justify her actions yet again, but the expression on his face froze her. It was pure rage, not the bluster of Wolstencroft, but a calm, silent disdain.

'There's nothing you can say.' He turned and walked away briskly.

Damn. She'd probably lost him for good now. She watched him talking to Wolstencroft. To her amazement, the soldier seemed to be listening. She walked slowly around the room, seeing what she could salvage. On closer inspection, the damage wasn't too bad. Mostly desks and papers; the broken glass partition made things look worse than they really were.

Her main concern was the generator itself. She walked up to the control desk and sat down. Error messages crowded the screen. She tapped a few keys, tried to cancel them. Nothing happened. She sighed, and took her glasses off. The world turned into a blur as she cleaned them.

The Doctor came to stand beside her, his manner still aloof. His long fingers danced over the keys. The computer gave a surprised sounding *bleep!* and the screen lit up blue.

Nagle put her glasses back on with shaking hands. She breathed in slowly, holding her breath. The main menu. The generator was still on line.

She turned to thank the Doctor, but he was striding towards the ravaged glass partition.

Nagle followed him, her shoes crunching on broken glass. She wanted him back on her side, badly. She looked up at the impaled creature. 'Wonder where it came from.'

The Doctor didn't acknowledge her presence. He just kept staring at the creature, his face shadowed and sad. 'Don't know. Pity, in its way it's quite beautiful.'

Booted feet crunched on glass behind them. Wolstencroft. 'Rubbish. It is – was – a hostile alien –'

The Doctor rounded on the major. 'There is no evidence at all that its intentions were hostile! How would you feel if you were snatched from your home world and catapulted across the stars to a strange and alien environment?'

It looked like a full-scale slanging match was developing. Nagle felt a headache coming on. She stepped over the remains of the glass partition to get a better look at the generator. If the frame supporting the silver prongs was damaged in any way, it would need to be realigned. Remarkably, it looked unharmed. She walked right into the generator, underneath the point where the prongs converged. She stared up. Yes, they were perfectly aligned – she'd have to run the troubleshooting program to be sure, but she allowed herself to hope.

Then something cannoned into her, sending her sprawling. She landed on her front, glasses slipping down her nose, chin butting the floor. There was a needle-sharp pain in her jaw and ear. She rolled on to her back, pushing her glasses back into place, drawing in breath to scream –

Standing over her was a green-skinned alien in shell-like armour, with a froglike head. She caught a glimpse of green wings, folded and rustling. It was aiming a black weapon, like a harpoon, right at her face. The jagged point filled her vision.

Nagle screamed, scrambling backwards, hands encountering bits of broken glass.

A shot, from behind her.

The thing fell, clutching its side, and she rolled out of its way. She felt a stinging pain in the palm of her hand; there was a triangle of glass hanging from it and blood everywhere.

The Doctor ran over, his face dark, his voice bellowing. Ignoring Nagle, the Doctor bent over the creature, his green velvet coat falling over its twitching green limbs.

She saw the tall figure of Wolstencroft striding towards her, gun pointed at the Doctor and the alien. A snarl of anger curled her lips. Was she invisible all of a sudden? 'Hey!' she yelled. 'Little help here?'

Fitz screamed. It felt as though his body were being pulled in all directions at once, and then compressed to nothing. His breath was torn from him and his vision seemed to revolve inside his head. Blinding, swirling lights stung his eyes, reaching in to fry his brain.

This was what Sam had gone through, in every sense. He fully expected to die at any moment.

And then, suddenly, he was in free space, spinning in blackness, the lights gone. Something thwacked against his back and he spun away. He looked up, saw a shining black wall, the lip of a swirling white whirlpool spitting and churning above him.

He hit the black wall and began to slide down, scrabbling at the sheer surface. His vision was fuzzy, out of focus. Below was something blue – the ground? He was sliding very slowly – was that because he was concussed?

Kerstin. He was sure she'd been with him when he'd dived through the node. Where was she? He looked up at the node – and it closed, suddenly and silently, like the switching off of a light.

He was trapped.

He continued to slide down the wall, turning to face outward, squinting. There was something golden and glowing in the distance, almost sunlike. He blinked. Yes, his sight was definitely improving. Now he could see the creatures above him.

He gasped. There were hundreds of them, their spiderlike bodies floating in the air of the… cavern, he supposed, though he couldn't see the ceiling for the mass of orange and black creatures. Had they seen him?

Fitz landed softly, on something soft. He reached down, his fingers touching sand. He looked up. The black wall towered behind him, and the creatures above looked as small as pennies.

He was not alone. Crouching on the blue dunes around him,

pointing deadly looking harpoons, were a group of green-skinned aliens with bulging blue eyes. They looked straight out of pulp SF and Fitz thought he was hallucinating at first.

'Hello,' said Fitz. His legs felt like jelly and there was a terrible pins-and-needles feeling over his whole body.

One of the creatures jumped down, aiming its harpoon at Fitz.

A wave of weakness washed over Fitz. Mad laughter bubbled up inside him. 'Take me to your leader!' he giggled. Then he passed out.

Kerstin screamed. It felt as though her whole body were being stretched into a thin line. She was massive, omnipresent; and then tiny, insignificant. All she could see was a golden-white blur. Fitz was gone, and, thankfully, so was the creature from the generator room. Just when she thought she was going to pass out, she felt her body swerve, as though she were on a roller coaster, and then everything *stopped*.

A moment of giddiness, of nausea – it felt as if her stomach were trying to climb up her throat – and she squeezed her eyes shut. The sickness passed, and she opened her eyes. And saw –

It was like looking into the biggest kaleidoscope ever made. A golden-white tunnel, rippling and surging in a way that seemed to tug at her mind. It was a calming sight. Somehow she knew it wouldn't hurt her. And at the end of the tunnel something tantalised her, never quite forming, first one thing and then another. Sometimes it was a field. Sometimes it was a pile of books. Sometimes it looked like nothing she had ever seen before.

She couldn't move, couldn't feel her body, didn't know if she was breathing, couldn't feel the beat of her heart. Couldn't feel where the soldier had hit her with his gun. Was she dead? Perhaps everyone who had ever died was here. She just couldn't see them, that was all.

Dazed by the golden light, her thoughts drifted back to the past. She'd been stationed with a horrendous family in the West Midlands of England on an exchange programme when she was eighteen. They'd used her as a slave, and the husband had made advances towards her. You could see it in his eyes, the petty lust; all Swedish girls were nymphos, weren't they? And this one was just a blonde bimbo without an idea in her head.

Disgusted with herself, she'd cut her hair brutally short and run away and lived in London with James, a sociology student a couple of years older than her. She'd met him on the train, when she'd had no idea where to go or what to do. Looking back, she'd been lucky. James was kind and considerate, and never even dreamt of taking advantage of her – it was Kerstin who'd made the first move.

He'd had wiry brown hair, the palest blue eyes she had ever seen, a quirky face and a skinny body; he'd been poor and lived in an awful bedsit in London; he drank sickly sweet tea and ate ghastly fried food. Living with James and mixing with his friends really opened her eyes. Before, she'd lived in the shadow of her parents' old-fashioned views, their inward-looking, overprotective natures hiding the real world from her. They believed that neutrality was all and Sweden was a cool and haughty outsider, its society a well-oiled machine, its culture and people rich. Peripheral to world affairs.

At home, Kerstin had fallen in line with this; it was easy, and excused her from having to care about anything or anyone outside her immediate family. But living with James, she'd gradually realised what she knew all along – she couldn't detach herself from the world; Sweden was as much a part of 'Western' culture as England and the USA. She had found in herself a yearning for travel, and a desire to put the world to rights.

So, after a month, she'd returned to Stockholm, vowing to return to James as soon as she could.

Her parents hadn't understood, of course. Her new views were alien to them. Her father had raged about her duty to her country, how she must study for her medical degree and oil the wheels of society.

She could have run away again; but she decided to bide her time. She concentrated on her studies, waiting for the day she could escape, truly escape, a fit and qualified woman, into the world. To do good or bad, she couldn't tell, but to do *something*.

She never wrote to James again. He'd been merely a catalyst, setting her on her way. She went to Uppsala and studied, studied, studied. Her father had wanted her to do a four-year medical degree and become, like him, a doctor – they'd argued about this, as everything, and in the end Kerstin got her own way. Linguistics, politics, sociology and psychology were her subjects. She wanted to understand how people worked, how the world worked.

And now she didn't know.

Or rather, she knew that this world wasn't all there was. There were other worlds, alien creatures, time travellers, and it was all frightening and exciting and she wanted either to forget it completely or become a part of it for ever.

But she couldn't do anything right now. She was stuck here, staring down this impossible tunnel, trying to make sense of what she was seeing, trying to make sense of her life.

Sam hung in the sky-sea, unable to move as the bullet-shaped thing drew nearer. It was approaching too fast.

The thing stopped in front of her. It was a very dark green, like some giant seed pod. She fully expected a mouth to open in the end and eat her whole, but instead a hatch opened in its side to reveal the yellow-clad figure of Itharquell.

Sam's heart lifted instantly and she kicked her legs, propelling herself towards the hatch.

Itharquell helped her inside.

'Am I glad to see you!' she said, sitting down on a leaflike seat. 'I thought you'd been nobbled by the Ruin.'

Itharquell shook his head. Sam heard his whispering voice in her mind.

I came across a patch of Blight. It's blocking the way in the opposite direction.

'So, how did you get hold of this dirigible?' said Sam.

I grew it. I always carry a spare seed or two.

'Oh,' said Sam. 'Right.' Then she remembered the whirlpool in the cavern. 'Itharquell, what would you say if I told you that I have seen the way out of the Dominion?'

There is no way out of the Dominion.

Sam sighed in exasperation. 'Look, you don't know where the Blight came from, right?'

Itharquell nodded.

'You can't explain it at all.'

It is beyond understanding.

Sam leaned forward, the leaf-seat adjusting to her change in position. 'Then why won't you accept that there may be other things beyond your understanding? Like me, for instance? And the possibility of life outside the Dominion?'

Itharquell sat back and pushed his feathery hair from his eyes.

I have been giving a lot of thought to what you have said. It is difficult for me to understand, but there may be something in what you say. Some of the words you used... What are planets?

Sam briefly explained what a planet was. 'I think this Dominion could be a planet – one so big that you just haven't discovered the surface yet.'

No. The Dominion is infinite.

Sam let it ride, for now. Her wishes had been answered and she now had a dirigible, a means of escape. Then she thought of the T'hiili Nest. There were hundreds, thousands of the creatures. 'Itharquell, we can rescue your people! If we go back to the Nest, we could bring them to the cavern I told you about, fight our way past the Ruin –'

A single word, crisp and chill in her mind.

How?

Sam told him about the winged T'hiili she had seen.

At this, Itharquell seemed to perk up a little.

T'vorha, fighting the Ruin... that means the new Queen could be nearby.

'So, we go back to the Nest? Try to save your people?'

The way is blocked by the Blight.

191

Sam ground her teeth. Things were closing in on them. 'Is there another way back to the Nest?'

There may be. We would have to search to find it. And there is not much time.

Sam stood up, and the leaf-seat furled closed behind her. 'Then let's go!'

In the generator room, Major Wolstencroft had taken charge – and, in his opinion, it was about time. The wounded alien had been taken to the laboratory. Damn thing must have been hiding in the generator room. Almost got Professor Nagle.

She sat on a swivel chair next to the Doctor, nursing her bandaged hand. Captain Rogers sat nearby, pistol held casually in his lap. Wolstencroft paced up and down in front of them, watching the Doctor carefully. Couldn't trust him an inch.

'I think it's about time we had a little chat,' he said.

'Why did you shoot that poor creature?'

Wolstencroft glared at the Doctor. 'To save Professor Nagle.'

'Yes, to save me,' said Nagle.

The Doctor just kept staring at Wolstencroft. 'I must examine the alien. It's our only link with the other end of the wormhole.'

'All in good time. Now tell me, what did you think you were doing in here?'

'He was trying to help us,' said Professor Nagle.

Wolstencroft gestured to the wreckage in the room. 'And do you think even in your wildest dreams that this has helped in any way?'

'Look,' said the Doctor. 'There's no need for us to argue. The situation is very simple: if the wormhole isn't closed, then Earth will be destroyed. We haven't got much time!'

Wolstencroft stopped pacing in front of the Doctor. 'I only have your word for that.'

Professor Nagle looked up at him, imploring. 'It's true,' she said. 'I've checked his calculations. The wormhole is consuming energy at a tremendous rate. It will soon be big enough to swallow this planet whole.'

Wolstencroft considered. If this was true, it put a whole new dimension on things. He'd acted responsibly as far as he was concerned, in shutting the operation down. Maybe the Doctor was right. Maybe that wasn't enough.

'So we can't just evacuate, and blow this place up?'

The Doctor laughed. 'Absolutely not! Did you seriously think that would solve everything?'

It usually did. Can't argue with high explosives. But Wolstencroft refused to be won over by the Doctor. 'So what's the alternative?'

'I must travel along the wormhole, find out what's at the other end,' said the Doctor. 'Could use the TARDIS – but she's still, well... she's not there.'

The TARDIS, the Doctor's infamous time machine. 'What do you mean?'

'I mean,' said the Doctor with a sideways glance at Nagle, 'it was invaded by an offshoot of the wormhole.' He glared at Wolstencroft. 'It's out of commission for the time being.' He broke into a smile. 'So, if you'll allow me, I'll fix your machine and pop through –'

Wolstencroft knew when someone was trying to pull one over on him. 'No, Doctor,' he said. 'You will not. You've seen those creatures. In their natural environment, they're probably very effective at killing.' He gestured at the Doctor's clothes. 'You're hardly suited for a foray into a dangerous alien environment. I'll send some of my men through first to establish an operations post.'

The Doctor looked appalled. 'You could be sending them to their deaths!'

Wolstencroft ignored him. 'Maybe at the other end the problem can be solved with explosives,' he mused aloud, watching the Doctor's face.

'This is madness!' cried the Doctor, standing up. Captain Rogers moved to cover him in an instant. 'Just what have you got against me, Major?' said the Doctor, ignoring the gun aimed at his head.

Wolstencroft remembered the first Auton invasion, back when

he'd first joined UNIT. Whole squads, their bodies melted and fused by alien weapons. And at the centre of events, the Doctor, always the Doctor, miraculously surviving each skirmish, each invasion. More than surviving: regenerating. Well, soldiers couldn't regenerate.

His lip curled in anger. 'People die when you're around, Doctor.'

The Doctor stared back at him. 'And if I wasn't around, there would be even more death.' He offered his palms to Wolstencroft in a pleading gesture. 'I'm on your side, Major.'

Wolstencroft smiled. 'No, Doctor. You're my prisoner.'

Fitz came round to find himself lying on something soft, staring up at a face from a nightmare. It was blank, pale green, and it had two bulbous froglike eyes with slit pupils. It had no visible nose, but a round, wet, red mouth at the bottom of its ridged face. And a mane of plaited white hair.

Where was he? London? China? The TARDIS? Sweden? It all came flooding back. He sat up. He was in a dark, cramped space with a dozen of the green-faced things. They were clad in some sort of armour, wings folded behind their backs.

The one who had been watching him turned to the others, muttering in a voice that was at once sibilant and deep.

The others crowded round to have a look at him, hooting in wonderment. Whatever they were, they didn't seem very bright. Their bulbous blue eyes, crowding in on him, made him feel nervous. After the trip through the wormhole, he could do with a bit of peace and quiet. And a cigarette. He felt in his jeans pocket beneath his biohazard suit; the lighter was still there, but not his Camels.

'Look,' said Fitz, pushing the creatures back from him. He appeared to be lying on a giant leaf, which moulded to his body as he moved, making it very difficult to get up. 'Who are you lot, and where are we going?'

More indecipherable muttering.

After a while the creatures lost interest in Fitz, and drifted away. As far as Fitz could work out, they were in some sort of flying machine. There was a horizontal slit in the brown fleshy wall next to him, and Fitz prised it open. Green light poured through. They seemed to be in some sort of glowing river, or sea. But the slit wasn't letting any water in, though he could poke his hand out. In the distance, he could see an inverted cone, which looked like a cross between a tangled vegetable root and a battleship. They were heading towards this.

Fitz's mind whirled with questions. This was obviously the place where all the creatures had come from. Where Sam had been taken.

Sam. If he'd survived the wormhole, then there was every chance that she would have too. He tried to sit up – only to cry out as ropelike tendrils snaked out from underneath the leaf-seat, binding him tightly. He yelled, but the creatures were obviously too busy flying this thing to pay any attention to him. Swearing, he lay back, watching green light filter through the slit. After a while, it went abruptly dark.

They had arrived. Fitz couldn't see a thing now, could only hear the voices of the things from up front. Couldn't move. It was like a nightmare. He struggled again, but the tendrils only hugged him harder, biting into his arms, his chest, his thighs.

They kept moving for a while, until Fitz felt a gentle bump. Muttering from up ahead. A lumpen shape in the dark. The tendrils binding him fell limp.

Rubbing his arms and chest, Fitz sat up. He cried out as clawed hands gripped him, propelled him to an oval mouth in the wall. Green light from outside. He was shoved down a ramp and into a glowing tunnel, the light coming from veins in the wall which seemed to be carrying flowing, green liquid. He walked as if he was in a dream, each step carrying him a few feet into the air.

A prod in the back. Fitz stumbled along the tunnel. It led into a large, domed chamber. The green veins ran around the walls and up to the ceiling of the dome, where they converged in a glowing lump.

His captors shoved Fitz towards the centre of this chamber, and then shuffled behind him, their heads held low.

Fitz stepped carefully forward. The floor was soft, and as he got used to the fish-tank lighting he could see that the entire floor of the circular chamber was covered with humps of a purple mossy substance. It exuded a heady, perfumed smell which made his eyes water and his head swim.

In the middle of this chamber was what at first sight was a naked, female human being. It rose as he approached. As he got closer he could see that it wasn't really the slightest bit human, though the skin was as pink and blemish-free as a newborn baby.

Fitz stopped when he was a few yards away. He heard a metallic click from behind him, and looked over his shoulder. The creatures had unshouldered their harpoons. Any sudden moves and he had no doubt what the result would be.

He turned back to the figure in front of him. She – it – was about Fitz's height, and completely naked. Along the front of the body ran a double row of budlike teats. There were no privates as far as he could see and the limbs were thin and shapely, ending in long-fingered hands.

The head was a smooth egg shape, the same oval mouth and round blue eyes as his captors; but the hair was different, a deep, shining red which fell in waves. Fitz was reminded of Botticelli's Venus and the girl who worked in the greengrocer's down the road where he grew up.

The strange creature stepped down from the raised dais in the centre of the chamber and approached Fitz, her movements languid and slow.

Fitz felt an itch, a tickle in his head, like a sneeze. The feeling grew and grew and there was a sound with it, a sighing, icy voice.

So it is true. There are caverns outside the Dominion.

Fitz glanced wildly around. What was this? He looked back at the creature. It seemed to be smiling, head tilted to one side.

The voice came again, hoarfrost in his mind.

What is the name of your Dominion?

Fitz became aware that he was cowering, his hands massaging

his head. With an effort, he stood up. He was scared, out of his depth. What would the Doctor do right now? Make small talk and ask for tea while figuring out a means of escape. No time for that now – Fitz needed answers. 'Who are you and what is this place?'

What is the name of your Dominion?

The voice brought tears to his eyes, and his vision became misty. 'Earth,' he gasped.

Is it free from the Blight?

Fitz clutched his head. 'I don't know what you're saying.'

Come closer.

'No.'

Come closer.

Fitz found himself kneeling before the creature, looking up at the pale body. She had produced a phial from somewhere, shaped like the bowl of a flower.

Drink.

Fitz took the phial. Inside was a dark-green liquid, thick and gleaming. He sniffed cautiously, expecting a head-spinning jolt, but it was odourless. He frowned up at the alien. 'What is it?'

Drink.

The voice was like the whisper of a conniving spider in a children's story. Fitz looked up into the bulbous blue eyes. The pupils were slits of deep, gleaming black. The round, red mouth moved and Fitz saw the wetness inside, like a wound. The face was alien, totally alien. Like something out of a nightmare. A pitiless demon woman, come to punish lecherous, lazy Fitz.

Drink.

The icy voice was unbearable now, like a migraine behind his eyes, and he was screwing his whole face up to try to stop the pain. It wasn't working. If the stuff in the phial was poison, he didn't care any more.

Fitz drew the phial to his mouth, and took a tentative sip. It was thick and cloying, the flavour shooting through his taste buds, fogging his head. His vision blurred and he began to feel very dizzy. The iciness melted from his mind and he felt as though he were floating on a soft, warm cloud. He tried to speak, but his mouth wouldn't form words. He dropped the phial, and watched it spin slowly to the mossy floor, feeling as if he were on top of a tall building. Then he was falling endlessly into a soft mossy heaven.

Chapter Sixteen
Someone Has to Take the Fall

Sam floated in the spherical control chamber of the dirigible, watching Itharquell make adjustments to its brain. He had found another route back to the T'hiili Nest, but it had involved many diversions around Blighted areas. They had been travelling for ages. Right now they were barrelling along a corkscrewing tunnel, which required maximum concentration from Itharquell. His hair floated around his head like fibre-optic filaments, and his round mouth was small and tight with concentration, like a bunched fist.

On the screen in front of them was the narrow tunnel, its black walls picked out in green by sky-sea lamps which glowed from the front of the dirigible. There were some areas of the Dominion that the light from the sky-seas could never hope to reach, and this was one of them.

At length, Sam noticed that it was getting lighter. Something very much like Earth daylight was swamping the dirigible's lamps. As they rounded a particularly narrow and tortuous bend, Sam had to shade her eyes as the light at the end of the tunnel poured right through the screen, golden and blinding, like the sun.

The dirigible emerged from the end of the tunnel, and Itharquell turned it in a wide arc. The sight on the screen was familiar – the cavern where Sam had seen the T'hiili children playing. She wondered gloomily what had become of them. Sacrificed to the Blight by their terrified elders, or used as hosts by the Ruin? She hoped they were still alive. Perhaps she'd find them, at the Nest.

It soon became apparent that the tunnel they had emerged from ran through one of the towers of black rock which jutted up into the cavern. They'd shot out of the end as if flying out of a chimney. Now, Itharquell was taking them back up to the cylindrical sky-sea, the golden glowing band which stretched from horizon to horizon.

'We're almost there, then,' she said to Itharquell. 'All we have to do is fly along that and we'll be at the Nest.'

Itharquell didn't answer. When they were inside the sky-sea, travelling along it, its golden light flowing from the screen, he floated back from the brain, letting out a long whistling breath, clearly exhausted by his exertions. Then he suddenly stared past Sam, at the passage that led to the cabin. She turned and looked. Nothing there. 'What's wrong?'

The light.

Sam frowned. And then she got it. The light from the screen had been sending a sliver of golden light along the passage. Now it had gone.

Sam raced along the passage, stepping off the edge and floating into the cabin, Itharquell close behind her.

They floated there, staring at the screen.

It was totally, completely black.

The Blight was here.

Itharquell kicked out and floated to the control brain, frantically twisting levers. Sam felt the dirigible lurch to one side, and on the screen, thankfully, the golden light of the sky-sea shone once more.

They emerged from the sky-sea, into the cylindrical cavern. The T'hiili Nest was above them, filling the screen, an impossible upside-down city, twinkling with tiny points of green light. The dark shadow of the Blight obscured more than half its surface.

Sam felt her insides turn to ice. 'We're too late.'

Itharquell guided the dirigible towards the city, widening the screen so they could see all around them. To their left, the cylindrical cavern was a solid wall of Blight, advancing across the sky-sea at one end and the Nest at the other. Flying into the black wall were tiny green motes. Sam looked up at the Nest, frowning, not quite believing what she was seeing. But it was true. As they grew closer, she could see them, in their hundreds, pouring from the towers and minarets of the Nest.

Hundreds of T'hiili, in dirigibles and leaf-flyers, drifting in waves towards the Blight and oblivion.

'Mass suicide,' she whispered, feeling sick. 'We have to stop them,' she said, the words choking in her throat. 'We have to tell them we've seen a way out!'

Itharquell didn't answer. His eyes were wide, his mouth gaping in terror, saliva dripping from his red lips to drift towards the wall of the cabin. His thin, white-clawed hands were working the controls jerkily, spasmodically. It took a while for Sam to realise what he was doing, and when she did she threw herself at him, trying to drag him away from the brain. But, in the low gravity, she couldn't move quickly enough and Itharquell managed to fend her off with ease. She spun up to the ceiling of the cabin, trying to regain her balance, staring at the screen, which was again completely black.

'Itharquell, no!' screamed Sam. 'Don't do it!'

A sepulchral whisper in her mind:

We must accept our fate.

Sam gritted her teeth. With an effort, she twisted round, placed her feet against the ceiling of the cabin, and launched herself at Itharquell, cannoning into him. She pinned him against the concave floor, holding his thin arms in her hands, her knees against his chest. He felt so light and insubstantial – one thrust and she would shatter his body.

'Look,' said Sam. 'You might want to kill yourself, but –'

Itharquell's head twisted from side to side, his slit pupils wide.

No hope, no hope.

Sam shook him, not caring if she hurt him. 'There *is* hope!' she hissed. 'We go back to the cavern. We fight our way past the Ruin and we get out of here!' She was sobbing now. She glanced up at the screen. The Blight was terribly close, its surface crawling like a mass of flies. She could feel its presence like a thunderstorm. 'Please, Itharquell, I don't know how to fly this thing. Please help me. You're a thinker, a scientist. Please think now!'

But Itharquell kept twisting and moaning beneath her, his voice rustling in her mind:

No hope, no hope.

Kerstin Bergman had come to a momentous decision. She had decided that she had had enough of life. Not of life in the sense of living and breathing, no – just her old life, before she knew that time travel and wormholes and aliens really existed. Stranded here, staring down the tunnel at something that would just not resolve itself however hard she stared, her old life seemed very far away indeed. Like a not-particularly-good film she'd only half watched. Her parents, her father, the university, all were falling away, like the mould around some fantastic new creation. Even Johan. She felt nothing, now.

To leave her old life behind. Hell, leave *Earth* behind.

Kerstin smiled to herself. She thought of the Doctor, his kind, handsome face. He had a time machine. A time machine, for God's sake! The ultimate impossibility, the biggest 'what if'. But it was true. Kerstin *yearned* to see it. Join the Doctor on his travels. Maybe even… if Fitz tidied himself up a bit…

Hang on…

The thing at the end of the tunnel. The thing that sometimes looked like a field, or a pile of books, or a fairground, or the glistening insides of some fantastic beast, was beginning to resolve itself. It was definitely a field, a green field, beneath a brilliant blue sky. Colourful splashes of flowers. As she stared, it became more real. Then she felt a tugging motion, an undercurrent, pulling her towards the field. The golden walls of the tunnel contracted and expanded like a snake swallowing a rabbit. Kerstin suddenly realised she could feel her body again. Pins and needles shot along her arms and legs, and she screamed with the sudden pain, though her voice had no sound.

She was spinning head over heels now, down a small tunnel, faster and faster, the sides wheeling around her in a whirl of colour, flashing and spinning faster and faster –

And then it all stopped. She was suddenly somewhere… else.

She was breathing, and the air smelled fresh and alive, like the fields around Strängnäs in springtime. She gasped as feeling returned to her body. The pins and needles in her arms and legs had dulled to an annoying fuzziness. And there was a dull pain in her head where she'd been hit. That meant she was alive, definitely alive. Slowly, carefully, she opened her eyes, sat up, and looked around in utter amazement.

She was sitting on the side of a grassy hill. The grass was the most perfect she had ever seen, a full, healthy green, cropped to a uniform length and totally free of weeds and worm-casts. At the bottom of the hill was a garden, flower beds arranged in a complex spiral pattern around a hexagonal plinth. Above it all was a perfect blue sky – perfect, that is, except for a television screen, floating above the plinth.

Kerstin sat there, hugging her knees. How did she wind up here? Where *was* here? What the hell had it got to do with anything?

She remembered the resolution she had made inside the wormhole. Leave her old life behind, travel the universe. It seemed ludicrous now. The thought of Johan made her feel wretchedly sad, and she'd give anything to be back home. The feelings warred constantly within her, so much so that she felt she was becoming two people: Kerstin, who was going to marry Johan, get a highly paid job and put the world to rights, and Kerstin-plus, who was going to travel with the Doctor and put the *universe* to rights.

She stood up. Perhaps if she did something it would stop her going crazy. She set off down the hill towards the flower beds. She noticed that there were other things scattered about. Bookshelves. A harpsichord. A maroon Volkswagen.

And then the butterflies came.

Professor Nagle sat on the lab stool, watching the Doctor mixing various chemicals in a boiling tube. Between them sat a glass jar on a stand, being heated mercilessly by the roaring flame of a Bunsen. She had no idea what the Doctor was doing, and half suspected that neither did he.

They'd been taken to the laboratory, and locked inside, with Boris Lindgard, who was sulking over the other side of the room reading yesterday's *Aftonbladet*. The creature that had attacked her was in the mortuary on the slab next to Johan. The Doctor had examined the thing, removed the bullet and tended the wound – not letting Lindgard anywhere near. Another reason for Boris's sulk. The Doctor had pronounced the creature's condition stable, and then he'd started fiddling about with the stuff in the chemical store. She wasn't a chemist, but she knew enough to be worried about the things he was mixing. Especially when he started adding strange yellow powder from a pepper pot he'd produced from somewhere inside his coat. The stuff in the jar was just coming to the boil, giving off vapours which made her head swim.

'Doctor, what are you doing?' she asked at length.

He glanced up. 'How's your hand? And your neck?'

'Um, fine.'

'Good, good,' muttered the Doctor absently, fishing a salt cellar full of tiny blue crystals from his inside pocket. He added them to the contents of the jar, which fizzed and churned furiously.

Nagle slid off the stool and wandered away. She didn't want to be anywhere near that stuff when it boiled over. She sighed. Wolstencroft had won, at least for now. He was going send UNIT troops through the wormhole and there was nothing she could do to stop him. In fact, she'd be forced to help him. The alternative was... well, there was no alternative. The base was under martial law. Wolstencroft had finally got what he wanted.

She tried to look on the bright side – or at least the slightly less gloomy side. The generator was still working. Her project was safe. Perhaps if the major did go through the wormhole, and never came back...

The lab was in a state of stand-down; things were packed in boxes, equipment disassembled. All the other C19 scientists had been evacuated to Stockholm. Still, someone had to face the music. Someone had to stay behind, to try to avert the End of the World.

It still felt unreal. She'd devoted two years of her life to the TC Warp to help all humanity. And now, according to the Doctor, it was going to *end* everything? She could see the anger in the Doctor's eyes, even as he'd inquired about her injuries. As if she'd meant to create a wormhole that could destroy the planet.

She walked over to the mortuary, looking through the glass at the alien. The oddest thing about it was its white hair, which hung straggling over its shoulders. She could see it breathing, its throat pulsing slowly.

Next to it, Johan's body lay out of sight under a grey sheet. Everyone seemed to have forgotten about it. Shouldn't it be disposed of in some way? She was about to go and ask Boris about this when the alien sat up and looked right at her.

'Doctor!' she cried. It was almost instinctual. Was this how his companions reacted? Calling out for him at the first hint of trouble?

The Doctor was at her side in an instant.

The alien was wailing, a thick sound, like an animal in pain. The Doctor opened the door and went inside, Lindgard and Nagle close behind.

The Doctor cradled the creature in his arms, and its wailing subsided into sobs.

It looked wildly around itself, its blue eyes wide. Its pupils were slitted, like a reptile's. Its face was oval, with a circular mouth at the bottom, a row of ridges along the centre of the face. It spoke, in a gruff, dry voice, but its words were complete gibberish.

The Doctor looked gravely at Nagle. 'I'm going to try something,' he said.

Nagle watched as the Doctor got on to the slab with the creature. He rested its head in his lap, cradling it with one hand, passing his other hand over its eyes. A milky membrane closed over them.

The Doctor sat cross-legged, a look of concentration on his face. He smiled once, said 'Yes,' and then his head slumped into his chest.

Nagle took a step towards him, but Lindgard held her back.

'What's he doing?' she whispered.

'I'm not sure,' said Lindgard. 'I think he might be trying to telepathically commune with it.'

Nagle jumped as the Doctor's head snapped upright. His mouth opened, closed, and then opened again, gabbling a confused string of words.

'Dominion is dying! Dying! Blight. Blight come, eating all. Soon no Dominion, all Blight. All Blight. Must protect Queen.'

Nagle suppressed a smile. 'He's making this up!'

The Doctor stopped speaking, his mouth and eyes open wide, and he emitted a shriek.

Then he collapsed on top of the creature.

Nagle was at his side in an instant, helping him down from the slab. He was muttering, his eyes unfocused.

She tried to lead him away from the alien, but he wouldn't let go. She noticed that its throat had stopped pulsing. It was dead.

Eventually, the Doctor let go of the alien, though he seemed to be in some sort of trance. With Lindgard's help she got the Doctor out of the mortuary and sat him on a lab stool.

The Doctor opened his eyes. He smiled, and then winced, massaging his head through his mass of brown curls. 'You'd think I'd be getting better at this...'

'What did you do?' asked Nagle.

'Soul-catching. I joined minds with the T'hiili. Poor creature. It can't survive long here on Earth.'

'T'hiili,' repeated Lindgard.

'It's actually a T'vorha, a warrior offshoot of the main race. Dedicated to protecting its Queen.' He frowned. 'Not very bright, I'm afraid.'

'Is that all you found out?' said Lindgard.

The Doctor gaped. 'I've just pulled off a very tricky feat of mental bonding; at least try to look impressed! Anyway, there's lots more. The things that besieged the farm we can translate as Bane – though they all seemed to have died now. And the others, the spiderlike things – they're more like Ruin. And they all live in a place called the Dominion.' He frowned again. 'Not quite sure where that is. And the Dominion is being destroyed by the Blight!' He jumped down from the stool, pacing about. 'Yes, yes, that would make sense; it *all* makes sense. Your wormhole has gone into a pocket dimension, you see?'

Hang on. This was theoretical physics, ropy at best. 'Doctor, slow down!'

He paid her no attention. 'That's where it's drawing its energy from and sustaining itself! The wormhole is causing some sort of entropic effect, draining away the substance of the Dominion.' He rounded on Professor Nagle. 'Do you realise that not only are you responsible for the imminent destruction of Earth, but for the genocide of an entire alien race?'

'Great!' snapped Nagle, refusing to give way. 'Next you'll be telling me I'm personally responsible for the Ebola virus, Hurricane Freya and the goddamn millennium bug!'

They stared each other out. The Doctor gave way first. He banged a fist down on the bench, making the test tubes rattle. 'Time is running out. I have to get to the other end of that wormhole!'

'Wolstencroft will have you shot,' said Lindgard.

The Doctor smiled thinly. 'I'm hardly going to walk into the generator room, now, am I? Now, are you with me?'

What choice did she have? 'Yes.' She turned to Lindgard. 'Boris?'

He shook his head.

Nagle sighed. 'Doctor, can you give me a minute?'

The Doctor nodded, threw up his hands and began pacing up and down.

Nagle drew Lindgard to one side. 'You have to help us.'

Lindgard rubbed his hands on the front of his lab coat. 'I want nothing to do with this. Fight it out between yourselves. I'm a scientist, and –'

'And we're supposed to be running this show,' said Nagle. 'Are you just going to let Wolstencroft walk all over us?'

Lindgard spread his hands. 'He *is* walking all over us. It is stupid, *suicidal* to argue with men who have guns.'

207

'Even when the fate of the entire planet is at stake?'

'If we're all going to die anyway, what's the point?'

'The point is, if we're all going to die anyway we've got nothing to lose.'

Lindgard shook his head. 'As I said, I am a scientist –'

'You're also a human being,' said Nagle in disgust. 'Or have you cut up so many bodies that you just don't care about that any more?'

The Doctor's voice rang out. 'If you two have quite finished!'

Nagle prodded Lindgard in the chest. Aware that this was a last resort, the sort of thing Wolstencroft would do, she said, 'I'm ordering you to help us.'

The Doctor came back over, beaming. 'All sorted out now? Fine!' He clapped his hands together. 'What I plan to do is go back to my TARDIS, use her to locate the Dominion.' He looked hard at Nagle. 'Usually all I have to say to my companions is "number forty-seven" and they know what to do, but I'm going to have to explain this to you in detail...'

Professor Nagle stood outside the door to the lab, a feeling of girlish excitement bubbling within her. The Doctor had outlined his plan, and it was fiendishly simple. He was standing on a lab bench, arms at full stretch, a test tube in one hand. It was belching acrid smoke up towards the ceiling, towards the smoke sensor. On the bench by his feet stood the jar, the Bunsen extinguished beneath it. Next to that lay a pad of cotton wool.

In front of the doorway stood Lindgard. They'd finally bullied him into helping.

The Doctor coughed, and Nagle held her breath. The yellowish smoke was wreathed around him. Why weren't the alarms kicking in? And then, all of a sudden, a shrill ringing noise burst into life. She jumped.

The Doctor bounced down from the bench, picking up the cotton wool and the jar, taking up position on the opposite side of the door so that, when it opened, he'd be hidden from view. He placed the cotton-wool pad over the top of the jar. 'It's a bit like chloroform,' he whispered. 'But nicer. In fact it might give him rather pleasant dreams.'

A few tense moments passed, and then the door opened. Nagle pressed herself against the wall. A UNIT soldier stepped in, rifle at the ready. He was lean and dark, with a thin moustache and brown eyes. 'What's going on in here?'

Lindgard stood before him, wringing his hands together. 'There's been a terrible accident.'

Not as terrible as your acting, thought Nagle. She stepped forward, holding her head and groaning, feeling stupid and terrified all at once. 'I – I'm dying,' she croaked.

There was an explosion of movement – the Doctor slammed the door, leapt on the soldier and pressed the soaked cotton-wool pad over his mouth.

And then everything went horribly wrong.

The soldier elbowed the Doctor in the stomach. The Doctor collapsed, dropping the pad. The soldier, eyes streaming, turned, slipped, and pulled the trigger of his rifle.

There was the sound of a single shot, horribly loud.

Lindgard staggered backwards, a look of surprise and bewilderment on his face. He reached up to his chest. A patch of blood was spreading out. He looked down at his fingers, red with his own blood.

Nagle went to Lindgard, holding him as he fell. She saw the Doctor sock the soldier on the jaw, with a crack that made her wince. The soldier fell to the ground, gun clattering beside him. The Doctor kicked it into the middle of the room.

She was kneeling now, Lindgard's head in her lap. She didn't know what to do. Was he dying? She felt numb, useless, as though this weren't really happening. His breath was coming in fast, uneven gasps, gurgling in his throat. His blue eyes were staring wildly as he clung to life. Blood flecked his lips. 'Jennifer,' he gasped. 'They were... meant to protect... us.' He coughed, his eyes widened and then dulled. His head lolled in her lap and she felt his body slump.

'Boris?'

A trickle of blood ran from the corner of his mouth.

She became aware of a sound from above her. The Doctor was staring down at Lindgard, looking through his fingers, his mouth open, a strange noise coming from his throat. It reminded her of a cat being sick. At first, she thought it was the effect of the stuff on the pad but then she realised he was reacting to Boris's death.

He took his hands away from his face and crouched down beside her. He suddenly looked so sad, so old. So frightened. 'I never meant this to happen,' he gasped, his voice fluttering, breathy. 'I *never meant* this. I never meant this!'

She laid Lindgard's body gently on the floor and led the Doctor away. 'It was an accident.'

'An accident,' he repeated. 'Nothing is ever an accident.'

She found herself hugging him. Hugging the Doctor, for God's sake. The stories she'd heard of him, she'd been expecting some kind of eccentric superman. Now she was seeing someone as vulnerable, as fallible as – well, herself. Here he was, totally thrown by the death of someone he didn't even particularly like, when the fate of the whole world was at stake. Two worlds, if you counted the Dominion. She realised suddenly why bastards like Wolstencroft saw the Doctor as a threat – he cared about everyone, everything. No matter who or what, all life was precious. And he wasn't afraid to show that he cared – if Wolstencroft was scared of the Doctor; it was because he was reminded of his own deadness, his own lack of humanity.

She remembered the Doctor's anger when he found out that she was responsible for the abductions, the deaths. How she'd been disappointed in him. How *she'd* been lacking humanity.

They stood apart. 'Are you all right?'

The Doctor nodded.

The alarms were still ringing, so the Doctor used the unconscious soldier's radio to report a false alarm, doing a very passable impression of his voice. Nagle was glad when the ringing stopped.

They carried Lindgard's body into the mortuary, on to one of the empty slabs, working in silence. Then they cleaned up the body the best they could. They tied up the soldier using electrical flex.

Now they sat down at a lab bench, facing each other. The shock of Lindgard's death was beginning to hit Nagle and her hands were shaking. They began discussing how to get out of the base without (a) getting shot and (b) hurting anyone else. She was telling him about the lift shaft that led from a disused part of the C19 base into the forest near Strängnäs. Ever security-conscious, Wolstencroft had always hated that little arrangement. He kept it closed off most of the time. But, once the alien manifestations had started, it became a convenient way to slip in and out of the base unobserved. It was their only chance.

The Doctor stood up. 'We'd better get going.'

Nagle stayed put. 'I'm staying here.'

The Doctor ruffled his hair, made an aggrieved sound. 'It's too dangerous! Look what happened to Lindgard. Imagine what Wolstencroft will do when he finds out!'

She folded her arms. 'I'm staying, Doctor.'

The Doctor's expression grew more pained. 'Why?'

She had to stay, try to salvage her project. At the very least, she could take her notes and disks and get the hell out. 'Someone needs to keep an eye on Wolstencroft.'

The Doctor sighed. 'And there's nothing I can say or do to persuade you otherwise?'

'No.'

'Well. It's up to you. But I have no choice: I have to go.' He walked towards the door, opening it and turning back to her. She thought he was going to say something more but his face was blank, expressionless. A hardness around the eyes. A reminder of who he was, what he thought of her project?

Nagle smiled, gave a thumbs-up. 'Good luck, Doctor.'

Then he was gone.

The lab seemed terribly quiet after the door closed behind him.

Chapter Seventeen
The Firemaker

Fitz dreamed. He dreamed of a place called the Dominion, an endless universe of caverns and strange glowing seas. It had existed for ever, and it was infinite, and it was full of life. The Bane, the Ruin and innumerable others, a vast panoply of life, existing in delicate balance.

And the T'hiili. A race of farmers, builders, spinning their giant Nests throughout the Dominion. Led by the Queen, who guided their thoughts, who planned their actions. The Queen, guarded by her fierce and loyal T'vorha.

The T'hiili life cycle unfolded in his dream. The Queen would be fertilised by T'hiili secretions. She would lay thousands of eggs, and live for many years. When the time came to die, she would lay a special clutch, which consisted solely of T'vorha and one new Queen. This was what Fitz had met. A new Queen, hungry to be fertilised, before the Blight came and destroyed her as it had destroyed the former Queen.

The Blight. Fitz felt the terror of it in his dream, the total despair of the T'hiili. He saw them piloting their dirigibles in hordes, into the swarming blackness. He saw the former Queen, unable to move as the Blight encroached upon her Nest. She was vast, bloated – a limbless bulk, all egg sac and brain. He saw masses of T'vorha flying about the Queen's vast body, using nets and dirigibles to try to move her out of the path of the Blight. But it was no use. He heard her dying scream, the miracle of the birth of her last clutch of eggs, a sorry dozen. He saw the T'vorha take these eggs to their battleship, nurturing them. He saw the birth of the new Queen.

He saw the T'vorha discover the node in the cavern of black rock, how the new Queen had reasoned that it was a way out of the Dominion. But what was the point of escape, if she was unfertilised? Were there any T'hiili left to fertilise her?

Fitz dreamed all this, and when he woke he was lying on the mossy floor of the Queen's chamber. He opened his eyes. The Queen was lying on the mossy ground next to him. It was for all the world as if they were lovers on Dartmoor.

'H-how was it for you?' gasped Fitz.

The Queen sat up.

'What was that stuff?'

The voice in his mind. It was less icy now, more of a skeletal whisper.

Part of me. I had to make you understand. There's so little time left.

Fitz was struggling to understand what had happened. Somehow, that mossy liquor had linked his mind to the Queen's, and she had filled him with a total knowledge of the Dominion. He now knew that it was a matter of hours before the Blight closed right in, allowing nothing to escape.

We must go through the node to your world. The future of the T'hiili is in our hands, Fitz Kreiner.

Great. Not only had he to find and rescue Sam, but the salvation of an entire species was now being foisted upon him. Maybe the Doctor was used to this sort of responsibility, but he wasn't having it. 'Oh, no,' he said, getting up. 'Sorry, but I don't think so. I'll take my chances on my own, if you don't mind.' And the knowledge you've given to me should help me find my way out.

The Queen also stood, her long red hair falling in waves down her back.

You have no choice.

The voice was cold and hard again, filling his head. He fell to his knees, silver light exploding behind his eyes. 'Stop! You'll kill me!'

You must help. I must survive.

Fitz nodded. Anything to stop the pain. 'Yes!' The pain went away, and Fitz rolled over on to his back.

The Queen stood over him. She had him totally in her power.

He had no choice but to help her. Still, at least, in helping the T'hiili, he'd stand a chance of escaping from the Dominion. Yes, that was it. Stay close. And, if the opportunity presented itself, leg it before the Queen could freeze his brain.

'OK,' he said. 'I'll help you.'

The Queen led him from the chamber towards the waiting T'vorha.

We have to get past the Ruin. They guard the node. They are many, the T'vorha are few. And with each attack, more die.

An idea popped into Fitz's head. 'Hey,' he said, turning to the Queen. 'Have you lot discovered fire yet?'

The Queen blinked.

What is fire?

The Doctor stood for a while, at the edge of the clearing, the shack behind him, breathing in the air, feeling it fill his lungs. It was good to be in the open again. He set off into the forest, deliberately not thinking about which direction to take, letting his feet and his hearts guide him. The musk of the pine trees tickled the back of the Doctor's throat. It was a beautiful morning. The sun shone through the angular branches of the trees creating pools of dappled shade in which clouds of insects droned.

He had escaped from the C19 base with ease. The whole place had seemed deserted, and he'd slipped along the corridors unchallenged. All the UNIT troops were probably preparing for their trip through the wormhole.

A surge of impotent anger. Nothing he could do about that.

He plunged deeper into the forest. He didn't want to admit it to himself in case it wasn't true, but there was a certain feeling, a presence in his mind. It was very faint, like a half-remembered dream which vanished on the instant of waking. Could it be the TARDIS? Or was it just wishful thinking?

And then he saw it, through the trees up above. A plain grey cube. The TARDIS. He quickened his pace, feeling suddenly cold inside. As he grew nearer, he saw something attached to the trees, surrounding the TARDIS. He stopped short and ducked behind a tree.

Police tape.

Inspector Nordenstam had been here – probably still was – watching, waiting. The Doctor closed his eyes and muttered soothing words to calm himself. The last thing he needed right now was to be dragged back to the police station in Strängnäs for an interminable interrogation. Opening his eyes again, he strained his hearing, listening out for the telltale sound of foot on twig.

Everything was utterly silent.

He had to risk it. Tensing himself, he stepped out from behind his tree, fished the TARDIS key from his pocket, and ducked under the police tape.

He stood still, looking, listening.

Nothing happened.

He stepped up to the TARDIS, placing his hands on the flat grey surface. She was cold. Cold as a Cyber-tomb. He walked around the TARDIS, looking for the keyhole. As before, there was none.

The Doctor sighed, stepping back from the grey cube.

So near and yet so far.

Sam held Itharquell against the floor of the dirigible. They were almost into the Blight, and the hairs on the back of her neck were standing up.

'Itharquell, you must help me,' she gasped. She was beginning to feel weird, as though she was being hypnotised.

That dry dead voice again:

No hope.

Sam thought desperately. 'You said that the presence of the T'vorha meant that there could be a new Queen nearby. You're the only one who can fertilise her. If we can find her, and then get through the node, the T'hiili would be saved.'

Itharquell blinked, milky membranes flicking across his blue eyes.

Impossible. I can't. No hope.

She shook him angrily. 'I thought you were a thinker!'

Itharquell was staring over her shoulder at the screen

The minds of the others – drawing me in.

They had to get away from here. No more time to talk. Sam dragged Itharquell upright and shoved him towards the control brain. 'Get us out of here,' she said. 'At least we can try. If we fail, *then* you can kill yourself. But we have to try.'

Itharquell began manipulating the stemlike levers, and Sam felt them back away from the Blight.

She let out a long sigh of relief, as they plunged back into the golden sky-sea, away from the doomed Nest.

When she was sure they were safe, she turned to Itharquell. 'What made you change your mind?'

He looked at her, black tongue licking his lips.

A single word flickered in her mind:

Fear.

Sam sank back against the wall, finding herself laughing, as they flew away from the Blight.

Professor Nagle had got tired of waiting for Wolstencroft to come and find her. How would it look if she was found with one of his troops trussed up like a Thanksgiving turkey? No, she had to go to him. Make up some lie about the Doctor escaping. Find out what Wolstencroft was doing with her generator.

So she dragged the soldier in his chair to the biohazard safe at the far end of the room. He came round halfway through and struggled like hell, and it took all her strength, but she did it. She didn't know what he was fussing about anyway – the safe was empty.

She shoved the heavy door to and spun the combination. She walked out of the lab and took the lift to the generator room level.

The generator room doors were standing open, so she walked straight in.

Wolstencroft looked up as she entered. 'Professor Nagle! I was just about to send for you. Where is the Doctor?'

Nagle took a deep breath. 'The Doctor's escaped. He's gone to try to close the wormhole.'

Wolstencroft's lips tightened into a thin line. 'Where's Lindgard? And Private Alomar?'

She thought of Boris, in the mortuary. She slumped down in a chair. The truth was probably the safest course; he'd never believe that the Doctor shot Lindgard, and she could hardly confess to it herself. 'Boris was shot in the escape attempt. It was an accident. Private Alomar is tied up in the lab.'

She closed her eyes, massaged her temples. She heard Wolstencroft order two soldiers down to the lab to free Alomar.

Then he strode over to her, scowling. 'This just confirms my suspicions about the Doctor. He's not going to help us; he's cleared off. We'll never see him again.' He crouched down, an earnest look in his dark-brown eyes. 'It's up to us to save the planet.'

'You're wrong. Anyway, how is sending a load of troops through the wormhole going to save the planet?'

Wolstencroft's eyes gleamed. 'They'll establish a bridgehead. Wipe out those… things. Once the area has been secured, you'll be sent through. It will be your job to close the wormhole.'

'What?'

'Now the Doctor's absconded, you're the only one qualified for the job.'

Nagle swallowed. Why hadn't she gone with the Doctor? 'You can't force me!'

'I can, and I will,' he snapped. 'If you don't obey, you'll be shot. Now, I've had a quick look at the generator myself. It seems to be intact, but you'd better run a quick systems check.'

It wasn't a request: it was an order. Nagle nodded wearily. She followed him over to the control desk. All the broken glass had been cleared away and the remaining bits of partition had been removed. In its place was a makeshift mesh fence, with a gate in the centre. 'It's electrified,' said Wolstencroft. 'In case anything nasty comes though when we switch on.'

She sat, initiating the systems check. It ran for a few minutes, and miraculously nothing seemed to be wrong. 'It's all on line,' she said.

'OK,' said Wolstencroft, waving a gloved hand at the shining steel prongs of the generator. 'Be ready to activate the node on my command.'

Fitz stood in the Queen's chamber, surrounded by a couple of dozen T'vorha. The Queen stood in the centre, her blue eyes never leaving Fitz.

He was giving his first combat-training lesson.

He'd changed out of the encounter suit, and was now wearing T'vorha armour over Björn's blue-checked lumberjack shirt. It was light and fibrous, but very hard. He had a pretty good idea of how foolish he must look, but the T'vorha didn't seem to mind.

He held aloft a stout stem, with some dried moss glued to the end. The T'vorha had used their saliva as glue, and it stank like rotting fish.

He took his lighter from his pocket.

He lit the end of the stem.

There was a roar and the moss burst into flame – a bright, yellow flame which shimmered and flickered brightly.

The T'vorha fell to their knees.

Fitz smiled. They had light and heat enough here, and they didn't need to cook their food, so they had never had a need to discover fire.

They'd certainly discovered it now, though.

They crowded closer, their ridged, masked faces reflecting the yellow flame, making grunting sounds of wonderment.

Fitz smiled to himself. This was going to work. It was actually going to *work*.

A few hours later, everything had been planned. It had taken Fitz a while to work out how to use fire as a weapon against the Ruin; everything in the Dominion seemed flammable, and Fitz didn't want to be responsible for torching the whole place. Not that it really mattered in the face of the Blight.

Another problem was that there was only one lighter, and about thirty dirigibles. If he went round lighting a fire in each one, by the time he'd set the last one, the first would have gone out. In the end, he'd found, more by chance than anything else, a narcotic drink the T'vorha used to prepare themselves for battle which burnt with a very evil-looking blue flame. Each dirigible would carry a bowl of this stuff, into which harpoons could be dipped, their points encrusted in flammable moss.

Everything was prepared, and Fitz was alone with the Queen. They were walking along a balustrade on the outside of her Nest. He'd got used to the low gravity now, taught his legs to make small short steps.

Something was bothering him.

'It's all very well going back through the wormhole,' he said, trying not to look at the Queen's glistening nakedness. 'But if you're not, erm, fertilised, the whole T'hiili race is doomed.'

He was used to her voice rustling in his mind now, though for some reason it tickled the inside of his ears. She hadn't used her ice voice since he'd agreed to help.

That is correct.

'So why are we attacking now?'

The Queen closed her eyes.

One is coming. One who can fertilise me.

Fitz wondered at the extent of the Queen's mental powers. Most T'hiili were telepathic to some degree, though they needed to exchange long protein strings regularly, through their salivary glands. That was what that mossy stuff had been. Essence of Queen, mixed in with a few narcotic herbs. 'So, we attack the Ruin, gain the node, and wait for Mr Right to turn up.'

The Queen stroked Fitz's arm.

That is what we must do.

They rounded a corner, from which there was a view of the cavern in which the Nest floated. Far below was a glowing sea, its green light filtering up in shafts through floating islands and rootlike growths.

But it was the thing on the far side of the cavern that caught Fitz's breath, making him gasp aloud.

Some of the ice returned to the Queen's mind-voice.

The Blight.

It was a giant black blister, spreading visibly on the dark-green wall of the cavern. Its edges were fuzzy, and looking at it made Fitz feel sick, scared. No wonder the T'hiili had decided on suicide as the only way out.

The Ruin are nothing, compared to the Blight. We can fight the Ruin. But we cannot destroy the Blight.

The Queen reached and held Fitz's hands in hers. They were damp and cold, like dead fish. He shivered. At times her long red hair falling over her shoulders made her look disconcertingly human.

Come. It is time for battle.

Chapter Eighteen
Time And Ruptured Dimensions In Space

The butterflies came in their hundreds, from all directions, until the air was full of the unhurried rustling of their wings. They came and danced in a multicoloured typhoon around Kerstin. She could somehow tell that they were pleased to see her.

Their wings were beating against the back of her head and neck, against her bare arms and legs, tickling her. They seemed to be guiding her, down towards the plinth.

She walked down the slope, arms outstretched, butterflies alighting and then taking off. She laughed – what else could she do in the face of all this?

When she reached the bottom of the slope, the butterflies retreated, some landing on the flowers, some hovering at a distance. She touched the plinth; it looked like some sort of control console, made of greenish metal. Six panels surrounded a perspex column, which contained pinkly glowing tubes. Each panel had a different array of knobs, dials and switches. The thing reminded Kerstin of the control suite of the hydroelectric plant she'd once visited near Gothenburg.

What was this? Was it part of the control for the wormhole? Had the butterflies brought her here so she could get Fitz back?

There was a little green butterfly hovering above one of the switches, now and then darting down towards it. Its intention was clear. It wanted her to press the switch. What would happen? What choice did she have? She pressed the switch and immediately the TV screen hovering in midair on the other side of the console crackled into life.

Kerstin gasped. It showed a view of a forest. A very familiar-looking forest. The forest around Strängnäs.

And there was the Doctor, staring at the screen, his blue eyes sad, his face concerned. Seeing him again lifted Kerstin's heart.

The green butterfly was now hovering over a big red lever, its wings fluttering in urgency.

Kerstin pulled the lever without hesitation and a white door appeared beside the flower beds.

The door opened, and all the butterflies took off with a roar like sudden rainfall.

Outside the TARDIS, the Doctor watched open-mouthed as one end of the grey cube swung silently open, revealing a shimmering white void. He laughed out loud, feeling like dancing. At last, things were going right. He had no idea how or why the TARDIS had opened up to him, and right now he didn't really care.

The Doctor walked into the white void, and the door closed silently behind him, leaving no sign that it had ever been there in the first place.

Kerstin got a brief glimpse of the Doctor as he entered. His face was alive with joy. And then, as one, the butterflies descended upon him, until he was completely obscured beneath a cloud of fluttering colour. She could hear his laughter. It was a boyish sound, the sound of freedom. Like Johan when they swam together. Kerstin gripped the edge of the console.

The butterflies lifted from the Doctor's body, and he watched them fly away with raised arms, a wide smile on his face. He walked dreamily over to the console, still unaware of her presence.

He started pressing buttons, muttering to himself. 'Poor thing. My poor, dear, *poor* thing.'

'I thought I was dead at first,' said Kerstin.

The Doctor did a double take, looking across the console, his mouth hanging open in surprise. 'How did you get in here?'

'I don't know,' said Kerstin. 'I just ended up here. Who were you talking to just then?'

The Doctor smiled broadly. 'My ship. My TARDIS.' He gave that boyish laugh again and all but danced around the console towards her. 'I thought she was dead!'

The TARDIS. So this was the Doctor's time machine. Kerstin felt a thrill run through her whole body.

The Doctor came up to her and put his hands on her shoulders, his face very close to hers. 'I'm very, very glad you're safe,' he said. 'How did you say you got here?'

For a moment she thought he was going to kiss her. 'I – I didn't.'

The Doctor took his hands away from her and turned to the console. 'Hmm. I think I know what happened. You and Fitz went into the node, must have come through the section of the wormhole that's snared up in the TARDIS. Fitz!' The Doctor whirled around, his voice hoarse, urgent. 'Where is he?'

Kerstin shrugged. 'I don't know.'

The Doctor turned away. She heard him mutter, his voice light and fluttery. 'No, no, no.'

Kerstin's mind was whirling with questions. One above all: Johan. 'Doctor, could we go back in time, rescue Johan before the wormhole took him?'

The Doctor smiled sadly. 'I wish we could. But there are laws of time which just cannot be broken.'

'Laws are there to be broken!' said Kerstin desperately.

'Not the laws of time. You see, Johan is part of this timeline. If I went back and rescued him, then you wouldn't have been caught up in all this. But here you are, bang in the middle of things. Cause and effect.' He shook his head and smiled sadly. 'I can't do it.'

It had been Kerstin's last hope, and now it was dashed. She let the tears come. She felt the Doctor's arms around her, the softness of his coat on her face.

When it was over, she stood back. She felt light-headed, and oddly relieved. Now that she knew Johan couldn't be rescued, maybe now she could lay him to rest in her mind.

The Doctor's eyes were sad, his face shadowy. 'I'm sorry.'

Kerstin brushed the last of her tears away. 'I'll be OK now.'

The Doctor patted her arm. 'Which is more than I can say for the TARDIS. I'll have to link with her.' He walked around console and placed his hands on two flat black plates. 'Bear with me,' he said. 'This shouldn't take long.'

He closed his eyes.

Kerstin stepped back from the console, her heart beating fast. What was going to happen? She glanced around fearfully. Would the wormhole come back?

A rising humming note emanated from the console and slowly, magically, everything changed. The green grass shimmered and coalesced into a wooden floor. The blue sky darkened. Walls erected themselves at a distance from the console. A whole library of books fluttered into existence. Next to them, a wall of wooden filing cabinets with brass handles and white name tags, towering up and up into the blue. Over the far side of the console, a wall of clocks appeared from nowhere, clicking and ticking busily. Before them, the harpsichord she'd seen earlier popped up. And on the floor beside that, a complicated-looking model train set, trains whizzing along the tracks at breakneck speed. Just beside the console, a very expensive-looking carpet, on which stood an ornate gold and red chair, a marble-topped table and a standard lamp. On the other side of the room, a huge double door melted into existence, underneath an arch crowned with a complex figure-eight symbol. Two lamp-bearing bronze statues stood, one at either side of the doors, at the top of a flight of shallow stone steps.

The console itself mutated slowly into a thing of beauty, all brass and wood and buttons and levers, the column in the middle telescoping into a vast tower which throbbed and hummed with potential. Cables and gantries ran high above, becoming lost to sight. And candles shone *everywhere*, their soft golden light contrasting with the harsh blue glow cast by the column in the centre of the console.

The transformation complete, Kerstin found herself standing in what looked like a cross between a castle, a Gothic mansion, a cathedral and the study of a mad inventor. She had never felt so excited. Kerstin-plus lived again.

The Doctor opened his eyes. He looked even more pleased now, if that was possible. 'You know, I could really do with a nice hot cup of tea.' Then he exploded into action, running round the console, pulling levers and twisting dials. 'But there's work to be done.'

Kerstin suddenly realised that everything he'd said was in Swedish, perfectly enunciated. 'Hey! You're speaking Swedish!'

The Doctor grinned. 'It's the TARDIS. The telepathic circuits are translating for you.'

'What?'

'Wherever you go in the universe, everyone will seem to be speaking your native language.'

Images of alien creatures threatening her in her own language popped into her mind. She fought down a rising sense of disorientation. This was a miracle, a wonder. She had to stay with it, whatever happened.

The Doctor bounded round the console, slipping on the polished parquet floor. He grabbed on to her to steady himself, then pointed, up.

'Look.'

His hair was tickling her cheek. She looked, into the night-blue dome of the ceiling. It seemed to go on for ever.

'There.'

Through the vista of blue, there was a golden thread, twisting and glowing. 'That's a representation of the wormhole. See, at one end, there's the Earth, and at the other – yes, I *thought* so.'

Kerstin looked at the other end. The golden thread just vanished. 'You thought what?'

'The wormhole's passed through a black hole,' he said. As if that explained anything. He walked over to the console. His face was grave again, dark shadows under the eyes. 'Possibly into a pocket universe. Part of it is caught up in the TARDIS like a temporal tapeworm.' He looked over at her. 'I can't take off.'

Kerstin's heart sank. 'What do you mean?'

'If I take the TARDIS through the wormhole, I'll be taking part of the wormhole with her. Like a snake eating its own tail. It'll cause terrible contortions in the space-time continuum. Unless…'

'Unless what?'

'Unless I can dislodge the wormhole offshoot.' He dived beneath the console.

Kerstin looked up at the golden thread. It was beautiful, she thought. To look at it now, you could never guess at all the death and pain it had caused.

The Doctor emerged from beneath the console, a battered brown leather toolbox clutched to his chest. 'Come on – Sam's room.'

He dashed out of the console room and along a tall, arched corridor, with white roundelled walls. He stopped outside a plain door.

'This is where the wormhole breached the TARDIS,' he said, motioning for Kerstin to stand back. He opened the toolbox and dug out a collection of small glass pyramids.

He opened the door.

The inside of the room was roaring with grey static, like a broken TV.

'It's ruptured the dimensional interface,' cried the Doctor. He stuck the glass pyramids around the door frame. They pulsed with a soft emerald light, and the roaring decreased.

'Dimensional inhibitors,' he muttered. 'They should stop it spreading.'

He dashed back to the console room. Kerstin stared at the static. It seemed to do things to her eyes, like a magic-eye picture. She blinked, shook her head and followed the Doctor.

They left the Nest behind, flying through the glowing green in the thirty-six dirigibles that remained. In each, bowls of narcotic fluid burned, T'vorha eyes watching the blue flames with superstition.

Fitz and the Queen travelled in the smallest dirigible, no larger than a small boat, near the back of the formation. The Queen was in a semi-trance, trying to trace the mind of the One who could fertilise her.

Fitz sat in a leaflike seat at the front, next to a large and fearsome-looking T'vorha called Gilthr, who manipulated the stems of the tiny, gnarled control brain with big, clawed hands. The T'vorha were telepathically retarded; their mindspeak was simple, wordless. He hadn't a hope of understanding it. Instead of the Queen's icy voice, all he got from Gilthr was the telepathic equivalent of caveman grunts and gestures – backed up with physical grunts and gestures.

On the screen ahead of them, Fitz could see the rest of the T'vorha fleet, sleek bullet shapes against the green glow. They flew down and down, keeping a safe distance from the Blight, until they plunged into the swirling green below. The screen became so bright it was hard to look at it.

They passed through several other caverns – once having to change course abruptly to avoid a thunderous wall of Blight, losing two dirigibles in the process – and then they plunged into a sea of golden light. It was almost blinding.

Fitz looked back to where the Queen sat on a bed of moss, cross-legged, her eyes closed, her red hair falling in waves around her. She seemed to sense his gaze.

We are very close.

Fitz waited. The tension was unbearable.

At length, they approached the edge – an oval-shaped curtain of colour the size of Wembley stadium, through which Fitz could make out the blue shimmering shape of a cavern. They drew nearer – nearer – and then they were inside. It was a vast womb of blue sand. On the far side rose a sheer cliff of black glass.

It was the cavern he'd arrived in. He'd slid down that cliff face, and the T'vorha had taken him.

But where was the node?

There were hundreds of Ruin massing around the black cliff, but no swirling white whorl in the black glass. 'Come on, Doctor,' said Fitz through gritted teeth. But he knew it might be a wasted thought. Was the Doctor still in charge of the generator? Was the generator still there? Anything could have happened at the far end of the wormhole since he'd left.

Fitz watched as the leading dirigibles neared the Ruin. The Ruin had noticed what was happening and were massing to attack, spiralling down towards the dirigibles.

A bolt of fire shot from the nearest dirigible right into the mass of advancing Ruin. They burst into flames, and the others spun away, away from the black cliff.

It was working. Jesus Christ Almighty, it was actually working.

Captain Daniel Rogers stood before the mesh fence. The prongs of the generator glittered through the dense metal. He was sweating inside his combat suit, the taste of rubber and metal in his mouth. Forget that you're a man, he told himself. You're a machine. A fighting machine.

He heard Major Wolstencroft give the order, and he led the men through the mesh gate into the generator chamber itself. The shining prongs towered above him. He tried not to think of the things that had come through. He tried not to think of what had happened to Johan Svensson. He and his team had a job to do to – protect Earth. It was what he believed in, what he'd signed up to UNIT for.

As he lined up with his men in front of the generator, watching the sun-bright glare form at the tips of the steel prongs, Rogers wished the Doctor was here – he couldn't believe he had left them in the lurch, as Wolstencroft seemed to believe. That wasn't the Doctor of UNIT lore.

Then, with little ceremony, the node opened. The shining prongs vanished, swallowed up in a tunnel of white light. Rogers's mouth was dry, sweat pouring down his back. The tunnel seemed to draw his gaze, make a mockery of his senses. He took an involuntary step back, but nothing came through.

He turned round. 'OK, first team, we're going in. Second team, fan out around the node and blast anything which comes back through that isn't us.'

He turned back towards the node. He didn't really understand how it worked – none of them did – and he found it easiest to imagine that the wormhole was just a tunnel that transported you instantly from place to place. Nothing fancy. Just a new method of transport. That was what C19 wanted it to be, wasn't it?

He stepped closer to the node – and was swept off his feet by a powerful force. He screamed as he tumbled head over heels, the glowing tunnel blinding him.

The Ruin were being beaten back by the flames. Many of them were ablaze, their burning bodies floating to the floor of the cavern.

And then, silently, suddenly, the node opened. Fitz gave a shout. 'Yes!' If they could get closer, hold the position... He looked back at the Queen. If he could get through, he'd be safe. The T'hiili were as good as doomed anyway, with an unfertilised Queen.

He realised guiltily that this was what he'd been planning all along. Leading the T'vorha into battle, just so he could get near the node, get back home. He realised with a jolt of shame that he hadn't even bothered looking for Sam. He'd forgotten all about her, until now. Perhaps it was the elixir he had taken, filling his mind with crap about the Dominion.

Then Fitz saw figures emerging from the node, floating out into the middle of the cavern. Soldiers in black combat gear. He gave a shout of joy – they'd come to rescue him!

He turned to Gilthr. 'Now's our chance! Head for the node, now!'

But the T'vorha shoved him aside, roughly.

Fitz looked at the screen, watched for a while and then averted his eyes, feeling sick.

It was a massacre.

Captain Rogers felt himself falling, incredibly fast. He tried to remain calm, but the feeling that he was going to smash against something became too much and he yelled out. Around him, his men tumbled head over heels, spinning black figures against the gold and white kaleidoscope of the wormhole. He gripped his machine gun, telling himself he was trained for this sort of thing.

Abruptly, the white tunnel vanished and Rogers found himself sailing into space, staring up at a powder-blue landscape, dotted with what looked like lumps of black glass. He swung round, saw a shining whirlpool in a black cliff face, his men tumbling out, arms and legs akimbo.

'Into position!' he yelled.

And then the creatures came. Huge, spinning wheels, their movements leisurely. A flock of them converged on three of his men, still disorientated. Swift, busy movements of the creatures' legs, screams, a spray of red, limbs floating down to the blue sand.

Rogers roared his anger, bringing his machine gun to bear on the creatures. He fired into them, watching the bullets tear into the hourglass-shaped bodies. The recoil from the weapon sent him floating backwards, into one of his men. A shape overhead – more of the things. Rogers fired again, shattering legs, tearing orange bodies. The sound of gunfire from all around. This would be easy. The things had no weapons, they could be smashed like insects.

Then he looked up, and swore. There were *hundreds* of the things, coming from all directions. He saw another of his men, firing at them, legs kicking in the air, sliced in half as one of the things wheeled past.

He looked around. Bits of alien creature, severed limbs, clouds of red mist everywhere. A gargling scream from nearby. A severed head floated past, trailing blood.

There were too many of them. Too many. Rogers fired blindly into the forest of legs and bodies before him. Something thumped into his back. He tried to turn and screamed out in pain. Something cutting, tearing – he coughed, blood spurting from his mouth on to the visor of his helmet.

He sucked in a gasping breath, letting himself feel the fear, the horror. He was going to die, torn apart by whatever the hell these things were. He'd failed. The world was going to be destroyed because he had failed.

He tried to bring his gun to bear but his arms felt heavy. He lost his grip, watched the gun spin away.

A flurry of black legs, an orange mouth yawning in front of him, a questing grey trunk. An explosion of pain, his body juddering as the thing sawed into his flesh. The pain ebbed and he felt himself falling into a black pit.

The last thing he saw was a dozen of the creatures, heading in formation straight for the node.

Professor Nagle jumped out of her seat as the monsters poured through the node, cannoning into the wire mesh.

Ruin, the Doctor had said they were called. Blue sparks crackled around them, a sizzling sound rent the air. The fence was holding. But more of the creatures were pouring through the node, cannoning into the fence, soaking up all the electricity. God, how many were there? How many monsters could a separate dimension hold? Too many for Wolstencroft's men to cope with, surely.

The second squad was outside the mesh fence, weapons trained on the creatures. Wolstencroft bellowed an order and the team opened fire, hails of bullets tearing through the fence, lacerating orange bodies. There was a tremendous, terrible shrieking above the chatter of gunfire. Then the fence stopped sparking. Something had gone wrong. And then, under the weight of the creatures, the fence split. Sickened, Nagle saw a soldier sliced clean in half by the flailing legs of a Ruin.

There was only one thing to do.

Nagle sat back down, though all her instincts were screaming at her to run, to get the hell out. With shaking hands, she typed a command into the keyboard.

She looked up. Like a folding flower, the node closed.

The battle began to turn. Fitz noticed that some of the Ruin were fighting back, leaping on to the dirigibles, spraying fluid at the flames. Some of the dirigibles had caught fire, and were nose-diving into the bottom of the cavern. Loads of Ruin had got through the node; none of the dirigibles were anywhere near. Gilthr swerved as a brace of Ruin headed straight for them.

Fitz kept his eyes fixed on the node. If only they could get to it –

Even as he formed this thought, the swirling white node puckered out of existence.

No point hanging around now to get slaughtered by the Ruin. 'Right, that's it. Get us the hell out of here.'

An icy presence in his mind:

No.

The Queen's eyes were open. Staring straight at him.

The One is near. The time of my fertilisation is imminent.

Fitz groaned. 'We have to get out of here!'

Gilthr shoved Fitz away from the control brain, grunting.

Fitz fell against the wall of the dirigible, staring up at the screen. It was filled with burning Ruin, the bodies of human soldiers, and T'vorha which had left the dirigibles, only to be killed by Ruin, or burned alive.

He noticed that they were changing direction, heading away from the battle, arcing round towards the golden sea. Why were they doing this? Then he noticed a small dirigible, a blip against the gold.

The Queen pointed

The One is there.

Now Fitz could see that it wasn't one of the T'vorha dirigibles. It was smaller, more delicate-looking.

Soon I will be fertilised.

Bully for you, thought Fitz. And I thought *I* had sex on the brain.

Then he saw the Ruin, tons of them, wheeling towards the tiny dirigible. It began to head downward, in a futile evasive action.

The golden light of the sky-sea played across Sam's face, and she imagined she could feel its warmth. Beside her, Itharquell manipulated the control brain. They had gone back through the cavern of the white sand, down the chimney of black rock, through the perilously narrow tunnel and into the golden sky-sea. They were about to emerge into the cavern of blue sand.

When they did, they found themselves in the middle of a battle. Sam could see dozens of dirigibles, heading for the cliff of black glass, firing burning bolts at the Ruin.

The dirigible lurched beneath them. Sam grabbed the stems Itharquell had been manipulating and they steadied. 'What's wrong?'

That light – it was alive!

Sam frowned. Had he never seen fire before?

The dirigible juddered under the impact of something heavy. Ruin?

They started falling, down towards the floor of the cavern.

Something burst through the roof of the dirigible. The leg of a Ruin. It began sawing back and forth urgently.

On the screen, the cavern floor was rushing up to meet them. Even in this low gravity, they were heading for quite an impact.

More Ruin legs burst through the wall of the dirigible. Itharquell was screaming. The ceiling of the dirigible caved in, pieces floating along the passage towards them.

In front of her, Itharquell screamed and pointed to the screen.

Sam looked. She gasped. A Ruin was splayed over the front of the dirigible, clasping on like a limpet. One end of its body was pressed against the screen, a gigantic orange sucking mouth, the grey trunk questing and poking.

They were completely surrounded.

Sam looked at the screen – the cavern floor filled it completely. She rolled into a ball, there was a thump, a flash of light behind her eyes and then –

Fitz watched the small dirigible hit the floor of the cavern. Most of the Ruin clinging to it were flung off, and sailed back into the middle of the cavern – but two of the things remained, sawing through the green flesh.

We must destroy them. The One must not be harmed.

Gilthr shoved past Fitz and picked up a harpoon, dipping the end into the flaming bowl of fluid. Fitz grabbed the stems of the brain. How would he know what to do? But then he found his hands moving, the knowledge suddenly there. The Queen? The elixir? He didn't know. He concentrated on keeping a straight course.

An aperture opened in the wall of the dirigible before Gilthr. He raised the harpoon, aimed and fired. The flaming missile hit the first Ruin right in the open tulip-like end of its body, and it burst into harsh yellow flame. The fire spread to the broken body of the dirigible. Another Ruin launched itself at them, its six legs splayed, rotating like a wheel of death, its body contracting as it jetted its way towards them.

Fitz twisted the stems and the dirigible swerved to one side. Gilthr quickly reloaded and fired a second burning harpoon – it missed, sailing off into the cavern to land on the blue sand, still glowing.

They were yards from the other dirigible now. Fitz twisted the stems and they slowed. He felt a bump as they landed, feet away from the stricken vessel. Gilthr squeezed through the aperture and took up position between the two dirigibles, scanning the cavern for more Ruin.

The Queen was swaying from side to side, her eyes distant, the slitted pupils almost invisible.

The One, the One. You must go inside. Rescue the One.

Fitz stepped on to the blue sand, and froze. Gilthr was grunting, pointing above Fitz's head. An image of a Ruin flickered in his mind and instinctively he ducked. A Ruin passed overhead, its cilia brushing his hair.

Gilthr fired his harpoon. It went straight into the central mass of the Ruin, blasting it back towards the centre of the cavern, its six legs closing around the burning wound.

Gasping, Fitz staggered to his feet, and stumbled over to the dirigible. The flames were on top, so it should be safe. There was a ragged opening in its side. He stepped in. Smoke filled the interior, Fitz could just make out two bodies. One T'hiili, clad in a costume of yellow leaves; the other human, female. With blonde hair. Kerstin? Sod the Queen, sod the One. He went to the girl first, rolling her over on to her back.

He cried out, hardly believing what he was seeing.

It wasn't Kerstin, it was Sam.

Kerstin crouched by the Doctor's side as he delved under the console. His toolbox was open on the floor before her, and he kept asking to be passed various tools: neutron ram. Atomic awl. She found that she somehow knew what they were, and passed him the correct tool each time. Was he telepathic? Or was it just blind luck?

From all around her, Kerstin could hear a rising and falling hum. The sense of power emanating from this machine was tangible. It made her feel safe and confident.

At last, the Doctor emerged from beneath the console, his face flushed and his hair ruffled. 'I can't do it.'

Kerstin's heart sank once again. This was like being on a fairground ride.

'I can't move the TARDIS without causing a massive dimensional tear.' He got to his feet and walked over towards the library, slumping down in the Regency chair.

Kerstin followed him. 'But you have to try to close the wormhole! You said it would destroy the world.'

He leaned his face on his hands. 'Very probably. But so might the TARDIS.'

He looked sad, and suddenly much older than he had first appeared to be.

Kerstin crouched down beside him. 'Maybe you can't save Johan,' she said, 'but you can still save Sam and Fitz.'

The Doctor sat in silence for a while. From the look in his eyes, she could tell he was thinking about Sam. It was the same haunted look that Björn had, when he talked about Nina. The same look that others would see in her own eyes, when she thought of Johan. Was the Doctor in love with Sam? She felt a burning curiosity. Hadn't Fitz said he was an alien? A thousand years old?

So many mysteries. 'Doctor?'

The Doctor started, as if being awoken from a dream. 'You're right. I have to try.' He smiled. 'After all, how bad can a dimensional tear be?'

He stood up and went to the console. 'Besides which I don't really have any choice,' he said. 'As usual.' A rueful smile. He looked up at the ceiling, where the golden line of the wormhole still glowed. 'If left unchecked there's no telling what damage that thing could cause.'

He looked over at Kerstin, who had joined him at the console. 'Hold on; this might be a bit of a bumpy ride.'

Kerstin gripped the edge of the console tightly.

The Doctor pulled levers, flicked switches and the blue fingers in the glass column began to mesh and unmesh, accompanied by a vast mechanical grating sound which made Kerstin's hair stand on end.

Above her, the blue ceiling exploded into a churning whirlpool of light.

In the forest, the TARDIS stood, a police box once more – tall, blue, totally out of place. There was a wheezing, groaning sound as it began to fade away like a departing ghost. But in its place, instead of the usual emptiness, it left a fold in the air, like a fault in a sheet of glass. Then everything went –

The generator room looked like a hospital in the middle of a war zone. Once the node had closed, it hadn't taken long for the UNIT guys to finish off the Ruin. Now they were clearing away the remains, taking the legs and saclike bodies out of the generator room, mopping up the fluid the best they could. The smell was almost unbearable. Four soldiers had been killed, and there were many injuries. Professor Nagle had tended as many as she could.

Now she sat at the control desk, tapping instructions into the computer. She knew that it was the end of her project. She'd never activate the node again. For one, Wolstencroft would shoot her if she did; for two, she didn't want to see anything like the Ruin ever again.

The Doctor *had* to close the wormhole. She prayed that the TARDIS would appear in front of her, the Doctor emerging, grinning from ear to ear. But what would happen if he failed? What would the end of the world be like? Would it be Armageddon – fire and brimstone and a painful death – or would the wormhole wipe the Earth cleanly out of existence with a silent, painless, clinical incision?

The computer bleeped. She looked at the screen. What the hell? Figures were scrolling down, too fast for her to read. She hit the ESCAPE button. Nothing happened. The figures were gibberish, machine-code madness. A flash of light made her look up. The points of the generator were glowing star-bright. Nagle stood up, not wanting to believe what she was seeing.

Wolstencroft rushed over, grabbed her arm and spun her round. His face was a grimace of anger. 'What are you doing?'

Nagle raised her hands. 'Nothing, nothing!'

She looked at the generator again. Suddenly, the node opened, its white throat swallowing the shining prongs of the generator. And then it expanded, beyond the mesh fence.

'Everyone out of here!' yelled Wolstencroft, shoving her away from the control desk.

She turned and ran from the generator room as behind her a white swirling whirlpool swallowed everything in its path.

Chapter Nineteen
Pocket Universe

Fitz and Gilthr carried the still-unconscious T'hiili and Sam into the Queen's dirigible. Fitz placed Sam in a tiny alcove between the spherical cabin and the Queen's moss bed. It was quite a crush, but Fitz tried to make Sam feel as comfortable as possible. She was out cold; there was a big purple bruise on her forehead. He still couldn't believe she was here, and wondered what she'd been through since her abduction from the TARDIS.

Gilthr floated over to the control brain and they took off, heading back towards the golden sea.

On the screen, Fitz could see clumps of smoke hanging in the low gravity, like giant wraiths, and the smell of burning was everywhere, even inside the dirigible. There were bright patches on the blue floor of the cavern. Some of them were Ruin. Other, bigger, ones were fallen T'vorha dirigibles. The Ruin were holding their position in front of the black cliff. They weren't attacking, but they weren't giving up either. They were massing, Fitz realised. Massing to go through the node when it opened. To Earth.

They plunged into the golden brightness. Four other dirigibles awaited them – sole survivors of the battle. Beyond them, a rippling swathe of Blight stretched from horizon to horizon, leaving only a narrow margin of sky-sea. Gilthr drew them to a halt.

The rescued T'hiili lay at the Queen's feet, breathing unevenly. Now they were together, Fitz could see the differences between the T'hiili and their T'vorha servants. The T'vorha were like combat versions of T'hiili – broader, taller, with more powerful limbs, and the added advantage of wings. The T'hiili's face was smoother than Gilthr's, the eyes wider, the hair finer. Between the eyes and the mouth there were no V-shaped ridges, and the

241

limbs were slender, more delicate. But this was the one who would fertilise the Queen. T'vorha were sexless, while the T'hiili carried the requisite secretions.

Suddenly, its eyes opened, and Fitz felt a rush of words in his mind:

No hope – Blight – Ruin – No hope –

Fitz closed his eyes and sank to his knees. 'Make him stop!'

The babbling flow ceased, and Fitz opened his eyes to see the Queen reaching down to the T'hiili, stroking his smooth green face, red hair falling over her shoulders.

Itharquell. The One.

The T'hiili – Itharquell – was staring up at the Queen, a look of awe on his leaf-green face. Fitz wondered how the telepathy would work – would he be able to overhear the Queen and the T'hiili? Or was it a more directional thing? They certainly seemed to be communing. The Queen was probably telling him that he was the lucky chap who had to 'fertilise' her. Where were they planning to do it? Not here, surely, in the cramped confines of the dirigible, with him and Gilthr looking on? After all he'd been through the last thing Fitz wanted to see was an alien sex show. Probably.

The Queen turned to Fitz

We should return to the Nest for the fertilisation ceremony. But there is not time. I must be fertilised now.

Fitz gulped. They really were going to do it in front of him.

She glanced around the dirigible.

I need more space than this.

Fitz was about to ask her for six bob to get lost for the evening when, on the screen, another dirigible loomed, its brown skin charred in places, a couple of burnt Ruin legs stuck to its underside. A hatch opened in the side of their dirigible and the Queen and Itharquell stepped out, floating across the short distance between the vessels.

'D'you think he's going to carry her over the threshold?' said Fitz to Gilthr.

Gilthr grunted in incomprehension.

Fitz longed to hear a human voice. Sam's voice. He squirmed past the bulky T'vorha and into Sam's alcove. She was curled into a ball, her hands protecting her head. Fitz squeezed in beside her, putting his arms around her. 'Sam,' he whispered into her ear.

She stirred, arching her back against him. 'Doctor?' she murmured.

'No, it's me, Fitz.'

Sam curled back into a ball, hiding her face with her hands.

Well, there's gratitude for you, thought Fitz.

Kerstin was kneeling on the floor, hanging on to the console for dear life, as the TARDIS juddered around her. She could just about see the Doctor on the other side of the console, though she couldn't hear what he was saying through the rising, roaring noise which was emanating from the tower above. It felt as though the TARDIS were going to break up. Everything was blurring, and the ceiling above was a churning ocean of light. After all she'd been through, could this be the end? She saw the Doctor stagger back from the console, throwing his head back and stretching his arms wide, a scream tearing from his throat, merging with the roar of the TARDIS. Kerstin screamed too, as reality bent and warped around her.

So this was the end of the world, thought Professor Nagle as she ran through the C19 base. A curtain of white energy billowed behind her, getting closer. She had no chance of outrunning it. She could only hope that the Doctor had been wrong, that the energy would run out, that the connection between Earth's space and the wormhole would be self-limiting. The remaining UNIT troops were pounding up the corridor in front of her, leaving her behind. She slowed to walking pace, exhausted.

A hand gripped her arm. 'Come on!'

Wolstencroft. He'd come back for her. Why? She laughed, waved him on.

He swore, sweat beading his bald head, and yanked her

towards him. She saw his dark eyes widen, his jaw slacken, as he looked back down the corridor.

She stared, feeling remote, detached.

The white wall of light was only feet away. She screamed then, grabbing on to Wolstencroft, hearing his throaty yell of horror. Then everything seemed to bleach white, a white that hurt her eyes, and then she felt herself lifting into the air – *but what about the ceiling?* – high above the world, still holding on to Wolstencroft's hand.

They spun together like sycamore leaves in a hurricane.

Wolstencroft was still yelling, but she couldn't see him. Only this endless white. So this was death. It wasn't too bad. It didn't even hurt.

And then, with a thump, Nagle landed chest first on a clump of ground, fingers digging in the mud. Wolstencroft landed beside her, cursing. Her hair was being whipped by a squalling wind and she'd lost her glasses.

'What has your blasted machine done, woman?' gasped Wolstencroft.

She squinted, brushing her hair from her eyes. Her nails clicked on something and she pulled it out. A miracle – her glasses, caught up in a tangle of hair. She slipped them on, and gasped at what she saw.

They were lying on the edge of a vast crater, almost half a mile across. The centre of it was a glowing mass, which pulsed and rippled. The node – distended, out of control. As they watched, hundreds of six-legged, orange-bodied Ruin began to pour through the centre of the node, spiralling up into the air, fanning out into the sky.

Wolstencroft took out his revolver. They looked at each other.

'Those things,' he muttered. 'I wish I had a name for the bastards.'

'The Doctor said they're called Ruin,' said Nagle.

Wolstencroft gave a harsh laugh. 'Where's your precious Doctor now, eh?' He aimed his pistol up at the Ruin. There were hundreds of them, and they were beginning to descend upon the forest. Nagle could see a few UNIT guys, haring about among the trees, taking up positions and firing at the things. She almost admired their professionalism, their apparent calmness in the face of this insanity.

Wolstencroft loosed off a few shots and Nagle covered her head with her hands.

Everything stopped. The roaring above them, the juddering of the floor. Kerstin opened her eyes. The Doctor was standing in front of the wall of clocks, clutching his sides, panting heavily. She stood up, stumbled and clutched the console.

The Doctor caught her eye, and smiled. 'We made it,' he said slowly. Then he burst into action, running across the room and taking her hands, spinning her around in a mad giddy dance. 'We made it! We made it! We made it!'

Fitz floated in front of the control brain, feeling utterly dejected once again. With the node closed, there was no way out of the Dominion. And the Blight was advancing behind them, so they had to keep moving. Soon they would have no choice but to enter the cavern – which was still crawling with Ruin. Blight behind – Ruin ahead. They really were caught between a rock and a hard place.

But when they emerged into the cavern, Fitz was greeted with a strange and welcome sight. The node had opened – only now it wasn't a tiny whirlpool: it was a yawning chasm, completely obscuring the cliff. Of the Ruin, there was no sign.

Fitz tried not to imagine what could be happening at the other end of the wormhole.

Gilthr was guiding the dirigible down to the blue sand, some distance from the glowing chasm. The other dirigibles were also coming to rest.

'What are you doing?' said Fitz. 'That's the way out! The way out of here!'

He felt a bump. They'd landed. Gilthr climbed out through the hatch, Fitz scrambling after him. The other dirigibles had landed in a circle around them, noses pointing inward. T'vorha emerged, staring back fearfully. The golden sea of light had disappeared, totally consumed by the Blight. In front of them, was the node, washing everything in harsh white light. Everything was black and white now. It was obvious what to do – get the hell out.

The T'vorha gathered outside the dirigible containing the Queen and Itharquell. So that was it. They didn't want to leave the Dominion until they knew that the fertilisation was successful. They'd better be quick about it. Fitz hung back, near the Queen's dirigible. If they took too long, he'd slip back inside, and take off – at least he and Sam might escape.

The T'vorha dropped to their knees as a hatch opened in the side of the dirigible. Itharquell stepped out, looking none the worse for wear. Fitz realised he had expected him to appear totally knackered. 'Rather you than me, mate,' he muttered. Then the T'vorha grew silent, their bulbous eyes fixed on the hatch.

The Queen emerged, her naked pink body glistening, her red hair falling in waves behind her.

The T'vorha stood, unfurling their wings, letting out a guttural roar of triumph.

The Queen spread her arms, and opened her mouth.

And sang.

Fitz would never forget the effect her song had on him, though for the rest of his life he'd try vainly to recall the tune. It cut right to his heart, bypassing rational thought, and he felt himself uplifted with joy, tears rolling down his face. Through the tears, he could see the T'vorha shuffle forward, lifting the Queen in their arms, their wings unfurling.

Itharquell ran over to Fitz, casting a fearful glance at the encroaching Blight. His voice whispered in Fitz's mind:

We must take the Queen through the node now.

'Right,' said Fitz, turning back to the Queen's dirigible. Now they'd get out of the Dominion. Hey, he'd be their saviour. Saint Fitz. Maybe it wasn't too bad, being a hero.

And then he heard a sound, a distant surging roaring which

merged with the Queen's song. Wait a minute, thought Fitz. Wait
– a – minute…

To Fitz's utter disbelief and joy, the TARDIS materialised right
by the side of the Queen's dirigible. The door opened and out
stepped the Doctor. He caught sight of Fitz and hurried up to
him.

'Fitz! You're alive!' cried the Doctor.

Fitz grabbed the Doctor's hands and shook them, glad the
Time Lord wasn't about to place another smacker on him. 'Not
for much longer.'

The Doctor looked up at the black wall looming over them. 'I
see. That's the Blight?'

'Doctor –' began Fitz.

But the Doctor had caught sight of the T'vorha. He walked
over to them.

They put the Queen down on the blue sand. The Doctor
started talking to her, his voice high and fluttery.

Although Fitz was glad the Doctor was here and back to his
old self, he felt an odd sense of deflation, as if his role in events
was over.

Itharquell was staring from the TARDIS to the Doctor.

What is that? Who is that creature?

'Your salvation,' said Fitz.

Now the Doctor was leading the Queen and the T'vorha to
the TARDIS. The Queen passed Fitz without even looking at
him. She could hardly walk – the T'vorha were supporting her.
They disappeared into the TARDIS. Itharquell followed them,
hesitating on the threshold.

'Go on,' cried the Doctor. 'It's quite safe!'

Itharquell stepped inside.

The Doctor came to stand beside Fitz. 'They can't go through
the node,' he said. 'Creatures from the Dominion can't exist on
Earth. The gravity is too high – it destroys their internal organs.
I've adjusted the gravity field in the butterfly room, so they
should be all right there.'

Fitz remembered the insect thing in the forest, the creatures

247

that had attacked the farm, the Ruin that the Swedish police had found. All of them had died.

And he'd been about to take the T'hiili through the node. To their deaths. 'Oh Christ. I was –'

A hand on his shoulder. 'You weren't to know. You were doing the right thing.'

Fitz looked at the Doctor's face, soft and compassionate. He shook his hand away. 'Good intentions aren't enough, are they? And now you've turned up everything's all right, isn't it? Bloody hell. You get all the glory.'

The Doctor flinched. 'You really think that I do what I do for "glory"?'

Fitz turned away. 'No. Course not.' Even there you're better than the rest of us, he thought. Then he smiled faintly. 'Thank God,' he muttered. He looked over to the TARDIS, wanting to change the subject. 'So, the TARDIS is all right now?'

'Sort of,' said the Doctor. 'The wormhole's snarled in her bowels like a tapeworm. It's caused the node to expand.' He suddenly looked haunted. 'I may have saved the T'hiili but at what cost?'

Then Fitz remembered the most important thing of all.

'Doctor,' he said, impulsively grabbing his arm. 'I've found Sam. She's alive!'

The Doctor turned towards Fitz, his jaw dropping open in complete amazement.

Kerstin watched as the procession of alien creatures scuttled into the TARDIS. First of all came a dozen bipedal winged froglike things in armour. Two of them were supporting what looked like a naked human woman. Following them was another, smaller froglike creature, in a leaflike yellow costume. They didn't even notice the grand panorama of the TARDIS interior. She supposed that if your world was coming to an end, nothing much would come as a surprise.

The Doctor had given her the task of showing the refugees to the butterfly room. She walked up the one in yellow. Was he their leader?

'Hello,' she said. 'Welcome to the TARDIS.' She felt like an air stewardess, or a holiday rep. She had to fight to stop the bizarreness of the situation getting the better of her. If she stopped to think, she would surely go mad. 'If you would please follow me.'

She led the creatures down a vaulted corridor which led from the console room, stopping outside a double door which opened at her approach.

Inside was the field and hillside, the place where she'd first arrived in the TARDIS. The butterflies were hovering in the air. They seemed to be floating about rather drunkenly; the Doctor said he had lowered the gravity. 'Please go inside; we've prepared this environment specially for you.' She stood to one side as they trooped in, counted them as they went past. Fourteen of them, in all. Fourteen saved from an entire universe.

The doors closed. Kerstin felt light-headed, excited again. Just how big was this place? She walked off down the corridor.

Sam's head hurt. She remembered ducking, as a Ruin leg swung for her – it must have banged her head, side-on. If that razor edge had made contact she would have been scalped. But her head still hurt, and she could still taste the smoke of the burning dirigible, coating the inside of her mouth.

She opened her eyes. Where was she? On something soft, something rubbery.

'Sam.'

A voice. A voice outside her head. *Human...?* Sam rolled on to her back, suddenly awake. There above her was the Doctor. He was smiling. He was holding her hand. 'Hello Sam.'

'Doctor!' She sat up abruptly, ignoring the throbbing pain in her forehead, and hugged him, breathing in the smell of him.

'Erm, I don't want to worry you,' came a voice from her side.

She turned to see Fitz, in a very strange get-up of lumberjack shirt and T'vorha armour. His hair was still short, but his chin was dark with stubble. It would still be some time before he was back to the Fitz she knew.

'The Blight's tickling the arse of this dirigible,' he said. 'I suggest we hotfoot it to the TARDIS forthwith.' He grinned. 'Hello, Sam.'

Sam smiled back. Hadn't they argued? It didn't matter. For now. She hugged him as well, and he swung her from the alcove.

Outside the dirigible, Sam's feet scudded on the sand. To her left, the Blight, metres away, gaining rapidly. She looked up. It arched overhead, like a pantomime cloak of doom.

To her right, a shining white chasm. Had the whirlpool opened again? What was going on?

Then she saw the familiar blue shape of the TARDIS, and made straight for it, the Doctor and Fitz close behind.

'How did you find me?' she asked the Doctor.

'It's a long story,' he said. 'Tell you over tea, if and when we have time for such a luxury.'

Sam stepped into the TARDIS, with a last backward look at the Blight. She walked down the steps, round the console and flopped down in the Doctor's Regency chair. She felt drained, but it was good to be home again.

The Doctor was haring around the console, pulling levers, snapping switches. The ceiling showed a view of the cavern they had just left, Blight on one side, node on the other, with only a narrow blue band of cavern in between.

'We'd better take off soon,' said Fitz, looking fearfully up at the blackness closing in.

'Yes yes yes,' said the Doctor. Then: 'Now that *is* interesting.'

Sam ran up to the console. 'What is it?'

The Doctor glanced up. 'I've just realised what's causing the Blight! It's not the wormhole at all!'

'Wormhole?' Sam frowned. What wormhole? She realised she had no idea what had been going on while she was trapped in the Dominion.

Fitz was removing his T'vorha armour, tossing it on to a pile of cushions. 'If it's not the wormhole, what is it?'

'No time for that now. Hold on – this could be a bit of a bumpy ride.' He flicked a switch, and the columns in the time rotor began to move.

A door opened on the far side of the console room and a girl entered. She was about Sam's age, with short blonde hair and tanned skin. She was wearing a black T-shirt and white shorts.

Fitz ran up the girl, exclaiming his surprise. 'Kerstin!'

Sam blinked. Obviously a heck of a lot had been going on. She had some catching up to do.

The girl – Kerstin – smiled weakly at Fitz. 'Good to see you too.'

'You could have told me she was safe, Doctor,' said Fitz.

The Doctor's head popped up from the console. 'Didn't I? Ah, Kerstin – are our guests happy?'

Kerstin had a foreign accent which Sam couldn't quite place. 'They're fine. I mean, as far as I can tell.'

Sam stood up. 'Er, anyone mind introducing us?'

'Kerstin Bergman, Sam Jones – and vice versa,' said Fitz. He shrugged and grinned. 'It's a long story.'

Sam shook the girl's hand. 'Welcome to the madhouse.'

The smile faltered on Kerstin's face. 'I've heard a lot about you.'

Sam looked narrowly at Fitz. What had he been saying?

Tears were brimming in Kerstin's eyes. 'I – I'm glad you're safe.' She turned away, beginning to sob. Fitz held her, and she buried her head in his chest.

'The wormhole,' said Fitz. 'It took her boyfriend away.'

Sam felt light-headed. She was dying to know what had been going on. 'Fitz?'

Briefly, Fitz told her everything that had happened since her unplanned exit from the TARDIS. Sam listened, trying to take it all in.

'How could a wormhole invade the TARDIS?' she asked. 'I mean, I thought she was – well, impregnable.'

'She usually is,' said the Doctor. 'And I don't know how.' He straightened up, hands on hips, frowning at the console. 'Almost as if she wanted it to happen.'

'Look – the Blight,' said Fitz, pointing.

The image above them changed. Now the blackness was almost absolute.

A thought struck Sam. 'Are we safe in here?

'We're in hover mode,' said the Doctor, his voice hushed. 'Temporally displaced. We're the only ones privileged to see the death of an entire universe.'

Sam grimaced. 'One privilege I'd gladly forego.' She looked away from the blackness. 'Anyway, I thought the Dominion was a planet.'

'No.' The Doctor shook his head, walking up to stand beside her. 'It is – was – a pocket universe. Imagine our universe as a balloon. Now imagine a small section "pinched off" from our universe, through a black hole.'

Sam imagined it. It seemed too simple. 'Is that what the Dominion was?'

The Doctor sighed. 'We'll never get to study it,' he said with genuine regret in his voice.'

Fitz had his arm round Kerstin. They were both staring up at the display. 'So, what is this Blight?'

'At first I thought was caused by the wormhole,' said the Doctor, pacing up and down. 'But it seems that has nothing to do with it.'

As Sam stared at the Blight, she could see tiny points of light within the blackness. Like stars.

Exactly like stars.

'Hey,' said Kerstin. 'That looks familiar.'

'It should do,' said the Doctor. His face was sad. 'It's our universe.'

Chapter Twenty
All For Nothing

Professor Nagle ran through the trees, not knowing or caring which way she was going. She only wanted to get away from the node, away from the Ruin. She'd kicked off her patent-leather high heels ages ago, and ran on her stockinged feet, her flesh scratched and torn by thorns. She ran awkwardly, one hand holding her glasses on, through clumps of ferns, occasionally stumbling into trees. She had to get away from here.

The glowing white node was a mouth that was going to gape wider and wider until it consumed the Earth. She knew there was nowhere to run, but still she kept running. She had to keep running because she knew it was all her fault and if she stopped she'd crack up.

Major Wolstencroft stood with his back against a tree, aimed his machine gun at the flailing creature and let out a short, controlled burst, the weapon juddering against his body. The bullets tore the bifurcated torso of the thing to bits and it sank to the ground, its legs and tentacles thrashing, then falling still.

A noise behind him. He swung round – there was another. He fired again, and it slumped to the ground, squealing.

The Ruin hadn't taken to the air for very long. They'd all spiralled down to the ground, where they scrambled about on their six legs, like giant spiders. Those legs were lethal, razor-sharp, and Wolstencroft and his men had a hard task keeping away from them. Still, he was glad they were on the ground. An airborne enemy was far more difficult to fight.

Wolstencroft dodged around the tree, swearing as he saw one of his troops on the ground between four Ruin. The man was dead. They were picking at him with their claws, their grey trunks probing his body. Tasting him.

Wolstencroft sprang out from behind the tree and yelled his rage, the chatter of the machine gun drowning out all other sound. The creatures fell, squealing, on top of one another and the soldier. Moore, his name was. Private Jeff Moore. Only twenty-three.

Wolstencroft ran to a clump of ferns, crouching down to check his gun. Some distance away, he could see the white glow of the node. The Ruin had stopped coming through, but the node was getting bigger. Was it the end of the world? He felt a strange and unsettling sense of liberation.

Footsteps behind him – human ones. He turned as a breathless soldier ducked down beside him. Private Schofield. He was wild-eyed, but still largely in control. This was only his second engagement against an alien enemy.

'How many of us left?'

Schofield shook his head. 'Don't know, sir.'

Wolstencroft swore. He noticed the young private was looking at him expectantly. Waiting for orders. 'Right. We'll try and contain the creatures inside the forest.'

'Just you and me, sir?'

Wolstencroft smiled. 'Yes, Schofield, just you and me.' He remembered the creatures in the generator room. 'These things don't live for very long, on Earth. All we have to do is stay alive until they die.'

Schofield suddenly leaned forward, shoved Wolstencroft to the ground and fired his machine gun. Wolstencroft looked up to see that one of the things had crept up on them. It danced in the hail of bullets, and then lay broken, twitching.

Wolstencroft scrambled away from its death throes.

'Well, they'd better hurry up about it,' said Schofield, scanning the trees ahead of then. 'Doesn't look like they're dying off to me, sir.'

They scouted round. All the creatures were heading in one direction. It took Wolstencroft a while to realise what was happening.

He stopped Schofield and pulled him into cover. 'They're heading back towards the node,' he said. 'They're trying to go back to where they came from.'

Sam stared up at the ceiling of the TARDIS. She was standing next to the Doctor. His hands were resting on the lever that would take them out of here for ever.

There wasn't much left of the Dominion now. All they could see was the glowing node, a white slash against the black glass of the cliff. Once the node had gone, that was it. No more Dominion. Sam wondered if she should go and get Itharquell, so he could be there at the end – but no. She doubted if she would want to watch if she were him.

The Blight surged once more, and, like a snuffed-out candle, the node was gone, and with it the Dominion.

Now the Blight was everything. Sam could see that, as the Doctor had said, it was *the* universe – *her* universe. The familiar sprinkling of stars, galaxies, the deep, deep black – the black of the Blight. She remembered being stuck to the stalagmite, the Blight advancing upon her. She'd had a feeling it was familiar back then, she'd thought it had been the way home. Well, it was, of sorts.

They all stood in silence for a while, as the Doctor pulled the lever. Sam heard the dematerialisation noise as if from a long way away, and watched the TARDIS ceiling swirl and coalesce – just like a sky-sea – into the familiar pattern of the vortex. That faded too to be replaced by the usual dark-blue expanse.

Sam realised that she was crying.

The floor beneath her was juddering slightly, making it difficult to keep her balance. The effects of the wormhole? She imagined it wrapped round the heart of the TARDIS like a boa constrictor.

'How long till we're back on Earth?' she asked the Doctor, brushing away her tears.

'A few minutes,' he said, pacing up and down. 'I've just realised – now that the Dominion is no more, there's nothing for the other end of the wormhole to latch on to. Look!'

They looked. Above her the TARDIS ceiling was a schematic, showing a golden line leading to Earth.

Fitz scratched his stubbly chin. 'Won't it just, well, close?'

The Doctor shook his head, ran his hands through his hair. 'No no no, there'll be massive feedback, probably enough to destroy the TARDIS *and* the Earth.'

Sam's stomach turned to lead – a familiar feeling. The End of the World. Again.

'We can stop it, right?' said Fitz. 'Doctor?'

'I hope so,' said the Doctor. He went over to the console and slid something out, putting it casually into his waistcoat pocket. 'You know, all this time I thought the cause of the Blight was the wormhole. Instead it seems that Nagle's meddling has enabled me to save the T'hiili.'

'Hang on,' said Fitz. 'If the wormhole didn't cause the Blight, what did?'

'Well, you see,' said the Doctor, gripping the lapels of his frock coat, 'our universe is continually expanding, drawing energy from outside itself.'

'But there's nothing outside the universe,' said Kerstin incredulously.

'Not quite,' said the Doctor, wagging a finger at her. 'Our universe takes its energy from pocket universes, drawing the energy through black holes or Charged Vacuum Emboitements.'

'And that's what the Dominion is?' said Sam. It all sounded so clinical. 'A pocket universe? But it was inhabited!'

The Doctor looked away.

She went up to him. 'Don't avoid this, Doctor!'

He looked over at her. With that look. 'Sam.'

She refused to be taken in. 'I know you're going to say that there was nothing we could have done about it, but that doesn't make it right.'

A hand on her shoulder. Fitz. 'No one's saying it's right.'

'What the T'hiili called the Blight,' said the Doctor, pointing up at the ceiling, 'was the very edge of the universe; or rather, the process of energy conversion.'

How was she going to explain this to Itharquell? That the Dominion, his universe, his home, was destroyed – consumed – by hers? Sam turned away. She heard Fitz's voice as if from a great distance.

'Doctor, could we have stopped it? I mean, if we had found it in time?'

Stupid git. How could you stop the universe from expanding?

The Doctor's voice echoed her thoughts. 'No, Fitz. Not even the Guardians have that power.'

She heard Fitz swear, and met his gaze. There was anger in his eyes, too. Between them, they'd been involved in the battle to save the Dominion. They'd failed; and worse, there had never been any chance of success. It had all been for nothing. If the Doctor hadn't turned up – at the last minute as always – they wouldn't even be here.

'Still, it's not all doom and gloom,' said the Doctor. 'We saved the T'hiili.' He gave her a hopeful little smile. Trying to appease her. Oh, she knew he wasn't to blame. She knew he had saved them all.

But she somehow didn't feel like giving him an easy ride. 'There were other races in the Dominion. It was an entire universe, Doctor. Imagine the billions of different races we didn't save.'

'The Ruin,' said Fitz, rushing up to the console. 'I almost bloody forgot. They've gone through the node – they'll be on Earth now!'

The Doctor glared at him. 'That's the least of our problems. They'll die before they can cause much damage.'

'What about the people from Strängnäs?' said Kerstin suddenly. 'The ones who were abducted when all this started?'

Sam remembered the body she'd seen, floating in the sky-sea, covered in purple growths. She decided to keep quiet about it.

The Doctor put his arm around Kerstin. 'They're lost, I'm afraid. They might not even have ended up in the Dominion – the wormhole had many offshoots.' He smiled at Kerstin. 'Luckily for you, you ended up in the bit that's ensnared in the TARDIS.' He frowned, putting his hand on his hips. 'Or maybe it wasn't luck – if it wasn't for you I'd never have got into the TARDIS.'

The Doctor walked up to the console, an indulgent smile on his face. 'What are you up to, old thing?'

As if in answer, the TARDIS lurched, and Sam grabbed hold of a nearby girder.

'Hold on,' said the Doctor, over an escalating electronic whine. 'This is it – crunch time.'

Again, thought Sam wearily, bracing herself.

The Queen was lying on the side of a hill, one hand supporting her head, her red hair arranged around her. Itharquell knelt before her, scarcely able to believe that they had survived. They had been rescued. They were… here.

Itharquell looked up at the sky-sea above them. It was very pale blue, like the eyelids of a sleeping child. He stroked the ground. Strands of green protruded from it, soft and damp. Insects flew in the sweet air, like airborne breathing-sacs, only smaller, more colourful.

All around, the surviving T'vorha lay sleeping.

Was this all? All that remained of the T'hiili?

His gaze fell once more upon the Queen. No. That was not all. Within her, a whole new clutch of eggs. A whole new generation that he had seeded. Soon, she would change. Now, though, she was beautiful, and Itharquell drank in her beauty in rapt silence.

Suddenly the Queen gave a little cry, like a child. She slumped, her head falling into her lap.

Itharquell knew. It was over. The Blight had consumed the Dominion. There was nothing left. Where would they go now?

* * *

Major Wolstencroft approached the Ruin, treading softly on the forest floor, machine gun at the ready. Schofield was a few metres to his left, also approaching the creature. It had been standing there for over ten minutes, occasionally squirting a clear fluid from its lower trunk. When they'd come upon it, Schofield had wanted to shoot it – but Wolstencroft had ordered him to observe. He wanted to see what it was doing. If it moved to attack them, they would fire.

But it hadn't moved.

And now it toppled, its legs giving way beneath it, the orange rubbery body folding, a strange hissing sound coming from the twin trunks.

'There you are,' said Wolstencroft, walking up to it. 'They are dying. That's why they're going back to the node – they've realised that they can't exist on Earth, so –'

Schofield pulled Wolstencroft back as the creature reared up, heaving itself forward, its uppermost trunk lancing out from the bell-like body. It had a surprisingly long reach and Wolstencroft staggered back. He fired a short burst and the trunk dropped to the ground, writhing like a dying snake. A black spike protruded from the end, whitish fluid dribbling from it.

'Remember what happened to the local lad who came back, sir,' said Schofield.

Wolstencroft turned away. The boy had been infected with alien eggs. He remembered Lindgard telling him about it, with ghoulish enthusiasm.

'It fancied you, sir,' said Schofield, smirking.

For once, Wolstencroft did not appreciate the private's humour. 'Shut up!' he said, bringing his machine gun to bear on the dead Ruin. 'Alien filth,' he growled, letting of a burst of fire into the dead body.

His anger spent, he turned away. Schofield was looking away, embarrassed. Well, he was young, idealistic. Hadn't seen the terrible things Wolstencroft had seen. The mutations, the madness. One day, Schofield would see it all, too. And then he'd become as dedicated to protecting the planet as Wolstencroft was.

'Come on, lad,' he said. 'We're going back to the node. Make sure those bastards get home.'

They set off through the forest, towards the distant white glow.

Sam clung to the girder, her teeth chattering, her vision blurring. This was one of the most traumatic landings she had experienced. It was as though the TARDIS were a Ventolin in the hands of a wheezy giant. Fitz and Kerstin were clinging to each other, stumbling over towards the library. The Doctor was at the console, total concentration on every line and angle of his face, seemingly oblivious to the chaos around him.

Sam kept her eyes on the blue fingers of the time rotor, though all she could see of them was a blur. Once the blur began to slow, it would almost be over. Hold on. Just hold on. Just don't think of the wormhole and what it was doing to the guts of the TARDIS. And her own guts, come to think of it. Her stomach felt as though it had come loose inside her body.

After what seemed like an age, the juddering began to ease off, and the blue fingers came into focus. Sam put her feet back on the floor. The Doctor ran around the console and yanked the chain that pulled the monitor down from its cubby-hole. Sam could see the screen clearly:

EARTH

SCANDINAVIA

HUMANIAN ERA 1999 AD

The Doctor gave a shout of triumph.

Sam let go of the girder and slumped to the floor.

Professor Nagle sat with her back against a tree, gently tending her wounded feet. Her tights were ripped and there were cuts all over her legs. Her feet throbbed with pain. She felt sick and tired and miserable and stupid and the Doctor had clearly left them all to stew.

Nagle closed her eyes. This was getting her nowhere.

She stood up, supporting herself against the tree, looking into the distance. The Ruin all seemed to have gone. Where, she did not know or care. Perhaps Wolstencroft had finished them all off; perhaps they had died naturally. Whatever.

The pain wasn't too bad, really. She stumbled through the forest, back towards the node. She could see it clearly deep within the forest, a glowing white wall, the light filtering through the branches, just as if the sun had fallen to Earth.

She had to go back. She gave a short, harsh laugh. The criminal returning to the scene of the crime. Perhaps she should throw herself into the node, see where it took her. Into the next world, if there was one. How many people had died because of her project?

No, don't think of that. Your aims and objectives were pure. You wanted to make things better.

But the roll call of the dead ran through her mind, unstoppable. The five locals who went missing – *she'd never even bothered to find out their names* – and the one who came back, Johan Svensson. The farmer, Björn something. Boris Lindgard. How many of Wolstencroft's UNIT troops? All of them? Was Wolstencroft himself dead? The tears ran freely from her eyes as she recalled the past few years, the rivalry between herself and Wolstencroft. The 'I'm in charge – no, *I'm* in charge' stupid macho bullshit. It had all been a game to her.

She was very close to the node now. She was amazed how quiet it was. Here and there, bodies of dead Ruin lay strewn, their legs tangled, their orange bodies deflated. She shuddered – so much like dead spiders. However alien and horrible, they counted among the dead she was responsible for as well.

Oh yeah, and the entire human race, gobbled up by the wormhole. That was to come, of course. There was no stopping it now. What had the Doctor said? 'You've raised a dragon you cannot feed'?

She stopped, a few metres away from the node. It was a solid white wall, reaching so high into the sky that she couldn't see the end of it. Its edge advanced towards her, consuming all in its way.

She felt a deadness where her heart should be. Hard to breathe. Her feet hurt. She'd just stand here, wait for the end of the world. Feed the dragon she'd raised.

Professor Jennifer Nagle closed her eyes, lifted her face upward. The glow of the node showed as a pulsing red beneath her eyelids. 'I'm sorry,' she whispered. She didn't know what else to say. 'So sorry. I'm sorry. I'm so sorry, sorry, sorry –'

Then everything went dark.

Sam got to her feet, rubbing her arms where they had chafed the girder.

Kerstin and Fitz were untangling themselves from a pile of books which had toppled over on to them.

Sam staggered over to the console. 'Is it over?'

The Doctor nodded. 'Almost. Bringing the TARDIS back here has sealed the rift between the Dominion and our universe. Like running a needle and thread through the vortex, stitching it together again.'

Kerstin and Fitz approached, supporting each other.

The Doctor looked at each of them in turn. 'It's going to be a close-run thing. All the energy in the wormhole is heading back here – there'll be a nasty implosion. I managed to buy us a few minutes, but that's all.'

'The feedback – you said it would destroy Earth,' said Fitz.

The Doctor nodded, talking fast. 'Imagine a huge elastic band, stretched out to its fullest extent, one end of it attached to Earth, the other to the Dominion.'

Fitz grimaced. 'I get the idea,'

The Doctor continued. 'It could destroy Earth but I'm going to try to adjust the parameters with the TARDIS's dimensional stabiliser so it will only affect this base and the area around it.'

'What'll happen to the TARDIS?' said Sam.

The Doctor looked grim. 'She'll withstand the impact. I hope.'

Oh great, thought Sam. 'What about the T'hiili?'

The Doctor winced, as if he'd been hit. 'They... *might* survive.'

Fitz swore.

A hard lump was forcing its way from Sam's stomach to her throat. 'What about us?'

The Doctor blinked, and looked away into the distance. 'I want you to get out of here. Get out of the C19 base, into the forest, and run. There should be enough time for you to outrun the implosion.' He operated the door lever.

'We can take the T'hiili with us!' said Fitz imploringly.

The Doctor shook his head sadly. 'They'll die in Earth's gravity, remember? They'll have to take their chances with the TARDIS and me.' He grimaced. 'I didn't plan it this way at all.'

Sam had never seen him so distraught. She could hardly believe it herself. After escaping the Blight, the T'hiili were facing destruction again.

'What about you?'

'I'll stay in the generator room, patch the dimensional stabiliser into the TC Warp control program.' Oh sod him, he was putting his life on the line again. 'I'll be all right. Now go on, run!' He shooed them out of the console room.

Sam knew that it was for the best, that he was right. There was no sense in their all dying. But, as she stepped out of the TARDIS behind Fitz and Kerstin, it felt like a betrayal. A betrayal of the Doctor, of Itharquell, of everything she stood for.

Professor Nagle opened her eyes, and her mouth, ready to scream.

The node had gone.

Before her, everything was normal. The forest, the trees, all as they were before.

263

She turned around, thinking she may have stumbled about a bit. But no – the node had definitely gone. The only signs that anything out of the ordinary had taken place were the slumped and broken bodies of the Ruin. And the bodies of UNIT soldiers, black against the lush green.

What had happened? Was Earth safe? She fell to the ground, her hands digging into the soil. 'I don't understand!' she wailed.

Footsteps, crashing through the forest. She looked up to see Major Wolstencroft's powerful figure standing over her, Private Schofield by his side.

She stood up, brushing leaves from her white lab coat. 'What's happened to the node?'

Wolstencroft's dark eyes glittered. 'You're asking me?' His voice was low and hoarse. He grabbed her arm and she stumbled.

'Hey, let go!'

His face was close to hers, and she could see he'd lost it. 'You're asking me what's happened? You built the bloody thing!' He was shouting, spittle flicking from his mouth on to her glasses.

'Sir!' cried the Schofield. 'With respect, sir.'

Wolstencroft let go of Nagle, and she stumbled back. She wiped her glasses.

Private Schofield was talking calmly, suggesting that they go back into the base, see what was going on. Wolstencroft seemed to calm down, and without looking back at her, stormed off through the forest.

Nagle followed. The node had closed. The Doctor had saved them, just as he said he would.

She allowed herself a tired smile. That would be one in the eye for Wolstencroft.

The TARDIS had landed smack bang in the middle of the generator room. Fitz looked around; it was a mess. There was torn and twisted wire-mesh fence in front of the generator, and tables, desks, chairs and computers were strewn everywhere.

Fitz felt Sam push him out of the room, into the corridor. He had one last look behind him – the Doctor sitting at the generator control desk, muttering soothing words, the TARDIS waiting nearby. Then he followed Sam and Kerstin out into the corridor.

He caught up with them. Sam was yelling that she didn't know the way out. Kerstin was just yelling.

'Follow me!' cried Fitz, and ran past them, hurtling round a corner straight into something tall –

He bounced back, gasping.

Major Wolstencroft. His uniform was grubby, there was blood on his arm and cuts on his face. His brown eyes were wide, staring. This was someone at the end of his tether.

Fitz could see Professor Nagle and a UNIT soldier, in the corridor behind Wolstencroft. Nagle was in a terrible state. She'd lost her shoes and her legs were covered in scratches. 'Let us past, we gotta get out of here!' he gasped.

Kerstin and Sam ran up behind him. He heard Sam's voice. 'No time for playing soldiers now! Let us past!'

'You're not going anywhere,' growled Wolstencroft.

Ignoring him, Fitz addressed Professor Nagle. 'Look, there's going to be an expl-, an *im*plosion or something. Bang! We have to get out of here or we'll all be killed!'

Wolstencroft had drawn his pistol. 'Schofield – cover them!'

The UNIT soldier raised his machine gun. Fitz felt a horrible sense of claustrophobic *déjà vu*.

Wolstencroft waved his pistol. 'Turn around. Back to the generator room.'

Fitz fell into step beside Sam.

'We're running out of time,' Sam said from between clenched teeth.

'We'll have to take our chances in the TARDIS with the Doctor.' At least they would all be together at the end. Fab.

They entered the generator room. The Doctor was still hunched over the control desk.

Fitz opened his mouth to shout out a warning, but Wolstencroft beat him to it.

'Doctor, step away from the control desk!'

The Doctor gave a surprised yelp and twirled round on his swivel chair. On seeing Wolstencroft he gave a groan of frustration. 'Not again! We've been through all this before!'

Heart in mouth, Fitz cried out, 'Did you do it, Doctor?'

The Doctor nodded. 'Yes yes yes, the Earth is safe – but we're not!'

'How much time have we got left?' yelled Sam.

The Doctor stood, spreading his arms wide. 'Minutes, at most!'

That was enough for Fitz. Letting out a yell he dived backwards, elbowing Wolstencroft in the stomach.

'What are you doing?' screamed Nagle.

Fitz fell on top of Wolstencroft, banging his gun hand against the floor. He was dimly aware of Sam prising the weapon from Wolstencroft's hand, the Doctor bellowing for everyone to get into the TARDIS. He was painfully aware of Schofield, standing over them, aiming his machine gun at his head.

Fitz stared along the barrel of the gun to the soldier's impassive face. 'You heard the Doctor,' he gasped. 'We're all going to die unless we get into the TARDIS!'

Then the soldier slumped forward.

Sam. She'd clobbered him with a chair. The love.

Fitz staggered upright. He yanked the machine gun from Schofield's hands and hurled it across the room. Schofield fell across Wolstencroft.

A hand on his shoulder. Fitz whirled round. The Doctor, his eyes wide. 'Fitz! Inside now!'

There was a mad scramble for the TARDIS. Fitz turned in the doorway and saw the two soldiers getting to their feet, groggily.

The Doctor ran across to them and pulled them towards the TARDIS. 'Don't argue – just get inside!'

Fitz stood aside as the Doctor shoved Wolstencroft and Schofield into the TARDIS.

Beyond them, Fitz saw Professor Nagle stumbling from the generator room.

The Doctor turned in time to see her. 'Where are you going?' he cried.

'My notes. Can't leave my notes,' said Nagle, framed in the doorway. Then she was gone.

Fitz stood on the threshold of the TARDIS, pressed into the door space with the Doctor. The Doctor's face was a grimace. 'So stupid!' he said. 'She doesn't have to die! I'm going after her.'

'No,' said Fitz, gasping with the effort of holding him back. 'We'll die if we don't get in there!'

Fitz shoved the Doctor into the TARDIS. The door closed behind them. Fitz all but fell down the steps into the console room.

Professor Nagle stumbled along the corridor towards her room. There was still time. The Doctor would wait. She had to get her notes – and the backup disks for the control program. C19 would want them. And, more importantly, she could start up afresh, create a new TC Warp Generator. Now that Earth was safe, she could start again.

Feet skidding on the tiled floor, she arrived at her room and tapped in the code on the electronic lock. The door fell open and she stumbled inside.

The familiarity of the little room calmed her. Neat and tidy and clean, just the way she liked it. The single bed, the chest of drawers, computer, desk, fridge, a few pictures on the wall. The big map of the solar system tacked to the ceiling. How often she'd fallen asleep staring up at that.

Her feet were really stinging now, as though she had walked through glass. Ignoring the pain, she went to her desk, pulled open the drawer that contained her disks. There they all were, numbered and indexed. She scooped them out and stuffed them in the pockets of her lab coat.

Almost two years she'd lived in this room. Not a sight or

scent of outside – until just now, and she'd been too freaked out to appreciate it. Two years devoted to the project. No lovers, no alcohol, no Thai cooking, no nothing. Her life was in this room.

Above the computer desk was a shelf, containing a row of box files. Which ones should she take? All of them? Or just the disks?

How much time did she have left? How much time?

Sam watched open-mouthed as Fitz and the Doctor tumbled into the TARDIS and the doors closed behind them.

'Where's Professor Nagle?' barked Major Wolstencroft. He seemed to be taking the TARDIS interior in his stride. The young UNIT guy, on the other hand, was standing around with a severe case of 'TARDIS-face' – open-mouthed boggle-eyed amazement.

'She went back to get her notes,' said the Doctor.

Sam closed her eyes. 'That's suicide,' she said.

The Doctor was practically tearing his hair out. 'I told you all to get away!'

Sam glared at Wolstencroft. 'We would have, if it wasn't for soldier boy.'

'It's going to hit in a few seconds,' said the Doctor grimly.

The TARDIS ceiling showed a schematic of the universe, a golden line zapping across space towards the solar system.

'Can't you take off?' said Fitz.

The Doctor shook his head. 'Wherever I take the TARDIS, the wormhole will be within her.'

Sam walked up to the Doctor and held his hand. He squeezed and she squeezed back.

Wolstencroft was staring up at the schematic, his jaw slack. He looked over at them. 'I – I didn't know.'

Fitz was holding Kerstin, a look of disbelief in his grey eyes. His travels with the TARDIS had only just begun; Sam knew what he must be thinking. *It can't end this way.*

'Any time now,' murmured the Doctor.

Sam reached up and held his face. He turned to her, and the look in his eyes almost broke her heart. He went to say something, but she silenced him with a kiss on his alabaster lips.

He tasted of coffee and cream and springtime and clean bedclothes and everything.

If she had to die, then this was the time.

They held each other.

And then a huge hand dashed her to the floor.

Professor Jennifer Nagle decided that the disks were enough. It was all there: her notes on the alien technology, the plans for the generator, the control program, everything.

She turned and ran from her room, her shoulder slamming into the door frame in her haste. She yelled out, a hopeless, lost sound, and skidded along the corridor. Her feet were bleeding. She was crying, her breath and heartbeat seeming to fill her whole body.

Part of her knew that it was too late. That it was the end, if not for the world, then for her. Humanity would never benefit from her genius.

When the end came, she didn't feel a thing.

Chapter Twenty-One
So This Is Goodbye

Sam opened her eyes.

She was lying on her back, staring up at something wide and deep and blue. The TARDIS ceiling, back to normal once more. There was something across her chest. She reached down, feeling something soft. Velvet. She moved her hand down, encountering flesh. Cool, smooth. A hand.

The Doctor's hand.

She sat up, wincing. Her back hurt where she had hit the floor.

Lying next to her was the Doctor, his face pressed against the floor, arms spread-eagled as though he were flying.

She held on to his hand, pressed it into her lap. She looked round. Fitz and Kerstin were sprawled amid an avalanche of books in the library. Wolstencroft and Schofield were prone on the floor near the console.

She had no idea if they were alive or dead.

She felt the Doctor's hand move in her lap, squeezing her own.

His eyes opened, his mouth moved. 'Spladoosh?'

Sam smiled, and helped him into a sitting position. He looked a bit dazed, but otherwise OK.

'We came through it,' he said, his voice a breathy whisper. 'I'm… quite pleased!'

A groan from the library. Fitz was extricating himself from the books, helping Kerstin to her feet. So they were OK. One soldier was sitting up, rubbing his bald head. A muttered curse from the other. So *they* were OK.

But what about –

'The T'hiili!' said the Doctor and Sam at exactly the same time.

In the butterfly room, it was a glorious summer's day. The air smelled fresh and clean, but then it always did. Fitz stood before the T'hiili Queen, the T'vorha and Itharquell kneeling in a semicircle around him. The Doctor and Sam were standing a little way away, watching, butterflies swirling around them.

The Queen was changing.

Her body was swelling, the limbs disappearing into the central body, the flesh darkening, hardening. The face was flattening, the mouth widening to a slit. She was turning into a giant egg sac. It both revolted and fascinated Fitz.

An icy presence in his mind:

I thank you for what you did for my race. We would never have escaped if it were not for you.

Fitz didn't know what to say. He'd almost led them to their deaths. He didn't deserve her thanks.

Now we must find a new Dominion.

Fitz bowed, feeling awkward.

Now you must leave, Fitz. You must all leave. My transformation is almost complete.

The icy voice melted away, for the last time.

Fitz turned away. Sam was waiting for him. There was a tenseness in her eyes, around her shoulders.

He remembered their argument, just before Sam was taken from the TARDIS. Oh blimey, surely she wasn't about to start it again?

She fixed him with a mock-serious stare. 'What's up with you? Not pleased to see me?'

Fitz winked at her. 'Sure am, baby. Boy, have I missed ya,' he drawled.

She laughed, and shook her head. They started back down the hill.

The Doctor ambled up, a dreamy smile on his face. 'You know, it's all worked out rather well, considering.'

Sam smiled up at him. 'You knew the TARDIS would survive, you sod!'

The Doctor shook his head. 'I didn't. I just hoped. I think it's about time the poor old thing had a rest.'

They walked down the hill together, half floating in the adjusted gravity.

Fitz frowned. 'I sort of understand why the T'hiili couldn't survive on Earth – but how come we could survive in the Dominion?'

The Doctor put an arm around his shoulder. 'Human beings are so adaptable, Fitz. That's why they have proliferated. Why do you think Time Lords and humans have such similar bodies – at least outwardly? Never waste a good design.'

An image of Kerstin popped into Fitz's mind. Now there was a human who was particularly well designed.

The door to the butterfly room opened before them. Fitz took one last look at the Queen, and then stepped through after Sam and the Doctor.

Major Wolstencroft was impressed by the TARDIS, even though he'd known what to expect. From where he stood, in the library, bookshelves stretched into dusty infinity. He took down a volume with shaking hands. The memoirs of Field Marshal Douglas Haig.

Suddenly the Doctor burst into the console room. Wolstencroft put down the book, composing himself. Didn't want to let the Doctor see how impressed he was. He folded his arms. 'Where are the others?'

The Doctor waved a hand. 'Bathing, changing. Making tea.'

Schofield was staring up at the blue dome of the ceiling. 'Where are we now?'

'Where the C19 base was.' The Doctor operated a lever on the console, and the huge doors at the top of the steps swung open. Daylight poured in.

Wolstencroft and Schofield followed the Doctor up the steps.

'What the –' began Wolstencroft as he stepped outside.

They were at the bottom of a huge crater a hundred feet deep and four times that across. At the edge, fir trees stood like soldiers on parade.

The Doctor looked around, grinning widely. 'A very localised implosion. Hopefully nobody got caught up in it.' His smile vanished. 'Except poor Professor Nagle.'

Wolstencroft tried not to think of what had happened to her. One more casualty… And at least the TC Warp Generator was finished. The C19 chaps would be hopping mad – millions of pounds gone, just like that. But it would show them the dangers of messing with alien technology. Perhaps then they would put more funds into UNIT, into protecting the planet.

He turned to the Doctor. 'Look, I'd… I'd appreciate it if you just – went away,' he said. He ignored the Doctor's look of slight injury. 'There's a lot to be done. D-notices. Reports to ministers. Letters to families.'

The Doctor held up his hands. 'I understand. You have your job to do.'

'How are we going to get out of here, sir?' said Schofield, indicating the almost vertical side of the crater.

The Doctor pursed his lips. 'It is a bit of a steep one. I could try a short hop.' He raised his eyebrows and gestured towards the TARDIS. 'Major? Private?'

Wolstencroft shook his head. 'No, thank you, Doctor. We're fit enough to climb.'

'Suit yourself.' The Doctor stepped into the TARDIS. There was an infernal roaring sound, and it vanished into thin air.

Wolstencroft turned and faced the wall of the crater.

'Come on, lad. We've got work to do.'

After Sam had bathed, changed and had a cup of tea, she felt a bit better. Her room was gone – there was simply nothing there in its place, just a blank wall. She wasn't that bothered. There were plenty of other rooms in the TARDIS.

Now she walked towards the console room, determined to get the Doctor to relocate the T'hiili right away. It was the sort of thing he could forget about unless he was forcibly reminded. Besides, the T'vorha had started eating the butterflies.

She'd left Kerstin in the wardrobe room. Although they were about the same age, the Swedish girl seemed so much younger, so much more vulnerable. Still, for someone totally unprepared for alien creatures, pocket universes and time travel, Kerstin was doing well. Maybe too well – Sam had detected a familiar light in her eyes. She'd seen it in Fitz's, when he'd first joined them. It said, *What a world I've stumbled upon. I don't want to leave.*

That might be a problem.

She found Fitz sitting in the Doctor's chair, his nose in a book. He'd changed back into more normal clothes – black trousers, boots and a white silk shirt. He'd even shaved. To impress Kerstin? She narrowed her eyes suspiciously at him. He returned her gaze, all innocence.

The Doctor was standing at the console, flicking switches and muttering under his breath. Every now and then he'd dart around to another panel, skidding on the floor.

She walked up to the console. 'Doctor, about the –'

He glanced up. His face wore the distracted look which usually spelled Big Trouble. 'There's something wrong!'

Sam sighed. 'Isn't there always?'

The Doctor ruffled his hair. 'This could be very bad. Very bad indeed. Look!'

Sam looked up at the ceiling. It showed a map of America. As she watched, it zoomed in to the west coast – California; she could make out Monterey Bay. Just above that was a glowing blue spot.

Fitz put down his book and came over to the console. 'What is it?'

'I don't know,' said the Doctor. 'Some sort of dimensional scarring.'

'Wormhole damage?' suggested Sam.

The Doctor drummed his fingers on his lips. 'Maybe. Maybe. But the location…'

Fitz frowned. 'What do you mean?'

Sam looked. The blue glow was directly over San Francisco. 'Where you regenerated?'

'Yes,' replied the Doctor, simply.

Oh, pants.

'We'll have to go there. Now.' The Doctor moved to the console.

'Hang on – what about the T'hiili?' said Sam.

The Doctor waved a hand. 'Oh, we'll drop them off on a suitable planet en route.'

To San Francisco via an alien planet! Only in the TARDIS, thought Sam. 'And what about Kerstin?'

There was a hopeful gleam in Fitz's eyes. 'Can't we take her with us?'

'Certainly not,' said the Doctor.

At that moment, Kerstin walked into the console room. Sam boggled. She was wearing a black dress, suede boots and a white cardie. The get-up showed off her figure to startling effect.

Fitz's face was practically falling over itself. She caught his eye. *Put your tongue back*, she mouthed. He grinned widely in return.

'Why can't I come with you?' Kerstin had obviously overheard the Doctor.

'Because you can't,' snapped the Doctor.

Kerstin looked stunned.

Grief. He could be so crap at this sort of thing sometimes.

Fitz went to stand by Kerstin, his face defiant. 'Yes, why not?'

The Doctor looked pained. 'I really haven't got time for this!'

'This is my life we're talking about!' said Kerstin. She looked scared.

What was it Fitz had said? Kerstin's fiancé had been killed? The strain was showing on her face. She would need normal things around her, whatever she thought now. Another trip in the TARDIS would probably unhinge her. She'd have to go, for her own good. Perhaps Fitz would decide to go with her – after all, he'd been ready to stay with Maddie in 1967. But Sam found herself rather hoping he wouldn't.

She walked over to Fitz. 'You'd better say your goodbyes,' she murmured.

Fitz scowled. 'Who to – you or Kerstin?'

Sam sighed. They were going to end up arguing. Again. Over a girl. She fixed Fitz with her most level, most serious, stare. 'Fitz, it's your life. It's up to you.'

Then she walked from the console room, in search of a new room to call her own.

Kerstin couldn't believe it. She'd found this wonderful place, but she wasn't allowed to stay. This fantastic machine couldn't save Johan, and now it couldn't save her from her own dull life.

She was standing with Fitz next to the train set. She watched the busy little engines whizzing round the track. Going nowhere. Just like her.

'He's made up his mind, you know,' said Fitz.

She looked him up and down slowly. 'What about you?'

Fitz leaned closer. 'If it was up to me...'

She reached out, held his hands, stared into his eyes. It was no use: Johan was still there, in the deep lake of her mind.

He must have seen something in her eyes, because his expression changed, grew distant.

Something flickered above. She looked up, and her heart sank. The TARDIS ceiling was showing a weird fish-eye view of Strängnäs, the familiar cobbled streets and tidy buildings, the lake and windmill.

She looked at Fitz, forcing a smile. 'Looks like my stop.' Not wanting to prolong her departure, she turned and walked towards the doors.

The Doctor was standing by the console, gazing up at the view of Strängnäs, his eyes alive with interest.

One last appeal. 'You haven't given me one solid reason why I have to go!'

The Doctor turned to her, shaking his head. 'Kerstin, Kerstin! I'll give you three. One, we have a job to do, there will be great danger. Two, you've been through a lot, and you need time to recover. Three, you're going to live a long, fulfilling life – on Earth. I'm sorry, but you have to leave. Now!'

He whirled away, began pulling levers, muttering under his breath.

Kerstin swallowed. She was already forgotten.

A hand on her arm. Fitz, propelling her across the floor and up the stone steps. The doors were open and she could see outside – the sun-bright cobblestones, a patch of grass, parked cars.

She walked outside and turned to face Fitz, the cathedral-like space of the TARDIS interior framing him.

Was this it? The end of it all? She couldn't imagine going back to her parents in Stockholm, back to Uppsala without Johan. She couldn't bear the dull, aching blandness of reality. 'So, this is goodbye.'

His face was shadowed. He nodded. 'Yeah. 'Fraid so.'

She thought of asking him to come with her, but she knew what the answer would be, so instead she smiled. 'Don't forget me.'

'I won't,' said Fitz. And with a wave of his hand and a smile, the blue door closed and the TARDIS faded away, accompanied by a surging, roaring sound which tugged at her heart.

When it had gone, Kerstin stood there for few minutes. Just in case it came back. Then she turned and walked towards a café on the other side of the street. In a few days, she would probably begin to doubt any of this had happened.

She ordered a pot of coffee, sitting down at a corner table.

She remembered the Doctor's words. A long and fulfilling life. How did he know? What did he mean? Right now, she didn't care.

The coffee arrived, and she sipped. It was bitter, sour. She sighed. Better get used to bitter and sour.

Kerstin stared out of the window, at the place where the TARDIS had been, wondering if it had ever been there at all, wondering what the hell she was going to do with the rest of her life.